Death Under Par

By Janice Law

THE BIG PAYOFF
GEMINI TRIP
UNDER ORION
THE SHADOW OF THE PALMS
DEATH UNDER PAR

Death Under Par

Janice Law

Houghton Mifflin Company

1981 Boston

Library of Congress Cataloging in Publication Data

Law, Janice.
  Death under par.

  I. Title.
PS3562.A86D4   813'.54   80-20307
ISBN 0-395-30227-7

Printed in the United States of America

BC 10 9 8 7 6 5 4 3 2 1

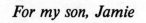

For my son, Jamie

Jack Nicklaus did win the British Open in 1978 in the manner described, although not against Peter Bryce. All other incidents are pure invention, and the Open at St. Andrews went off uneventfully, doubtless because the real organizing committee bore no resemblance to the group imagined in this book.

Death Under Par

1

I PICKED DRIED BLOSSOMS off my begonias and watered their three square beds and the cluster of potted geraniums. While I pinched back leggy specimens and uprooted weeds, I considered certain activities in the shipping office of a D.C. department store. As of this afternoon I was pretty sure I knew what went on there. Now came the matter of securing proof for my client and his lawyers, and I was deciding which of several investigative avenues to pursue, when Harry stepped out onto the tiny brick-paved yard.

"What would you say to a honeymoon?" he asked.

"I thought we'd gone far enough already with the wedding."

To some minds, we'd gone entirely too far with that. After years of urging respectable matrimony, Harry's mother had ultimately decided she preferred the impermanence of sin to the finalities of marriage—at least where I was concerned.

Harry smiled and produced a fat envelope. "I'm all for tradition at someone else's expense."

"That sounds promising."

"It is. I've scored a coup. I'm doing a series of illustrations for *Sports Illustrated.*"

"Marvelous! They're going first class."

"Thanks. It's purely commercial, but there are fringe benefits."

"What are you to do?"

"Scenes from the British Open. Background stuff, atmosphere, capturing the sense of the event, the human dimension." He gestured expansively. "According to their art director, that is. Actually, I have carte blanche so long as the course and golfers are recognizable."

"Well, congratulations. When are they due?"

"The week after the Open. I can get all the preliminary stuff done beforehand, but I'll have to stay for the last day to get sketches from the final round." He looked slightly disappointed. "You haven't asked where we'll be going."

"Where will we be going?"

"The Home of Golf."

"I'm touched and pleased. Where's that?"

"The Old Course at St. Andrews. It's supposed to be beautiful: seaside resort, medieval ruins. Full of charm."

My memories of Scotland are distinctly mixed. My professional initiation there left a lingering impression of rain and fear. "When would we have to leave?"

"The first week in July. I could leave it that late if you have a case to finish." Harry looked hopeful. I could see this trip was something important.

"Let me see. I'd better check the calendar upstairs. I have a couple of things in the works."

Harry nodded and slid open the glass door that he'd installed during the conversion of the duplex, long before our recent legal amalgamation.

"You've got Baby, now," he reminded me as we entered my study. Acquired from Harry's graphics concern, Baby was a topic of mild reproach; and both he and his partner, Jan Gorgon, resented her loss.

"She still needs supervision. But Harriet's holiday isn't until

2

the first of August, and George—" I tapped the book. It looked feasible. "No more than two, two and a half weeks. I couldn't manage a day more."

"We can get a flight out on the second."

Not much time for the shipping office! "That will be a rush—"

"But you do want to come?"

It would be a shame, I thought, to spoil his surprise and the first vacation we'd taken together in years. Executive Security, Inc., could run itself during the July doldrums, for even the swindlers take holidays, and the corporate piranhas could be allowed to flourish a few weeks longer.

"Call the airline," I said.

"Wonderful!" He gave me a kiss. "You'll love it."

"I'm sure I will. And remember, I'm being a dutiful wife."

"There's something to be said for tradition," he replied smugly, as he picked up the phone to make reservations for our flight. I opened the atlas to inspect the fretted coastline of the U.K.

"All set," Harry announced shortly. "We're on the seven-thirty night flight." Then, noticing the map, "Were you there before?"

"No. Up above Aberdeen. And in the West."

"No bad vibes, I hope?"

"None whatsoever. I'm sure it will be lovely."

*   *

It drizzled the night we left Washington, and the thick mist of hydrocarbons and water vapor that hung over Dulles blotted the city with its haze. It was raining when we arrived in Prestwick. Glasgow, if anything, was wetter— and sooty as well, while the gutters ran like freshets in Edinburgh. But as we approached St. Andrews, the clouds broke, pouring golden light on the spires and towers of the old gray town, which rose silver and gleaming from a flat stretch of green farmland. To the north, the town and the golf courses fronted the sea, while close against the other three sides pressed green and yellow waves of pasture, potatoes, and barley, their colors brilliant against the slate and purple clouds.

Directly before the town was a stretch of lawn where tents were being erected. "Are those for the Open?" Harry asked.

"For the exhibition," the cabbie explained. "Fife Region puts on displays during the week. The tents for the golf will be farther over, there where the bleachers are being set up along the course."

"Quite a job."

"For a little place this size," the man agreed.

"Imagine you'll be busy over the tournament."

"Run off our feet. They'll put on extra buses, though, for the spectators. Here you are," he added, pulling up to a cream-colored stone hotel with a pub attached. The main cobblestone street widened before this building to accommodate the monument and flowers of the market square and a pre-Open crowd of visitors and golfers. There were a few drops of rain in the air, and, after Washington, the Kingdom of Fife felt frigid.

"You're not here for the golf, then," the driver remarked, noticing the absence of clubs.

"We're on our honeymoon," Harry said pleasantly.

"Oh, congratulations. You've come at rather a busy time, though. Town's prettier when it's not so crowded. Thank you. Enjoy your stay."

"Incredible, isn't it?" Harry said as we carried our luggage into a narrow lobby with a large paneled cubicle pierced by a high window like a bank teller's cage.

"Yes, I hadn't realized it was this small a place."

"Oh, that, yes. I meant the light. Wonderful cloud formations. Have you a room for Radford?" he asked a small, dry-looking clerk who consulted the register with an expression of profound pessimism. "Changeable, though. I'll have to go out right away to get that effect over the beach."

4

"Room fourteen. Lynn will show you upstairs," the deskman announced and, ringing a bell, summoned a young woman in a blue cleaning smock who led us to our room. Harry disappeared almost immediately to buy an umbrella to protect his sketching equipment, while I recuperated from twelve hours of constant travel with a nap, a pleasant activity interrupted at five, when the town's bells set off a great pealing and clanging. Outside, the clouds were dark, but the sun was shining and the street below our windows was jammed. Battalions of British visitors in tweeds, a few older Scots in kilts, several women in vivid American polyesters, a group of elegant Japanese, hikers with faded backpacks, and just on the edge of the square, a young man in what appeared to be a full-length cloak and sandals. I leaned out the window to get a better look at this apparition, but he vanished down a narrow lane just as the door behind me opened, and Harry entered, carrying an immense multicolored umbrella and the knapsack that held his sketching materials.

"Returned to life, I see."

"Very much so. You look a little damp."

"I was caught in what the locals call a 'showery interval.' They can be expected for the next few days."

"How's that portable tent?"

"Ideal, but down on the course the wind is terrific. Comes in right off the sea. I made a few sketches between the showers, though. Beautiful shore. Watercolor's the only thing to capture it." He fussed with his paints and sketch pad, loath to put them away for the evening. I watched him adding notes in pencil for a moment, before I asked if we could get mobilized for dinner.

"I thought we could eat here," he said.

"Fine."

"And then walk down toward the castle and the harbor?"

"Sounds good."

"It is nice, isn't it?"

"Beautiful," I agreed. "A honeymoon is a super idea."

"And you can really relax," he said, putting his arms around me. "This time, you've got nothing to worry about."

"Except dinner," I reminded him. "Let's eat and enjoy some of that terrific light you've been telling me about."

*   *   *

After supper, we walked the cobblestone streets past the ruins of the cathedral toward the archbishop's palace, a crumbling façade on a cliff overlooking the sea. The front and apse of the cathedral and the wall around its burial ground were the only remnants of what must once have been a spectacular building. Now, with the single intact wall of the castle and a thin solitary tower from yet another ecclesiastical structure, the cathedral made an austere backdrop for the plain stone houses of the town. Beyond these ruins was the harbor, with a long mole jutting into the bay, and between the dock and the castle, a stretch of seaweed-covered rocks, alive with sea birds. The sun had dropped into a golden haze above the western horizon, and to the east hung a stretch of pellucid silvery lavender, mingling air and water and marked only by the black lines of the rocks and the white wings of the gulls. We leaned against the fence that divided the path from the edge of the bluff and stared over the vast stillness of the sea. After a few minutes, Harry opened his pad and began to cover the pages with quick sketches, oblivious to all else. He was not, perhaps, the conventional companion for a honeymoon, but I knew his habits too well to find them irritating. While he was absorbed in his work I inspected the castle and the sand, enjoying an unaccustomed freedom from chores, responsibilities, and deadlines; and when the light began to fade, I returned to where he still scribbled industriously. Below, some children and a dog were leaving the narrow beach and the strollers passing between the town and the harbor had gone. Only one figure remained along the water, a man sitting halfway out on the rocks. He had unruly black

6

hair and an odd, dark shirt, which, when he stood up, was revealed as a full-length black cape.

I nudged Harry. "I noticed him earlier today."

"Original outfit."

The man carried a long staff and, instead of slacks, sported buff-colored leggings.

"Town eccentric?"

"Actor, probably. There's a theater here."

"Very appropriate for the setting, anyway."

"A touch too romantic for my purposes," Harry said, closing his notebook. "Ready? Light's gone."

"Sure." I couldn't help taking another look at the unusual figure, standing now, at the end of the rocks, watching the oncoming tide. "Odd face."

"Not typical," Harry replied, thinking of his assignment. "Not really suitable. I've gotten some good ideas already," he added as we started back along the sea front, talking of his project and stopping to admire things he'd spotted during his afternoon excursion. While we were loitering in front of a pretty Victorian bandstand, two men emerged from one of the restaurants. The taller one hesitated when he noticed us, then approached rapidly.

"I beg your pardon. It *is* Miss Peters, isn't it?"

I recognized his sandy hair, colorless eyes, and thin features: a Scottish salmon magnate who had employed me a year before in a little matter involving the fraudulent use of his firm's name and logo. "How are you, Mr. Sutherland?"

"Fine, fine. Over here for the golf, are you?"

"Only indirectly. This is my husband, Harry Radford." There were mutual introductions, and I thought Sutherland gave Harry a very sharp, close look.

"Harry's here for *Sports Illustrated.* Doing illustrations for a special section on the Open."

"Are you? Quite an assignment! I should have remembered that, but there have been so many requests for credentials. We on the organizing committee rather have our hands full."

"It's a beautiful course—from the aesthetic point of view," Harry said.

"From every point of view, I can assure you. Was it you I saw out on the links this afternoon?"

"Yes. I hope that was all right. I needed to make some preliminary sketches before the practice rounds begin."

"Certainly, certainly. No golfing, of course. We want the greens and fairways to be in the best possible condition." He smiled and looked, I thought, rather relieved. "I saw you from the upper windows of the clubhouse."

"I'll stop in tomorrow and make all the arrangements," Harry promised, "but the light was so good this afternoon—"

"The artistic eye! Miss Peters, Mr. Radford, we have an engagement, unfortunately, but I'll look forward to meeting you both during your stay. See me if there's anything you need for the tournament. Are you fond of the game?" he inquired, looking directly at me.

"I'm afraid I don't play."

"A pity, but no obstacle to enjoying the Open," he said, shaking our hands. "A fascinating event, Miss Peters; I promise you will find it interesting."

2

WE SPENT THE NEXT FEW DAYS doing nothing, which, since this was a vacation, meant we did inhuman amounts of walking: up and down towers, through churches, historic homes, and ruins, and, more pleasantly, to lazy picnics on the lonely shores beyond town. Harry's assignment easily stretched to include these activities, which produced piles of drawings. On the morning that practice rounds started, however, he had to get himself out to the links. The alarm rang early, and I opened my eyes to a chill, dank morning: The brilliant skies of "Costa Fife" were today but a publicist's memory.

"Feel like coming with me?" Harry asked.

"Is it raining?"

He got up and consulted the window. "Not yet."

"Where are you going to be?"

"All over the place. They want pictures of the different holes."

I could envision a wet morning tramping after high-strung golfers. "Why don't I meet you for lunch?"

"All right. Going sightseeing?"

"No, to the Laundromat."

Harry made a face.

"The fate of unemployed wives," I said. "Besides, we've about run through our clothes."

This was the conclusive fact, and after a late and leisurely breakfast, I bundled up the laundry, located the shop, and had begun negotiations with the woman in charge when a bearish man with a halo of wiry black hair and heavy rounded shoulders arrived. He carried his laundry in a sheet and immediately started to load one of the self-service machines. He was dressed in a plain tweed jacket and a pair of corduroy slacks that were conventional enough, but there was something distinctive about him. It was not just that he struck one as being bulky and a little ungainly. No, despite his lack of grace and any sign of conventional good looks, he made an impression. Even burdened with that most depressing of props, dirty laundry, he managed an "entrance," and it was this theatrical air that convinced me I had seen him before. Small town, I thought, and turned to collect my change. "And they'll be ready this afternoon?" I asked.

"Any time after four, Miss."

As I was leaving, I glanced at him again; he had small, very dark eyes set in a well-fleshed face with a high forehead and heavy jowls.

"New England," he said to me, "with a touch of the urban South. I'd guess Washington. Before that"—he hesitated again and looked at me appraisingly—"Connecticut," he announced triumphantly. "Am I right?"

"Yes, you are. That's remarkable."

He smiled and took out his wallet with a flourish. "Will you put them in the dryer for me, Mrs. McKay? I'll be back after lunch."

"Aye, I'll have them ready, Dr. Thorston."

"I'm uncertain as to the precise location in Connecticut, but I'd guess you were born there."

10

"Right again." As parlor tricks go, this one was impressive. "Center of the state. I couldn't go much closer than that." "Dead center. Hartford."

The conversation skipped a fraction of a beat. "Oh, Hartford. I should have known."

"Still, remarkable."

"Oh, aye. The doctor can tell doon to the name of yer farm," the proprietress remarked.

"Now, Mrs. McKay, only in the East Neuk—and I've had practice."

"Pretty good for an American, I can tell you," she said.

"By the speech?" I asked.

"That's right. Melvin Thorston," he added, and stuck out his hand. He had a loud, resonant voice and distinctive, sweeping gestures. My original impression of ungainliness had not been quite accurate. For a fattish man, he was light on his feet, and he had small, neat hands like a tailor or a conjurer. He would have made, as I think back on it, a wonderful patent medicine man. "Have you been here long?"

I introduced myself and explained I'd only recently arrived. "I thought you looked familiar, though," I said.

"You'll have noticed Wulf, of course," he replied as he started to the door. He pronounced the w like a v in the German manner, and I was curious enough to inquire who this was.

"A little project of mine." Thorston held the door open and bade Mrs. McKay good-by with another flourish. "He's made quite an impression here. I could present papers that would shake up the psychologists and sociologists."

"This is some sort of study?"

"No, I said 'project' advisedly," he corrected in a professorial tone. "I meant that I had gained additional insight and information into human psychology. A mere by-product." He waved his hand. "Rewarding but tangential."

We were by this time in the street, which, like all of St. Andrews' thoroughfares, was jammed with slow-moving crowds of tourists, shoppers, and locals. Dr. Thorston took no notice and began in his resonant voice to discuss his specialty. "My field is linguistics and philology," he said, "obsolete Germanic and Anglo-Saxon dialects, in particular. I'm here studying and teaching early and middle Scots literature. Fascinating, you know. Lowland Scots is a separate language, related to English but as different from it as, say, Norwegian and Danish are today. There were interesting things written in it. From a linguistic point of view, it was a misfortune when the countries united."

I nodded politely, conscious of the curious stares of the shoppers.

"Here to play some golf?" he asked abruptly.

"Just for a vacation."

"Long way from Hartford and D.C."

"Best feature of the place."

"Yes. I have to get a paper," he said, holding open the door of the newsstand for me. Curious and a little overwhelmed by this surprising personality, I went in and picked up a *Herald Trib*. Thorston did likewise, selecting the *Guardian, The Telegraph,* and *The Times,* as well. I noticed he greeted all the clerks by name like a regular customer and that they seemed quite unperturbed when he launched into another discussion of his linguistic pursuits. "I introduced my specialty," he said, "as a means of explaining Wulf. I am Wulf, or more precisely, he is my alternate persona."

This took a certain time to digest.

"I'm developing him on a grant from the Gruen Foundation," he added airily. "They found it a most original proposal."

I could only agree.

"Are you familiar with the Gruen Foundation?" he asked sharply, but when I confessed I was not, he offered no explanation. "Odd, that it hasn't been tried before. Of course it's a matter of temperament. Not everyone has a sense of theater."

12

He swept up his newspapers with this remark and glared around the store with a haughty expression, as though daring contradiction. "I see that the idea makes you uneasy," he said.

In truth, it was his manner that made me uneasy—his sudden shifts in emotional gear and his tendency to declaim even the simplest statements as though he were behind some imaginary podium. "No, but I know now why I thought I recognized you."

"Exactly. Most afternoons, I'm Wulf. Classes are over then for the day. The summer Scottish Studies Program I do meets only in the morning. Of course, they enjoy meeting Wulf when we're doing poetry, but as a general thing, I'm only Wulf in the afternoons."

"He has a distinctive costume," I remarked, as we left the shop.

"Medieval. Wulf is fourteenth century. The name is a difficulty. I began developing him in German. Yes," he said and nodded rapidly, "Wulf started out speaking a West Germanic dialect, but somehow it wasn't quite right. It didn't really fit me. The ambiance was wrong." He darted another quick, sharp glance at me, and this time I sensed that there was a good deal of intellectual power behind that montebank façade.

"This is certainly an attractive place if rather a"—I hesitated. *Conventional* wasn't exactly the word, nor, so far as I could see, was *conservative*. Rather, St. Andrews revealed a kind of prim independence, bracing or confining, no doubt, depending on one's perspective.

"Far from the metropolis, far from street theater? That's what makes it ideal. And my appointment here is convenient. The Gruen Foundation's grants are considerable but not lavish." His heavy face assumed a sour expression, and one of his small hairy hands inscribed a dismissive circle in the air.

"You're working for the university."

"That's right."

13

"Wulf must present something of a novelty for them."

"Like most administrators, they're afraid of real innovations."

"I imagine he would raise complications—"

"But Wulf is the whole point," Thorston said with considerable animation. One of the professor's distinctive features was his compulsion to instruct, to clarify. In this, he was totally unselfconscious, and however awkward I might have felt listening to a dissertation in the middle of South Street, Dr. Thorston was completely at home. "It is a commonplace," he began, "that every language presents a new perspective on reality. Reality, in every case, being filtered through the cultural and linguistic assumptions of the grammar and vocabulary. Who was it said, 'a new language, a new soul?' I'm conducting a practical experiment. I'm finding out how far that goes. Not with a living language, but with a relic of another time. By learning and using Wulf's language, I am enlarging my insights into the medieval mind." He nodded rapidly, as if continuing this monologue internally. After a moment, he spoke again. "You will say this is an artificial construction. That has its advantages, too. The lack of a bona fide surrounding medieval culture forces me to create a new character from within. My literary colleagues in the English Department are always talking about 'personas' in writing," he added in a belligerent tone. "I think I can say I have real insight into that part of the creative process."

"An intriguing experiment." I was beginning to lose interest in the professor and his eccentric theories, and when, with what I now realized was habitual bluster, he asked what I did, I told him. "I run a security business."

This brought Thorston up short. "Securities?"

"No. Security. And investigations. I'm an up-to-date private detective." That is a phrase which has been known to end unwelcome conversations. It worked.

"In Hartford?" he asked quickly.

14

"No. In D.C."

"Of course. Southern speech pattern overlay quite noticeable in spite of definite urban characteristics. Nice to have met you." He nodded his large head, swung on his heel, and stalked away. At the corner, he turned, oblivious of the crowds, and called, "Be sure to introduce yourself to Wulf. Naturally," he bounced off a shopper, made his apologies, and continued, "naturally, he's puzzled by modern life, but for a humble swineherd, he's not uninteresting." With this, the professor strode off toward the university buildings. I put him down as an uncommonly aggressive and original academic hustler and, wondering whose money was being cast abroad by the Gruen Foundation, set off to meet Harry.

I found my husband leaning against the stone wall that separates the seventeenth, the famous "Road Hole," from the little narrow street along the fairways. His face was red and his hands, white, for the wind sweeping in off the magnificent beach was definitely cold. We adjourned for lunch, then to a studio he'd rented from the art department at the university, and, except for a pleasant hour spent in our room before dinner, the day was uneventful. When the phone rang as we were dressing for dinner, I was surprised.

"Can you get that, Harry?"

He straightened up from the washstand, dripping water everywhere. "What are you doing?"

"Repairing my eyelashes."

"Good lord. I'm getting the full treatment."

"I'm only going on a honeymoon with you once, you realize."

He interrupted the next ring. "Hello? That's right." A brief pause. "Just a moment. It's for you, Anna."

My caller came directly to the point. "James Sutherland, here. It's important that I talk to you right away, Miss Peters."

"What about?"

"Not over a hotel switchboard, please."

"If this is a business matter, Mr. Sutherland, I'm afraid—"

"I know you're on holiday, Miss Peters, and I do apologize, but this is urgent. Could we have a drink somewhere? What I have to say won't take too long."

"My husband and I were just on our way to dinner—"

After a slight hesitation, Sutherland recovered with imposing cordiality. "We'll all meet for a drink. How's that? I'll pick you up and bring you back in plenty of time for dinner."

"Well—"

"Say ten minutes?"

"All right, but just for a talk. I'm in no position to take on anything at the moment."

"Just listen. That's all I ask, Miss Peters. I'll meet you out front, then."

"Very well, Mr. Sutherland." I hung up.

"The fish man?" Harry asked.

"With a fishy request. We've been invited for a drink."

"Gaelic hospitality?"

"He's after something."

"More trouble with his labels?"

"I don't think so, somehow, but it doesn't matter. I'm not going to work on this vacation."

"Absolutely right," Harry said, catching me in his arms. "Why don't we stand him up?"

"Lovely idea," I said, disengaging myself as slowly as possible, "but not polite."

"So we'll drink his Scotch under false pretenses."

"Exactly." I pulled on my dress and completed a few last minute repairs. By the time we walked downstairs, the rounded bottle-green nose of Sutherland's Jaguar was parked in front. The salmon magnate uncoiled his agile frame from behind the wheel and opened the doors.

"A pleasure to see you again, Mr. Radford. And, of course, Miss Peters, whom I shall have to call Mrs. Radford now."

"I'm keeping my own name for business," I said firmly.

16

"Ah, yes, this is business, no way around it." He settled behind the wheel and started the powerful engine. "We'll drive down the road, if you don't mind. Have you taken any drives around?"

"This is a working holiday for me," Harry said. "I've been out sketching most days."

"As I've noticed. You're employed by *Sports Illustrated,* Mr. Radford?"

"Only to do this set of illustrations."

"Harry runs a graphics workshop," I added. "This is an extra commission."

"May I assume, then, that you have no journalistic ambitions?"

"Journalistic?" Harry asked with a laugh.

"I mean, you have no interest in securing material for that American sports magazine?"

"I don't interfere in my wife's business, if that's what you mean, Mr. Sutherland. Whatever you have to discuss with her is quite confidential."

"No offense meant, Mr. Radford. You will understand my caution when I explain the nature of our conference." He had turned onto the main road by this time, and after driving a few moments in silence, he announced, "It concerns the Open."

"Therefore, a drive out of town," I said.

"Exactly. St. Andrews depends on two things, the university and the golf course. Such a dependence makes any information about either a matter of vital interest." He glanced up into the mirror. "And hence my concern about your employment, Mr. Radford."

Harry nodded, mollified.

"I am one of the members of the Royal and Ancient involved in the organization and conduct of this year's Open. For a number of reasons it has turned out to be an unusually difficult and delicate charge."

He slowed the car at this point. Misty fields and forest

17

stretched on both sides of the road, but at a junction ahead stood a black-and-white timbered inn. "We'll have a drink here," said Sutherland, "and talk about it."

He did not begin until we were settled in a dim corner. "We on the committee have had a number of discussions about how we should proceed," he said. "There have been various opini ns and quite a number of names put forward. Some very good ones, I might add, but there was always a problem: in a word, the necessity for secrecy and discretion. The people we could get agreement on were apt to be too well known for the job, and then there was no consensus on whether or not anything at all should be done." He made a sour face. "I trust you are familiar with the difficulties of doing anything by committee."

I nodded. This was pretty vague, but Sutherland seemed disinclined to come immediately to the heart of his problem.

"Your arrival," he continued, "provided a means of breaking a deadlock on the committee."

"In what way?"

"It was decided, on my strong recommendation, that a group from the R and A should meet with you, ask your advice about certain incidents which have occurred over the last few weeks, and if we can come to an agreement, employ you to make what I am sure will be very brief inquiries."

"Under any other circumstances, Mr. Sutherland, your request alone would be sufficient, but Harry and I are not only on our first vacation in years, but on our honeymoon. Naturally—"

"My apologies. This is very awkward, but—Mr. Radford has his drawings to keep him occupied, and this is of some interest even to him."

"How's that?" Harry asked.

"There is a threat to the Open."

There was a pause as a sort of mental hush enveloped Sutherland.

18

"I'm not entirely clear how that concerns me," Harry countered flatly.

"Surely for aesthetic and professional reasons, Mr. Radford, you would like to see this event proceed successfully. I have noticed your admirable application to your work. Having your pictures appear in this sporting journal will be something of a financial boost to your artistic career. Am I correct?"

"It won't hurt."

"Certainly not. Now I think I know journalists and editors well enough to say that should there be any"—he hesitated, seeking, I suspected, the least offensive word—"difficulty, any scandal, any sort of disaster, well, what would be the first to go? Hmmmh? Art would be sacrificed to press photography."

"Possibly," Harry said noncommittally."

"Definitely. Even Michelangelo's drawings would have been bumped for the fuzziest telephoto from the Munich Olympics."

"Surely," I interrupted, "there's no question of some sort of terrorist attack?"

"No, no. Believe me, we'd have the army out if there were even a hint. I merely chose that as an illustration for Mr. Radford."

"You've made your point," Harry said.

"I thought so. No, our difficulties are, in contrast, trivial, almost juvenile, but their potential is uncertain. We would be very grateful, Miss Peters, if you would meet with us tomorrow morning at the R and A. We would explain the matter in detail, outline our own theory, and request you to look into the matter a bit further. In all honesty, we are quite sure it will not prove a complicated matter."

I glanced at Harry, who shrugged.

"You make it difficult for me to say no. But I still don't understand. You have your local police, you have all manner of private investigators, you have Scotland Yard. I find this appeal frankly peculiar."

"The ever-cautious Miss Peters. Will it reassure you to know that the police are involved and are convinced the matter is too trifling to pursue?"

"Only slightly."

"My feeling as well. The real reason is perfectly simple: We've got our eye on an American."

3

WE ARRIVED THE NEXT MORNING at the clubhouse of
the Royal and Ancient, a steel-gray Victorian edifice sprouting
chimneys, pediments, and dormers, a large bow window, and
a dainty balcony from which the members can watch activities
on the first tee and on the eighteenth green directly below. I
parted company with Harry, who joined the flock of journalists
and photographers waiting for the demigods of golf to begin
their practice rounds. He was there to sketch the young American, Peter Bryce, currently hailed as the greatest new talent
since Jack Nicklaus, and while the bustle and pressure of a
major sporting event rather amused Harry, it was taking him
time to adjust to the working conditions. I saw his quizzical
glance at the mob, then watched him take out his sketching
materials and station himself along the fence away from the
crush. "Good luck," he called as I headed to the main door, and
I waved in response.

We had spent much of the previous evening on Sutherland's
proposal, speculating about it at dinner before we strolled re-

flectively through the long northern twilight. I wasn't enthusiastic; yet there were certain interesting things in the salmon magnate's discreet references to a problem at the R and A. As for Harry, I understood he wasn't averse to my having some occupation. His work was taking up more of his time than he had anticipated, and I think he felt a trifle guilty that so much of our vacation was being spent trudging across golf courses and collecting sketches along the sands. But that was not the deciding factor. The deciding factor was something else entirely.

Our walk took us, as it usually did, toward the sea. We passed the high wall that had once formed part of the cathedral cloister and headed toward the ruins overlooking the water. The oncoming darkness had chased the last golfers and swimmers home, and the silent gray stones exhaled the tranquil aroma of great age. The town was, I think, the prettiest place of its size I've ever seen, the open sweep and beauty of its setting saving it from the merely picturesque and the ruins lending a certain gravity of aspect. No one, the guides report, escaped from the castle's dungeon, a bottle-shaped pit carved through the bluff to sea level and horrid enough even under electric lighting. Religious wars burned both the once splendid cathedral and the castle, the archbishop himself having first been hurled from his apartments. Several martyrs later, the madness of humanity migrated to other unfortunate towns, leaving its relics to attract the admiration of travelers from places too young to boast of ancient wars. Harry and I sat on a bench and watched the first lights from Dundee and Carnoustie flickering across the bay. In the beauty of the evening, it was an unlikely setting for crime, and to my perverse taste, the improbability of it cast a certain fascination.

"Well?" Harry asked. "What about Sutherland's request?"

"I'm curious."

"I thought so."

"It wouldn't take too much time to talk to them."

22

Harry smiled faintly. "Probably not." He nodded toward the sky. "And the working conditions here are exceptionally nice."

* * *

They were in the morning, anyway. The sun was out, the sky was gloriously blue and clear, and the treeless courses rolled brilliantly green, their emerald satins accentuated by dark clumps of gorse. From the upper room at the clubhouse, the four courses rippled like an inland sea until stopped by the silver line of the Eden river with the pine forest at Leuchars behind it. RAF planes tore off the runway at the base to roar into the sea haze, returning to swoop before the black line of the forest like silver wasps. I moved the telescope slightly and picked up a group moving down the fairway to the second tee. Harry walked alongside a large man in a vivid sky blue sweater. "Is that Peter Bryce?" I asked.

Sutherland put his eye to the glass. "I believe it is. So you're beginning to follow the game?"

Sports Illustrated had provided Harry with reams of information on the players they especially wanted. Bryce led the list.

"One of my husband's subjects."

"One of the draws of the tournament. A very exciting player."

"Charming young chap, too," a low voice interrupted.

Sutherland relinquished the telescope and gestured toward the three men in club blazers who had appeared from the hallway. "Miss Peters, I believe we can begin. Let me present the committee: Sir Malcolm Greene, who is chairing our group, Robert Frazer, who will present the report of the groundskeeper, and Walter Irving, who has been overseeing our security arrangements. Gentlemen, Anna Peters, who heads Executive Security of Washington, D.C."

There were greetings all round. Greene spoke first. He was a sturdy, almost heavy, man of medium height with a large intelligent face and long gray hair swept straight back from his forehead. Whenever he consulted his notes, this mane flopped forward into his eyes, to be rearranged irritably, cigarette in hand, a proceeding that threatened to set him alight. Although knighted for his distinction in ancient Near Eastern languages, Sir Malcolm looked like a shrewd old bird. He was, as a matter of fact, a most practical man, and he began by outlining the general situation.

"James will have explained our desire for some discreet advice and our possible interest in a few personal inquiries?"

"Subject to the outcome of this interview," I replied.

"Quite. Our concern, Miss Peters, is predicated on two things, the first of which is the smallness of the town, which as you can observe, is in unusually close proximity to the course. We are, I think, unique in our total integration with the town and the sands. This lends a certain flavor, but it means that the R and A must exercise all its diplomatic skills during an event like the Open. It also means that periodically our abilities to handle what has become a sporting event of international interest and magnitude are called into question." He paused and the men beside him nodded. "James tells me you are not knowledgeable about golf, but I assume you can assess the points at which the Old Course might be questioned?"

"Crowds must be difficult to handle and control," I answered. "Then, transportation, parking, lodging—"

"Precisely. There is no room of our own to expand. For the exhibition the Fife Regional Council is running concurrent with the Open, the Madras College fields have had to be used. Discontent there."

"Mature turf lost," Frazer added. "The playing fields will undoubtedly have to be reseeded." He furrowed a pair of ample tufted eyebrows. "The rugby enthusiasts are concerned, and just yesterday the games mistress cornered me—" Our expert on grounds and grasses would undoubtedly have digressed had Greene not cut him off.

"The point is, we must deal on two fronts: the golfing world

24

with newer courses ambitious to hold the Open, and the town of St. Andrews, now administered by the Fife Regional Council, which has goals not always in the best interests of the Old Course."

"The course has an immense reputation, though. Is there any serious danger of losing the tournament?"

"The Old Course is the greatest in the world. I speak now of its age, tradition, and when the winds are right, its difficulty. If we are lucky with the weather and if all goes well, I think we will be able to challenge the success of any course in the kingdom. It looks very good, anyway. All the big Americans are coming this year. Your PGA schedule broke right for us: Watson, Nicklaus, Palmer, both of whom are still immense favorites here, Green, the younger Snead, this new man Bryce; two very fine Japanese golfers; Gary Player, of course; all our British chaps. It's a dream field. This year's Open should be a very exciting tournament, and we want our course and our town to show at their best."

"But there is a problem?"

"Let us say there have been problems. But I must mention a final aspect of our situation: our vulnerability to development. You've noticed the Old Course Hotel, I'm sure."

This was a modern hotel owned by British Railways. Known locally as the "chest of drawers," it looked exactly like an immense bureau dropped on the edge of the sixteenth fairway.

"Everything possible was done to preserve the course at the time," Frazer put in. "Even the silhouettes of the sheds."

"I'm afraid—" I began, puzzled.

"The netting," Sutherland explained. "By the Old Course Hotel. There used to be railway sheds when the line ran along the course. The nets reproduce the shape of the buildings so that the character of the hole remains the same."

"I see."

"Recently," Greene continued, "there have been various schemes to put up holiday chalets in the area. We have defeated

25

these plans, most recently one to develop a stretch of farmland along the Eden course. A certain amount of bad feeling was stirred up about that."

I sensed, at last, an approach to the problem of the moment.

"Robert, I think you should now give our guest the greens-keeper's reports," the chairman concluded.

Frazer cleared his throat. He was a slight, wiry man of about fifty with black hair, neat, almost Oriental features, and the delicate, precise gestures of a well-bred mouse. He raised his sheaf of papers and summed up their content in a word, "Vandalism."

Something more seemed necessary. "Around the course?" I asked.

"Aye, and the clubhouse. Now, Miss Peters, here is the situation. Since three weeks ago, we have had tampering with the course and with the groundskeepers' equipment, beginning, mind you, with the outer courses and on holes farthest from the R and A and the town. June 11, sand dumped on the ninth of the Jubilee. June 15, hose turned on the green at the Eden seventh."

I interrupted at this point. "Have you a map of the courses so that I can see where these incidents occurred?"

A large chart was produced, and Frazer marked the sites as he read off a considerable list of petty mischief. The trail of damage ran in an irregular line nearer and nearer to the Old Course and the clubhouse.

"The most serious, from our point of view," he concluded, "are the most recent. On the first of July, the grounds staff found that someone had hung a skull and crossbones from the pin on the Old Course eighteenth. Luckily the groundskeeper arrived early and removed it before any press photos were taken."

"That suggests a juvenile imagination."

"Possibly. That was our immediate thought. We've had to re-evaluate that notion as of this morning."

26

Irving, the last of the trio, nodded and prepared to continue the presentation. He was a fat, handsome man with very white hair and very blue eyes. "There was an explosion this morning," he announced.

Sutherland and I were both surprised.

"A device went off in one of the members' lockers."

"What sort of device?"

"That is something we must yet determine. It was a small explosive about the size of a medium firecracker, and it blew up a cream tart."

"A cream tart?" Sutherland asked incredulously.

"Made quite a mess," Irving replied imperturbably. "You can see, Miss Peters, there is a peculiar mind at work here."

"I do, indeed. The aim seems to be to make the R and A feel nervous and look ridiculous."

"Well put," Greene said. "We are being given a message of some sort. The question is its precise import."

"What was done with the firecracker or whatever it was?"

"The mess," Irving answered, "was cleared away. I have the remains of the explosive device in my pocket." He produced a small box containing paper, metal fragments, and a few wires flecked with whipped cream.

"Was it on a time fuse?"

"I would think so."

"This wouldn't have done anyone any harm, would it?" I asked.

"Not likely."

"Have you called the police?"

"That is one of the things this meeting must decide," Greene replied. "We would rather not attract publicity with this particular event."

"Undesirable, I agree. But it might be useful to know what this device is, where it came from, and who would be likely to acquire one. Is there no one you could consult?"

"There might be a chap at Leuchars," Sutherland said.

"They have different people in and out all summer—liaison from the various services for the annual Battle of Britain Day."

"It would need to be an explosives expert. At home, I'd know just whom to call, but—"

This defect in my expertise did not seem to phase the committee. "If you would set it up, James, Miss Peters could consult with the proper chap. Keep us out of direct contact, don't you know?" Greene said, endangering his coiffeur with another flick of his cigarette. They all nodded at this and waited expectantly.

"We may be able to find out the timing on the fuse; we may not. If we can, you'll have an idea when the device was planted. In any case," I continued, "I would suggest hiring a night watchman for the clubhouse and checking the various entrances to learn how this person got in."

"A sensible plan," Irving said, "but the protection of the clubhouse is not our first concern. Our first worry is the course. The real solution is to find out who is playing practical jokes of such an elaborate nature."

"When Mr. Sutherland first broached the subject, he indicated you had your eye on an American," I said.

"In the sense that we know a person with a motive, yes," Greene explained. "Unfortunately for easy solutions, it isn't likely he'd have opportunities for this sort of mischief."

"Do you care to tell me his name?"

The committee members exchanged glances before Greene spoke. "His name is Wilson Daintly. He inherited an interest in a building corporation here, and it was his scheme for the chalets that was recently defeated."

"I see. And is he the owner of the land in question?"

"Part owner. The other interests in the group may, frankly, be discounted. Daintly is the main holder and, from our dealings with him, a most aggressive young man."

"Successful, would you say?"

28

"Seemed to be. He had no problem with raising capital, certainly."

"He would have had to file numerous papers in connection with his business and the abortive development project?"

"Most certainly."

"If you can get me a little more information on him from those, I will contact my office in Washington and see what they can find out about him for you. It seems to me, though, that a successful young businessman does not play schoolboy tricks when a deal is blocked. Granted that there is a kind of method in this"—I traced the line of damage marked on the diagram of the courses—"you might do better to ignore the publicity, turn the matter over to the police, and let them check people with a history of petty vandalism. In the meantime, hire a few extra people to watch the course at night."

This did not meet with favor. "We don't want publicity," Sutherland declared, "and you will see the problem with a too great concern for protecting the course from the public. This is the town's course; it belongs to the people of St. Andrews. There has never been any question before of its being damaged."

The others concurred. "And you must understand," Irving elaborated, "that from now on till the end of the Open, our local police will have their hands full with traffic and visitors. Besides, this doesn't point to your ordinary youthful offender, does it?"

He had me there. "No, I must agree this looks like the work of an adult."

"It's vital that we find him," Frazer said. "The fact that he has caused minor damage at will—even inside the clubhouse —suggests that he could easily accomplish something serious, and I'm certain that's what we're supposed to understand."

"Well, if you don't want to begin looking for residents with destructive tendencies, then you'll have to begin with the explo-

29

sive and with the man with a motive. In all honesty, though, I'm not sure that will give satisfactory results."

"But it is what we want," Greene said flatly. "I believe the committee will agree that you should look into this for us." He glanced around the table and the other members gave their assent.

"As far as it goes, it's easily enough done," I said. "I'll be happy to see what the office can turn up on Daintly."

"And inspect the doors and windows in this building," Irving added.

"That, too, if you don't think I'd attract attention checking them."

"The eccentricities of visiting Americans are well known," Frazer said drily.

"All right, if Mr. Irving will take me around."

"And I will ask if there is anyone knowledgeable about explosives at Leuchars at the moment," Sutherland said. "See me before you leave, Miss Peters."

"Right." I looked at the chart of the courses, marked by Frazer's neatly penciled crosses. "Very odd."

"I think we're on the right track," Greene said briskly. "Walter will fill you in on the security plans for the Open. Perhaps you'll have some advice."

"I'll do my best."

"Fine. I've a feeling we'll soon have this cleared up."

I smiled. Customers like to be reassured. The right sort of smile goes a long way in a business where intangibles are often as important as hardware, and I didn't see any reason to alarm the R and A committee. They were paying to have someone else do their worrying, and that was smart. Trivial or not, there was something very peculiar about the joker on their fairways.

4

THE CUSTODIAN HAD UNLOCKED the doors of the R and
A at 6:00 A.M. in anticipation of the morning practice rounds.
None of the entrances had been forced, and in opening the
doors, he had obliterated any sign that a lock had been picked.
The windows on the lower floors were routinely shut and
latched at night, and the custodian, a thin, sharp-faced chap
named Fred, was confident that everything had been properly
secured. He worried that point like a terrier with a pet slipper,
until Irving conceded defeat with a shake of his handsome
white head and led me back upstairs.

"Any chance of an inside job?"

"Ach, I can't imagine it. Our staff's been with us for years.
Same with the caddies. I wouldn't even suggest that without
absolute proof."

I nodded, and we proceeded in silence, Irving needing all his
breath to raise his bulky frame to the upper story. "A weird
sense of humor," he added as we reached the landing. "Something far off there."

"That's my feeling."

"Hmmmh. Not staff. Not golfer, either, I'd say." The last

was very positive. Members and guests were clearly to be out of bounds.

"We'd better check the windows on this floor. Fred said they aren't usually locked."

"You'll be thinking it's a climber, eh?"

"Climber?"

"Favorite university sport, that. When they built the new gym, they finally put up a practice wall to keep the lads off the buildings and the ruins." As he opened the first room, he gave a reminiscent chuckle. "Used to climb myself as a boy. In the old days, we'd do the cliffs after the birds' eggs. Many's the scrape I got right over there." He pointed toward the line of rough brown rock rising from the beach to the turf and the road above.

With this local pastime in mind, I examined the windows and their catches with unusual care, but all was in order until we approached what appeared to be a closet door at the far end of the hall.

"A wee storage room," Irving explained, taking out his key. I reached over and turned the knob.

"Usually unlocked?"

"Not that I know of. I shall have to check with Fred."

"We can leave that for now." The room held various bits and pieces of furniture, extra pins and flags and several file cabinets. There was a single window, open a crack. I threw up the sash. The broad granite ledge was clean, but running my hand along the outer edge, I found a clod of grass and mud. "Here we go."

Irving wrapped our discovery in a handkerchief and frowned. "Odd this was still on his feet if he scaled the wall."

Below, the bleachers for the crowds at the eighteenth were almost finished. Workmen swarmed over spidery frames of steel and aluminum, affixing molded plastic seats. Some ladders lay on the ground, and others were stacked against the side of the building. I nodded toward them. "I don't suppose he had to bother."

"Ach, of course not. It's no human fly we're after anyway."

"That's some consolation."

"These windows will all need to be kept locked from now on," Irving said briskly. "And the ladders put away at night. I'll tell the crew." Our discovery seemed to cheer him, for he added, "One mystery solved. Come away and have a drink, Miss Peters. I'll explain our security arrangements for the Open."

"Just as a matter of interest," I said. "I'm sure you've had much more experience with athletic events than I've had."

"Thirty years, now, I've been working with the golf tournaments here." He wheezed slightly as we started down the wide stone steps. "Never had a cream tart explode on me before, though."

"I don't like that," I admitted.

"I'm glad we agree. I would rather have called in the police, to tell you the truth—even at the risk of looking foolish."

He had taken a different tack at the meeting, but I just nodded; customers are entitled to change their minds.

"I lost a nephew two years ago to explosives. He was with the Seaforth Highlanders in Belfast."

"Oh, I'm sorry."

"Perhaps it's made me overreact to this little firecracker thing, but—"

"Here's Mr. Sutherland. Maybe we can learn something about the device. Depending on what it is—"

"Getting a committee to change its mind," Irving said with a touch of asperity, "is harder than getting it to make up its mind in the first place. Any luck, James?" he called down to Sutherland, who was watching our stately progress with barely suppressed irritation.

"Yes, but we'll have to leave at once. They've a chap on his way to some big military affair in London. Black Watch explosives expert. He can take the later train, but he'll be cutting it rather close."

"Away you go, then, Miss Peters. Fred and I will take this under advisement," Irving said, and put the handkerchief with our evidence into his vest pocket.

The Jaguar was waiting close to the building, and Sutherland pulled it sharply around the scaffolding into a narrow street cluttered with bikes, beer trucks, and pedestrians. "So you found where he got in," he remarked.

"Second floor window."

"That should keep Walter busy." Sutherland's tone was patronizing.

"He seems pretty well organized."

"Good old duffer, but he hasn't changed a thing in thirty years. Thinks the tournament's no different than it was just after the war."

"He apparently grew up here."

"Raised in the clubhouse. He's a fixture," Sutherland replied, as he let the powerful engine out a little. We shot along the smooth wide curves of the road that ran across the meadows north of town. Beyond the pastures, the shining mudflats of the estuary were speckled white and brown with sea birds and waders. The opposite shore held the squat ugly hangars of the RAF base.

"This is my first Open in St. Andrews," Sutherland remarked. "I must confess I find some of the proceedings—old fashioned."

So that was it. New boy versus the old firm. I had the feeling that I was delicately being enlisted in some tiresome organizational squabble. "I suppose every course is different," I replied noncommittally.

"Left to himself, I think Irving would have called in the police," Sutherland continued. "I think we've brought him round—"

"I must say this firecracker business makes me a bit uneasy."

"Well, it's important not to panic over trifles, isn't it? That's why we called you in." He gave me a sharp look and a smile

34

without warmth. "The sooner this is cleared up the better."

The Leuchars RAF base is set smack in the village, the hangars and runways bordering a cow pasture across from the railway station. The road wound through the base, passing neat lawns edged with tangles of barbed wire, and Sutherland slowed the Jaguar to avoid the airmen and officers wheeling around on ugly black bicycles. "Stationed here for a while," he remarked as he pulled into one of the lanes. "I still know quite a few of the people." A sentry directed us to a row of nondescript white buildings with wire across their windows. When we got out of the car, Sutherland handed me the box with the wires and fragments. "Nothing about where it came from, of course."

"Don't worry."

"The danger of publicity has almost escaped some of my colleagues." I could see that this was going to be a chronic source of irritation.

"I understand."

"Quite." He compressed his thin lips and abruptly led the way to a small bare office. On his home turf, Sutherland seemed more aggressive and high-strung than at our previous meeting in Washington, a consequence, I assumed, of the rigors of Scottish social climbing. Inside, a good-looking major with a smooth manner and dreamy speculative eyes was waiting for us. I explained how kind James had been to drive me over and feigned distress about an explosion in one of my trash bins. The major sympathized and touched his intercom. Our expert appeared.

Sergeant Graham was short and broad-shouldered, with an almost immobile face. Dressed in khakis with a camouflage shirt and a soft cap bearing a tuft of brilliant red feathers, he looked tough but personable. He was currently on recruiting duty, giving demonstrations to civilian audiences; and when I opened the small cardboard box, he seemed disappointed that his expertise was being so inadequately challenged. He laid the pieces out on a paper on the major's desk and made a soft

35

clucking sound. He sniffed the fuse. "Wid this be cream?" His burr was soft but pervasive.

"Yes. It was thrown into the trash. Blew the lid off."

"Wasna thrown in. See this? This is a time fuse."

I looked as blank as possible.

"How long would it have been there?" Sutherland asked.

"Hard to tell without seeing the exact setup," the sergeant replied cautiously.

"Put in sometime during the night?" I asked.

"Aye. If it had gone off early this morning. Much as six hours if it was rigged right. Seems like a long time for a kid's prank. If that's what it was." The sergeant's face was expressionless, but his eyes were intelligent.

"Well, what else," I asked, "with a firecracker?"

"I'll tell you, lass, this is no firecracker."

Sutherland and I exchanged glances.

"This is a type of detonator. And ye didna need me to tell you that. Any lad on the base would have recognized it."

"This is a military device?"

"Aye. What they couldna have told you is where it came from. This is U.S. Army equipment."

"Not used anywhere else?"

"Not officially. In certain quarters they're quite popular," Graham said drily. "With plastique, this would blow up a lot more than a bin lid."

"How easy are they to come by?"

The sergeant shrugged. "Depends who you know, right? Lot of U.S. military in and out. They sometimes keep odd souvenirs. And, as I've already said, this type of thing has its uses." He looked inquiringly at the major as he spoke, and when he was finished, the officer said, "All right, thank you, sergeant. Graham here has to get to London."

Sutherland and I apologized for delaying him, thanked both men, and to evade the major's curiosity, departed immediately.

"Still suspect Daintly?" I asked when we were outside.

36

"An American explosive just the same." He sounded a trifle defensive.

"A warning for sure."

Sutherland didn't respond. I thought it unfortunate that the police hadn't been called while there might have been finger-prints available and other, now lost, clues undisturbed. If Suth-erland thought the same, he didn't let on. All he said was, "Sir Malcolm will have some information for you. I just hope your staff gets cracking on it."

Half an hour later, I sat on my bed, reading out information from a sheet of lined paper and hoping the same thing. On the other side of the Atlantic, Harriet interrupted her lasagna din-ner to scribble down the vital statistics of Wilson Daintly. "Thirty years old. That's from a newspaper report, may not be accurate. Gives two residences, Houston, Texas, and Simsbury, Connecticut. Check those, will you? Find out if he went to school near one or the other. His business is described as real estate and development, so you can begin with the directories."

"I'll start with the Babb and Dordeck first thing tomorrow," she said with remarkable enthusiasm. Harriet is a genius. She is fat, fiftyish, tedious about her children, and myopic almost to the point of blindness, but she is still a genius; she can make her way through the paper mills like no one else I've ever known. "Anything else?"

"Find out if he was in the military. And if there's any crimi-nal record. I'd really like to get a handle on his character. That's the main thing." At the moment, it was the only thing.

"And where his money comes from?"

"Sure. All I know is that he inherited an interest two years ago in a Scottish construction firm, Tayside Homes. What? T–A–Y. He's been here on and off for weeks at a time, appar-ently staying in a rented place outside of Dundee. It would be nice to know if he's been back to the States in the last month or so. The right dates would eliminate him."

"I'll get right to it."

"Good. Thanks, Harriet. Call me as soon as you learn anything."

I put down the phone and tapped impatiently on the table. A few days at best—and for what? The Daintly angle had seemed far-fetched from the first, and our interview with the explosives expert had convinced me that we were on the wrong track. The committee had been insistent, though, and that raised some new questions. Was it just a case of having it in for Daintly, who seemed to have impressed the R and A in the worst possible manner, or was this whole business just a wrong-headed refusal to come to grips with the situation? Either way, I could see nothing in it for me but trouble. Then there was the question of the course. Meeting Daintly would have to wait until I had some clue to his business; the course could be tackled immediately. I decided the best idea would be to spend some time around the fairways at night. In preparation for that, I put on a pair of slacks and walking shoes and headed for the links, figuring I should reconnoiter the layout in daylight.

5

RAFTS OF HIGH, COMPLEX CLOUDS scudded from the
western horizon to create vistas of light and vapor, like the
background of a baroque painting. All that was needed was a
wigged prince on a beribboned charger, but only crows and
wood pigeons rose over the flat green sweep of the potato fields.
I had walked out along the shore road, risked nameless perils
to cross the fairways of all four courses, and emerged on a track
left by the old roadbed of the rail line. This, as far as I could
determine, bordered the middle holes of the Eden course, a
bunkered stretch of greensward that ended at the grassy earth
dyke on the edge of the estuary. I waded through brambles and
thistles to the top. The tide was in, the mudflats sunk beneath
a shallow lake reflecting the clouds. Seals lay on a splinter of
sand like dirty sacks, and as I made my way back to the flints
and cinders of the path, two huge swans flew overhead with
thin, eerie whistles. I followed them for a moment through
Harry's binoculars, then dutifully turned the glass back to the
fairways. Without trees, they were open to observation, but
there were too many points of access and pretty good cover in

the clumps of gorse and in the dunes along the estuary and the shore. I would speak to Irving, I decided, and knowing the layout, would myself take a turn about the course that night.

Halfway back to town, a gated lane led me to the highway and on to the Madras playing fields, which were covered with blue-and-white striped exhibition tents and crisscrossed by studded metal walkways. Bleachers were rising on the Eden rough behind, while farther over, close by the R and A, the press tents were already open for business. On the opposite side of the road lay the newer campus of the university, a number of modern laboratories and a large residence hall that sprawled down the steep slope like a concrete spider. There was a fenced-off stretch of ground at the foot of the hill and, fluttering on the wire, a black wool garment. I crossed the highway and looked for Wulf. He was farther down the lawn, dressed in his leggings and a coarse tunic, practicing with a javelin.

I stopped at the fence to watch. Beside his cloak was a large cudgel, appropriate, no doubt, for his imaginary duties guarding swine, and a leather pouch, open to reveal the incongruous presence of Dr. Thorston's grade book and a paperback anthology of Scots poetry. At the end of the field, Wulf plucked the javelin from where it was stuck in the turf and, holding it parallel to the ground, began his run, stopped, whipped back his arm, and sent the blue-and-silver shaft hurtling forward. A modern javelin seemed a bit of a cheat, but Wulf was certainly adept, and judging from the length of the throw, I realized that a good deal of the professor's weight was muscle. The weapon landed neatly in the earth about twenty yards from me, and he came trotting up to retrieve it.

"Nice throw," I said.

The swineherd turned a pair of expressionless eyes in my direction and said nothing. The professor wore glasses, but his "alternate persona" had blank, naked eyes, small and black, which looked me up and down in a frankly unsettling manner.

"I met you at the Laundromat," I said. Had Thorston not

explained his alter ego, I would never have believed they were the same person. While the professor was full of bluster and bursting with his own theories, Wulf seemed withdrawn and intensely peculiar.

"Whit?" he asked.

"In town. I've seen you in town." His pretense of not understanding modern English was a trifle much.

The reply was all but unintelligible, his dialect full of words I had never heard, and his pronunciation beyond comprehension. He had indeed been in the "toon." That was the extent of it. I thought it advisable to nod politely. The professor was obviously set to maintain the joke, and as Wulf, Thorston seemed not only a larger man, but one who exuded a very definite air of hostility. I realized that I was poorly acquainted with the manners of fourteenth-century pig tenders. "Just practicing?" I asked with a glance toward the javelin.

"Aye. For the wars."

"Ah." I didn't know which wars but doubted I would understand an explanation. I nodded in what I intended as a conciliatory manner and stepped back a trifle from the wire, as Wulf picked up the javelin and hurled it nearly the length of the field. Then I walked down along the road to see the university buildings before starting back toward town. As luck would have it, Wulf had returned to his satchel as I passed, and I stopped to see if he would have anything more to say. This time, he motioned me nearer and slipped under the wire. I waited, wondering what bit of small talk we could exchange about pigs, when he lifted his cudgel, a very stout hunk of oak. A ripple of a smile tightened his phlegmatic expression, and without a word, he swung the heavy shaft at my head, missing my face by the merest fraction of an inch. I flinched back in alarm, and Wulf leaped onto the roadway, catching me against the fence. Then he began rotating the cudgel in a complex and rapid pattern, making quick little shifts and feints, bringing the weapon teasingly close to my head. I backed hastily against the fence, well aware that with the slightest advance, he could lift my head off. He smiled faintly now and again, but otherwise his face revealed nothing except an intense concentration on the task at hand. Yet, when I started to move sideways, he shifted his feet rapidly to block my escape; no doubt about it, Dr. Melvin Thorston's experiment in creative linguistics was trying to frighten me. I glanced up and down the road, but the campus was virtually deserted, except for the tennis courts, and if Wulf were indeed a fixture, no one would take any notice. Of course, nothing serious could happen, but as the shaft swung closer and closer, it grew harder to keep that rational assessment in mind. I sensed I had only two choices, terrified tears or bland persistence. The latter seemed slightly less humiliating, and I bit my lip, stepped forward a fraction and fixed my eyes on Wulf's. He did not move this time, but spun the weapon faster and faster, occasionally breaking its rhythm for sudden feints as if to ward off a sword or a stick. Behind this whirling barrier, his small, fathomless eyes remained still, alien, and unrevealing, watching me with absorption, yet with complete human indifference. Then a horn honked, as a blue minibus pulled out of the parking lot below the residence hall. The cudgel stopped in midrevolution, and Wulf turned and waved.

"Tomorrow night?" the driver inquired.

"At eight," Professor Thorston answered.

"The Arts Building?"

"That's right. On North Street."

"We'll be there," the driver replied, and tooting his horn again, drove away.

I took a deep breath and stepped away from the wire and onto the roadway. Wulf picked up his leather sack, slung it over his shoulder, and collected the javelin as though nothing had happened. Although he did not seem the slightest bit embarrassed or awkward, he did not even glance in my direction. The performance was over; it was time to exit. His weapons in hand, he crossed the road and set off toward the university buildings,

42

and I was disinclined to stop him. Conversation with Wulf had not proved fruitful, and our little encounter had given me the eerie conviction that when Wulf was in residence, Dr. Thorston was somewhere else, altogether.

On the way back to town, I wondered about that and also whether Wulf often showed his more primitive side. "Who's the fellow with the sandals and the black cape?" I asked the desk clerk at our hotel.

"Ach, a harmless laddie. One of those American professors over-keen on things Scottish." The deskman pursed his mouth and crinkled his nose until he acquired a striking resemblance to the locality's squat, wiry terriers.

"I saw him today with a javelin, and I couldn't help wondering—"

The desk clerk dismissed this concern. "Nay thing to worry about. A very brilliant man, I'm told, but peculiar in his ways. He wanted to carry a spear, wouldn't you know, but the police couldn't allow it. Perfectly harmless," he added, torn between his desire to be reassuring and an understandable civic embarrassment, "shows the bairns all his gear."

The chambermaid had a similar response. "Na need to worry aboot him, missus. He's always got a stick or something. Going to Bannockburn, I shouldn't wonder," she said with a laugh. "Aye, but it's a shame to make fun of him. He's no worse than some ye see around in their kilts and them no more Scottish than I'm Chinese. They say he gives a grand lecture, though. My sister's heard him. He knows all the old speech. She said he sounded just like the old fish wives—and him a Yank, too! It just shows you what education can do for a man," she concluded, perfectly straightfaced.

"Lectures? You mean his classes?"

"Aye, but he gives lectures for the public, too. You should check with the information center. The university gives programs over the holiday."

So the fellow who'd nearly brained me was a harmless eccentric who liked kids; either the locals had exceedingly lax standards of behavior (which from the quiet and good order of the town seemed unlikely) or something about me had triggered a nasty streak in Wulf. It would be interesting to find out a little more about Dr. Thorston, and interesting, too, to see how he'd explain that little display by his "alternate persona."

But first, I had to spend some time consulting with Irving, who, although slow and ponderous, was a decent, genuine sort of person. Then between 3:00 and 6:00 A.M., I put in a damp, frozen stretch wandering the roads along the golf courses. This dawn watch revealed absolutely nothing. I went back to bed, woke at nine almost as chilled as when I'd lain down, and got up to fortify myself with breakfast.

Harry was lingering over his coffee downstairs. "No luck?" he asked.

"Nothing."

"Scared off, maybe?"

"I don't think that's likely. What time is it in D.C. now?"

He checked his watch. "Two-thirty."

"Probably nothing till tomorrow—if then."

"I'm meeting Nicklaus this morning. Care to come?"

"I'll be over in the afternoon, how's that?"

He was puzzled.

"Scottish Studies," I said. "I think they'd bear looking into."

I began at the information center: Thorston's lecture had already been given. Then to the university where in one of the high stone buildings, I located the Scottish Studies office. The program was filled and half over, but my disappointment at missing Professor Thorston's appearance brought a concession. "Oh, if you've met him, I don't suppose he'd mind. Everyone does enjoy his lectures," the registrar admitted. "A theatrical sort. What I'd call a really good classroom presence."

"Where do they meet?"

"Lower College Hall. Just behind us, through the arch and

across the quad." She looked at her watch. "If you're interested in today's talk, it begins at eleven-fifteen."

That was ideal. The university library was half a block away and after a few moments' consultation with the research desk, I was seated at a bleached wood table with a directory of American educators. The volume revealed that Melvin G. Thorston, Ph.D., taught at Duke, where he was an associate professor of languages and linguistics. Born in 1949, he had earned his B.A. in languages at Michaelmas College, his M.A. and Ph.D. from the University of Chicago. He had served in the army 1969–70, between college and graduate school. Then came assorted prizes and honors, including a Woodrow Wilson Fellowship, and publications in abstruse journals: "Troilus and Cressida—by Chaucer, Henrysoun, and Shakespeare," "Verb Forms in Lowland Scots," and "Palatinate Dialects," and an oddly titled book, *The Hidden Potentials of Linguistic Transformation.* All very impressive and legitimate. And that set me wondering why a research-minded professor would be spending time at an ancient, honorable, and picturesque institution catering basically to undergraduates. Or why he would give up the salary due a prof at Duke for the presumably slender stipend of the Gruen Foundation and a summer job in "Scottish Studies." That was intriguing, as was the fact that Thorston had evidently passed up an educational deferment to enter the army. Clearly he was a character of some complexity, and when I entered the large comfortable hall that served as his classroom, I was curious to see what his public personality would be like. He was arranging his papers when I approached the desk to ask if I might sit in on his lecture.

"Peters? Oh yes. From the Laundromat." His black-rimmed glasses almost, but not quite, domesticated Wulf's hard stare. "You're not pursuing me, are you? I mean in the strictly professional sense." With this he gave a loud, hectoring laugh.

I assured him I had been drawn only by his reputation as a lecturer.

"Oh, you're very welcome," he said, instantly genial. "You've come on a good day, in fact," he added as I took a seat. "We're doing border ballads. These were written on both sides of the Tweed, so this is reconciliation day for those of you who are English." Thorston paused with expert timing, and the class responded with the mild titter that passes for laughter in Academe. "We've even enlisted a visiting American to help out my side," he continued with a gracious nod to me, "because I've brought in some tapes of American ballads. These are mostly from Appalachia, the southern mountain region so heavily settled by Scots, and they'll illustrate the sea changes the stories have undergone. In terms of content, the alterations are easily explainable, but these mimeographed sheets will alert you to the linguistic changes." Thorston passed out handfuls of his papers, before beginning a learned, but entertaining, examination of several concise and powerful little narratives. He had a beautiful reading voice, rich and vibrant, a complete mastery of both Scots and American southern mountain speech, and a dramatic sense that emphasized the weird poetry of the tales. The personal quirks that made the professor seem eccentric in normal social contacts and the emotional forces that powered Wulf came into harmonious balance in the classroom. Even his rather unattractive physical appearance was transformed by its proper setting. His heavy torso was the resonating chamber for that remarkable voice, and his otherwise ponderous gestures became dramatic. There was no doubt that he was a performer and teacher of the greatest gifts, and I began to understand how the university could overlook Wulf for the sake of this unusual talent, or conversely, how they could attribute Wulf's appearance to Thorston's theatrical abilities alone.

I lingered after the rest of the class to congratulate him.

"Thank you. Kind of you to say so, but the material's wonderful. These"—tapping his volume of border ballads—"these, Miss Peters, are brutality in suspension with poetry. Nothing like them for hundreds of years. Some think the violent crime

46

novel approaches them, but never, never for brevity and precision. Brevity is the soul of violence, as well as wit." He paused here in his rather oratorical style and added quietly, "The act is short, the consequences endless. Our present narratives conceal that fact." He went on, resuming his booming delivery, "Our modern preference for long stories is the enemy of poetry and recollection. Who would begin to memorize *Gravity's Rainbow?*"

"You certainly make the old ballads remarkable."

"I'm so glad you enjoyed them," he replied formally.

As we walked out, I mentioned I had seen Wulf.

"Oh?" Thorston's black eyes swam behind his thick lenses and registered nothing.

"He seems to have a military bent."

The professor nodded rapidly. "Yes, essential for his time. Scots armies were full of Wulfs. The army was comprised of spearmen, basically, with only a sprinkling of archers and light armed cavalry. Scotland was an isolated and backward nation in those days. The Scots were already far behind in military technology in Wulf's period, and of course, the resources of the country were slender. Both cost them heavily and repeatedly, but they went surprisingly far with what they had. From a military standpoint—"

I interrupted what threatened to develop into a lecture on military techniques. "I wondered about Wulf, Professor Thorston."

"Wondered? Wondered what?" he asked in his sharp, rather hectoring style.

"Wondered if he was reliable. Dangerous."

"Dangerous? What nonsense. How could he be dangerous? He's a creation, Miss Peters." Thorston sounded very confident, but perhaps he was not as sure as he seemed, for he added, "Why do you ask?" and waited with what seemed to be a genuine curiosity. This, at least, did not strike me as playacting. I had the distinct and unpleasant conviction that so far as memory and knowledge went, Thorston and his creature, Wulf, were very nearly two different people.

"Well, he's armed, isn't he? And he's not particularly friendly. I had the feeling he was threatening me with that big stick he carries."

For the first time, Thorston seemed taken aback and off guard. "Just his manner," he said rapidly. "The pressures of the time. One wonders how they kept sane." He began to enumerate the uncertainties of Wulf's existence, pillage, invasion, famine, disease, unrest. "How different their viewpoint must have been. Their tolerance for violence and misery. You have to ask how they gave any meaning to life. How they coped with the violence, with the destruction." He elaborated on this theme for several minutes, and I was only too well aware of the currents running beneath the surface of his conversation. My remarks about Wulf seemed to have stirred a troubled place in Professor Thorston. I wondered what was the matter with him and whether, considering his talk about the devastations of war, he had served in Vietnam.

He broke off abruptly as we left the quad. "I live just down here."

I repeated my pleasure at his talk.

"So glad," he replied as he unchained his bicycle and dumped his books into its capacious basket, but there was another flash of suspicion. "You've come a long way just to hear a talk on mountain ballads, haven't you?"

"Yes," I said, "odd how you meet people."

"Next time you meet Wulf—" he began.

"Yes?"

"Never mind," he replied shortly, and throwing his leg over the bar, he pedaled off toward the cathedral. I watched until he turned down the narrow street and disappeared behind the wall of the graveyard. It would be easy enough to find where he lived, but I shrugged off this notion and returned to the hotel. It would be better to pay attention to the investigation at hand

48

than to potter off after Thorston, no matter how fascinating his personality.

*   *   *

That evening, Harriet called from Washington, but the connection was poor, and she seemed to be burbling as she spoke, like the Jabberwocky. "Nothing untoward," she said as she read me data about Daintly's education, his background, his excellent credit, his list of clubs and charities.

"Where'd he make his money?"

"Houston. A construction firm."

"Inherited?"

"No. He started with a bar near the docks and parlayed that into a food service for some of the oil rigs. That money went into development and real estate."

"I see. Why did he pick Houston?"

"Don't know. He showed up there two years after college."

"What?"

"Two years after college, he showed up in Houston. You were right, by the way: He went to school in Connecticut. Small male liberal arts college. Michaelmas in Hartford."

She gave me the dates. For a small institution, Michaelmas seemed to have had some interesting folks in its class of 'sixty-eight. "Any idea what he did after school?"

"Not yet. Probably further study. He wasn't in the service."

"See if you can find out."

"Right. Let me see what else—"

Daintly had been married—and divorced. His ex-wife had custody of a daughter, three. He was an enthusiastic sailor. He had stayed in his Connecticut house in June.

I interrupted. "Were you able to get the dates?"

"I talked to the housekeeper. He arrived the fourteenth and left on the seventh of July."

"She's sure about that?"

"She keeps a log because she's paid on an hourly basis."

49

"That's what I needed." Even if he were somehow involved, Daintly certainly wasn't physically responsible for the course damage, something I could almost have told the committee right from the start.

Harriet had a few other items, trivial bits and pieces adding up to a picture of a hustling businessman not very different from thousands more. "That's it, I think," she concluded.

"Thanks, Harriet. Good job," I said. I was about to hang up, when she asked me about some office problem. When we had it straightened out, I remembered something else. "Ever hear of the Gruen Foundation?" I asked.

"Oh, sorry, I meant to mention that. Yes, it's right here. Daintly's one of the trustees. May be his money, for all I know. It's a new outfit. A tax dodge, I'd—"

"Trustee? For how long, Harriet?"

"Two years. I'd never heard of the Gruen."

"Find out for me, O.K.? When it was founded, whose money, what they award grants for."

"All right."

"And one thing more." If I was going this far, I might as well go the whole way. "I want the military record of Melvin G. Thorston. He's a Duke professor of languages and he was in the army in 1969 and 70."

"Are we interested in him, too?"

"We're becoming more so. See if you can find anyone at Duke who'll talk about him."

"Will do."

We said good-by, and when I put down the receiver, I picked up the picture of Daintly I'd gotten from the local paper. He was quite a good-looking man, well put together, with wavy hair, round face, touch of weight under the chin and around the beltline. Full of confidence, too, if that white-toothed grin were any indication. He was shaking hands with a woman from some local charitable organization who looked as if she had just landed a big contributor. Probably she had. That was the period just before the defeat of the land-development scheme when Daintly was cultivating the townsfolk. I glanced over the story again. Daintly was quoted as having a deep interest in St. Andrews and Fife and great confidence in development possibilities for the whole east coast. His experience with the oil industry in Texas was cited, and on that basis, he predicted North Sea Oil prosperity all the way from the Shetlands to the border. I wondered if that booming Texas style was what had turned off the canny Fifers. And why Daintly had put an obviously considerable effort into what sounded like a fairly small-time project. The Michaelmas alumni were nothing if not surprising, and I propped the photo up against the telephone and studied it while I thought about approaching Wilson Daintly. Just when I figured he was quite out of the picture, he had suddenly moved back into contention.

6

"It seems odd to me," I said. "Too much of a coincidence."

"Uh-huh." Harry responded without real interest and continued to float plumes of Prussian blue and burnt umber across a damp sheet of watercolor paper. The intense blues and the deep, blackish browns coalesced to form mounting, stormy clouds like those in the darkening skies above the town. When the wash dried, he would pick out the forms with some lighter blues and faint yellows. The brilliant green of the course would appear in heavier paint below; then the various golfers would be pasted up against the background, their clean silhouettes like the sharp lines of Harry's usual prints. In the magazine, the effect ought to be very handsome. Several pictures in the same style were already on their way to New York, and Harry was working ahead on backgrounds and golfers in preparation for the events of the tournament.

"It's a small school," I continued. "And in the same class, they must have known each other." From where I lay sprawled on the bed I could see the deep gray-blue evening sky, and the sun touched chimney pots and roof slates. The round red dial on the church steeple read 8:45.

"Stranger things have happened," Harry said. He was adding light touches of lavender and pink and, occasionally, thin washy lines of burnt sienna, which reddened the line of buildings in his painting until they glowed like the evening stones outside. The management of the hotel had found him a plain table and a straight chair. A large drawing board propped up on two books served him as an easel.

"Oh, every day," I agreed. "But here we have someone with a grudge against the course, against the R and A. And plenty of money. Then who should show up but a penniless old college classmate with a crazy alter ego? The Gruen Foundation clinched it. If that's not a payoff—"

"I thought you said Thorston had been on this fellowship for a while?"

"That's what *he* said."

Harry shrugged and applied himself diligently to working in a foreground of rough and sand.

"I wish I was home," I said in exasperation. "This doing things over long distance—"

"Last time I take you on a honeymoon!"

"You *know* what I mean." Nonetheless, I got up and kissed him. "Almost done with those?"

"I have to put in the figures. The courier expects a couple tomorrow," he said apologetically.

"That wash has to dry."

"So it does," he said, reaching up to embrace me, and the evening proceeded in a very satisfactory manner until the phone rang.

"Damn," said Harry, "that'll be the idiot from the magazine. Yes? Who?" He raised his eyebrows in exasperation and covered the mouthpiece with his hand. "It's your rich fisherman."

"What does he want?"

"His hand held." Harry set down the receiver and returned to his paints.

"Hello?"

"Anna?"

"Speaking."

"James Sutherland, here. We've had a bit of a disaster. I think you'd better stop by the clubhouse."

"Another—"

"No, nothing like that. We'll explain when you arrive. Say a quarter of an hour?"

"Nothing that can wait till the morning?"

"We'll meet in the members' room. Come to the side door; Fred will be expecting you."

"All right," I said, and hung up. "Damn."

"The wash is dry now, anyway," Harry said.

"Great. Hand me my blazer, would you?"

"Another bit of slapstick?"

"Doesn't sound like it this time. 'Disaster,' he termed it." I put on my shoes, ran a comb through my hair, and kissed Harry good-by. "I may be late."

He began stretching another sheet of paper. "Remind them you're on overtime," he called.

* * *

The mood at the R and A was distinctly less jocular. "They're all here," Fred remarked as he opened the door for me. "A detective inspector, too. From Cupar. They'll have the detective superintendent from Dysart next thing you know."

"Who called the police?"

"Sir Malcolm, himself."

Then it was serious.

Fred read my expression. "They're in a fair dither," he remarked, enjoying the excitement, but too experienced for real anxiety. He'd "seen all the great ones," and from a previous conversation with him, I gathered that Nicklaus's driving the green on the eighteenth had placed all subsequent events in manageable perspective. He opened a door and stood aside.

"Thanks, Fred."

54

An immense bay window occupied the front of the long paneled room, flooding it with the golden haze that hovered beyond the course and the wood. Large portraits of golfers in antiquated dress shared the walls with a portrait of the building and a likeness of the Queen, caped and ribboned. The committee were gathered about a fireplace directly beneath this royal effigy, and a red-faced police officer was taking notes, while his superior questioned Sir Malcolm Greene. On the edge of the group stood a big, handsome man in full PGA plumage. He wore red-and-gray plaid trousers, a gray shirt, and a brilliant red golfing sweater that flattered his fine tan and his sun-bleached hair and matched his temper. I knew who he was, despite the angry distortion of his features. His portrait had been scattered in its various stages all over our hotel room for the past several days. Whatever the disaster was, it had encompassed the tour hotshot, Peter Bryce.

"Ah, Anna. Just in time." Sutherland broke off his conversation with the pro, making a quiet clucking sound as if consoling a nervous horse. "You must speak to Miss Peters," he said. "She's been looking into this whole matter for us."

"The hell she has," Bryce said. He had a low, harsh voice, which, if not modified, was going to cost him residuals. "This whole thing is completely out of hand. One crank note and you people—"

Greene stepped out of the circle to take charge. "We regret this inconvenience, Mr. Bryce," he said firmly, "but as I have tried to explain to you, the 'crank note' is but one in a series of unfortunate incidents. This is Anna Peters, inspector," he said, motioning for me to join the group. "Her office turned up the somewhat suggestive information we've already discussed."

"Gordon Stewart. This is Sergeant Barnes."

"How do you do."

"Miss Peters knows the whole story, inspector. I think she should have a look at the note."

"This arrived at the Royal and Ancient this evening," the

inspector said. He took a plain white envelope from his sergeant and passed it to me. The typed note inside came directly to the point:

> If Peter Bryce competes in the Open, he will be killed.
>
> An interested Friend.

"An old Royal, probably."

"I beg your pardon," Greene said.

"The typeface. It looks as if this was typed on an old Royal Standard. They're a very common American machine."

"The first one we'll check," the inspector said.

"Do you know what time this arrived?"

"It had been slipped under the door," Greene explained, shaking his head. "Fred said it wasn't there when he went out for his tea at six. I arrived just shortly before seven and found it on the floor."

"Someone may have noticed it being delivered."

"Might have," the inspector said, "but with the bucket-and-spade brigade coming back from tea—"

"The whole area is crowded," Greene agreed. "Short of asking people to come forward—"

"That raises other problems," Sutherland said sharply.

"Oh, aye." The inspector sympathized. "With the first round starting—"

"Precisely," said Greene.

"I can't believe you're taking this seriously." Bryce broke in. "Listen, anybody who gets his name in the papers attracts cranks. You know that, huh? Let's just forget it. If it had come to me, I'd have pitched it into the trash. It's going to take a lot more than some nutty two-fingered typist to keep me out of my first British Open."

"We certainly don't want to see you out, Mr. Bryce," Greene said. "Nothing could be further—"

"Why did you say 'two-fingered typist'?" I interrupted.

56

Bryce plucked the note from the inspector's grasp and thrust it toward me. "Anyone can tell," he said. "The letters are all struck the same. No variation in blackness."

He was absolutely right. Such accuracy of observation in an angry man rather surprised me. "Sharp eyes."

Bryce saw my interest. "No sweat," he said, "when you've been around as many sportswriters as I have." He made a series of sharp, staccato sounds and hammered out a story. " 'Peter Bryce astonished the field in the Masters' today with a sixty-seven in the final round—' " He smiled.

"But I don't suppose you think our correspondent's a sports-writer."

"Who the hell knows? Or cares? I've gone over this with you guys. I've told you all I know. If you want to pursue crank notes, that's your business."

He straightened his shoulders and started for the door.

I looked at Greene, who hesitated only an instant before nodding. "Have you mentioned the developer?"

"No. Not at the moment."

"I'll call you later," I said, and with a hasty good-by, followed Bryce out the door. He was well down the road by the eighteenth before I got outside, and if my call had not alerted a pair of young autograph hunters, I don't think he'd have stopped.

"What do you want?" he asked as the children left. "I've gone over everything with those old farts on the committee, and once is enough."

"They've had their problems," I said.

"Damn right. Greens are slow. Too much rain."

"The grass must be in nice shape, though," I said, drawing upon my feeble knowledge of the game to build a little rapport.

"The fairways are okay. Helluva rough, too." He discussed the course for several minutes, which seemed to settle his nerves. By the time we reached the street leading to the Old Course Hotel, he was taking a lighter view of the whole proceeding. "Great way to start your first Open, isn't it?"

"The price of sudden fame. How long have you played on the circuit, anyway?"

"I've played seriously for the last five years. I was a slow starter. But all of a sudden, my game's come together. Here I am."

"Play in college?"

"Sure. Captain of the Michaelmas Golf Team."

I felt an unpleasant sensation, a premonition of complications. "In Hartford?"

"You know it?"

"Sure, I know Hartford. I lived there years ago."

"No kidding. When did you leave?"

"Early sixties."

"Before my time," he said. "I graduated in 'seventy. Knocked around for a while. Went back to golf. Played a couple years as an amateur. Then I decided, this is it. I can afford the gamble. So I joined the tour."

"It paid off for you."

"Sure has."

"You didn't make any enemies along the way, did you, Mr. Bryce?"

"You're not back on that!"

"Probably you're right, you know, that that was a crank note, but a few precautions can't hurt. Is there anyone who might have it in for you?"

"This is a crank note. I know. Just lay off the subject."

"How do you know?"

"Because it's not the first," he said in a bored, sulky tone. "That's why."

"Where are the others?"

He shrugged as if it wasn't worth his time. "I threw them out."

"The same sort of note?"

58

"Yeah. Typed, you mean? I recognized the style right away."

"Were they hand delivered?"

"Naw. They came in the mail."

"From where?"

"Wherever I was playing. I got one last year at Augusta. My first really big tournament." He stopped and considered. "Where the hell was the other one? I got one in Hartford at the Sammy Davis. Then nothing until now. I'd forgotten all about them."

"You mentioned this to the inspector, though?"

"They would just have gotten him all excited. You know small towns. This will be the biggest thing since some drunk knocked over a lamp post. I don't need it. I mean, I'm trying to prepare for one of the world's great tournaments. I don't need the hassle."

"There's some reason to believe that your crank might be serious this time."

"You don't believe that."

"Someone has spent the last two weeks tampering with the courses here. Petty damage. They told you about that?"

"Crazy kids."

"I don't think so."

"Listen, if I find the guy who slows the greens down, he'll be getting threats from me."

"Just think it over, would you? Try to think of someone who might have a grudge against you. Merited or unmerited."

"I can tell you right now, forget it."

"Well, let's hope we can," I said. "Good luck, Mr. Bryce." I shook his hand. "You ought to have a bit of a gallery," I added. "Home town, I mean."

"Why's that?" It might have been my imagination, but I thought his large, warm hand stiffened.

"There are some Michaelmas alumni in the area. I don't suppose you knew that?"

"No. How'd you come across them?"

"I read the papers. Wilson Daintly is in Dundee at the moment. Developer, Class of—uh—"

"'Sixty-eight. Ahead of me."

"You knew him?"

"Everybody knew him. Ran the campus."

"And a professor. A Melvin Thorston. I heard him lecture just the other day. Quite a surprise to find he'd been educated in my home town."

"Yes?" said Bryce. He had hard eyes. "I didn't know him."

"About five-ten, five-eleven, dark hair. Language student, amateur actor, I'd guess."

Bryce shook his head. "I told you before I don't remember him." His face was stiff.

"Perhaps he's not a golf fan," I said. "Good luck tomorrow, and if you should remember something, I'm at the Centre Hotel."

"There's nothing to remember," Bryce said. "Nothing at all."

When I returned to the R and A, I told Sutherland I needed a car.

"You mean right now?"

"Yes. Can I borrow yours?"

Sutherland hesitated. "It's not too convenient at the moment with all of this going on."

"I won't be long."

"What about a cab?"

"I wouldn't advise it. I need to see Daintly."

"Oh." He raised his eyebrows and thought a moment. "Hold on," he said, and disappeared back into the members' room. Ten minutes later, equipped with a serviceable old Rover, I set out for Tayport on the St. Andrews side of the firth. Ahead, the railroad bridge and the motorway cut neatly across the silent water, while on the other side, the gray expanse of industrial Dundee twinkled and glistened like a lump of fool's gold. The

60

pinkish glow of the northern night sky made it easy enough to find the lane that led from the main street to the harbor, where the sea and river mingle at the mouth of the Tay. Daintly's house was farther along, a neat two-story building with a pair of oval flower beds at the front. Isolated from the neighboring cottages, it sat near the water, with barley on one side and a stretch of rough pasture on the other. As I stepped from the car, a flight of oystercatchers piped noisily overhead; and closing the door quietly, I started down the steep gravel drive to the house. The front of the building was unlit, the rooms quite dark, but as I approached the door, I could hear voices.

". . . tell me, who's taken the risks?"

The reply was indistinct, a low murmur, as if the speaker feared being overheard or habitually pitched his voice at a near whisper.

"Just leave it to me," the first man said.

"I'm warning you—"

His companion laughed scornfully. "You're panicking. I never thought I'd see the day. There's no problem, I tell you. Just give me time to work things out. You know how the market's been." I decided this was Daintly and moved along the shrubs at the side of the house. "After the first of the year—"

"Who do you think you're talking to? Our friend? I know the state of the market, and I know your habits. It would be a mistake for you to lose my trust. Do you understand—"

"This is ridiculous. Do I look worried?"

"It's different for you."

"That's your trouble," Daintly interrupted. "You always think things are different for you."

This brought a murmur of protest.

"You've always thought different rules applied," he continued. "Ever since—"

"That's irrelevant. I want to know . . . done now."

"It takes time. Nothing in this life's perfect, you know," Daintly replied.

"That's not good enough. I'll tell you—"

I edged forward, my curiosity aroused by the obvious tension between the two men, and nearly stepped on a large yellow cat. It bounded to the back of the property, upsetting a potted plant in the process.

"Is that someone coming?"

"It'll be my neighbor after the bike pump," Daintly said. "I'll go see."

His feet approached rapidly on the gravel, and I had no choice but to introduce myself as innocently as possible. "Mr. Daintly?" I called.

"That's right." A dark, husky figure materialized against the mirrored surface of the firth. Behind him, another—taller—man vanished through a hedge at the side of the property, but even the white northern night was not bright enough to illuminate his features. "What do you want?" Daintly demanded.

"I'm sorry to bother you. I really should have rung the bell. I was just about to leave when I heard voices."

"No bother. Just my neighbor." He glanced over his shoulder, then, satisfied that his visitor was out of sight, assumed a more genial expression. "Trouble with my roses," he said, nodding toward a healthy looking bed of hybrids. "Great gardeners, the Scots. I'm trying to acquire a taste for the art."

"A good climate for roses," I agreed.

"Yes, indeed. About all it's good for, I'd say." And Daintly gave a short laugh. His picture had not lied. He seemed cheerful and self-confident and about to fulfill the hints of oncoming corpulence. In person, though, there was a distinct hardness about him. Genial as he appeared, Wilson Daintly seemed unlikely to mature into a jolly fat man. "I don't imagine you came here to discuss roses, Miss—"

"Peters. Anna Peters. No, I came on another matter altogether. I wonder if we could have a little talk?"

"On what subject, Miss Peters?"

"Michaelmas College."

62

"My dear Alma Mater! I didn't think the Alumni Fund had such a long reach. Come in, it's getting a shade chilly out here by the water." And he looked over his shoulder at the dark line of the hedge, but there was nothing visible except a soft humped vegetable outline against the silver Tay.

"Thanks."

"Right in here." He opened the door and switched on the light. The living room was at the rear of the cottage, a pretty, pale room overlooking the firth. Daintly gestured toward a blue velvet sofa, then reached for a collection of bottles sitting on a chest.

"A drink, Miss Peters?"

"A small Scotch, please."

"Coming up." He smiled, apologetically. "We're out of ice."

"Perfectly all right."

"I'll get some. I can't stand lukewarm drinks. They're positively unAmerican." He smiled again and hurried into the other room. I didn't find this show of hospitality particularly convincing, and under the pretense of admiring the evening, I stood at the window, examining the silent lawn and garden. Unless Daintly's visitor were even now crawling through the potatoes or swimming in the Tay, he was still secreted behind the hedge, and I thought it interesting that the developer, far from rushing me out the door, was going to some pains to keep me around.

"Ah, here we go. Scotch on the rocks."

"Thanks. Cheers."

"Likewise. Like the view?"

"Yes. Beautiful scenery."

"I wish I owned a few more acres here. There's money to be made off this property." He sipped his drink reflectively. "I don't, unfortunately, so less for me—and less for the Alumni Fund."

"I'm sure you're always very generous," I said, "but I'm not fund raising."

"Just a joke, Miss Peters."

I took out one of my business cards and passed it over.

"Washington?"

"That's right."

"Is some corporate head-hunter after me?"

"Nothing so exciting, I'm afraid. I actually came for some information on an old college classmate of yours."

"Oh?" Daintly spoke casually, without quite managing to conceal his interest. "Who might that be?"

"Peter Bryce—the golfer."

"Oh, yes. He was on the team in college. Quite good, but none of us would ever have predicted his current success. Astonishing. They're talking here as if he may have a shot at the Open."

"So I understand."

"I remember him from school, naturally, but you probably know more about him than I do." He looked again at my business card, before slipping it into his vest pocket. As he did, he disturbed a very elegant watch chain, embellished with a handsome antique coin.

"Yes and no," I said. "As you've noticed, Bryce has captured a lot of attention. He has that elusive star quality. Wouldn't you agree?"

Daintly shrugged. "The press loves him, anyway."

"The fans, too. I'm told by the people interested in him that he's a great draw. I'm not a golfer myself, but—"

"An exciting player," Daintly agreed.

"Yes, and as a businessman, I'm sure you're aware that popular athletes are a commodity of some value. Sporting goods companies are always anxious to sign up the best and brightest."

"Ah ha," said Daintly. "And fearing to accept anything less, they've asked you to make some inquiries."

"That's about it. Bryce's athletic endowments are beyond question, of course, but those endorsing a product need to be beyond reproach. I happened to be in town, heard there was another Michaelmas graduate around and thought I'd stop and ask you what sort of man he is."

Daintly gave a soft laugh, at once reminiscent and ironical, and refilled his glass. He stood rattling the ice cubes a moment before the window, then he turned. "Peter Bryce is a son of a bitch," he said.

"In any specific direction?"

"I see moral turpitude is not in itself sufficient to disqualify him as an endorser."

"That depends. There's a certain cynicism in the business," I said. "What in the average person would be ruthlessness or egotism, appears like the winning drive in a pro athlete."

"How right you are. Well, by those standards, whoever it is should go ahead and hire him. Peter always got what he wanted and always knew who to get it from. A man with a limited, but efficient, knowledge of human nature."

"Meaning what, precisely?"

"Meaning he got on very well with practical types. Your businessmen will love him. And for that matter, he is clean, thrifty, and brave."

"Quite straight?"

"No problem there."

"Then there's the opposite extreme. Scandals with women are out, too."

"He keeps a cool head where women are concerned," Daintly said drily. "At least he did."

"I can almost foresee success in his chosen profession."

Daintly's thin smile might have been touched with envy. I wondered if the former BMOC rather regretted his classmate's success. "Almost," he said.

"You mentioned a limited knowledge of human nature."

"He understands only his own kind," Daintly replied. "No grasp of people with different—values, aspirations." He shrugged. "Classic jock, I suppose. Freshen that drink, Miss Peters?"

"No, thank you. I really must be going. You've been very helpful."

Daintly rattled his ice again and stared out toward the garden. "My pleasure. You brought back old college memories."

"I'd have thought you were too young for nostalgia."

"Until very recently," he said with a laugh, but I had the feeling that he was listening for something. He was reluctant to see me leave, which made me wonder if he had reason to be anxious about his earlier visitor. "How did you find out I was in town?" he asked, sipping his drink.

"Coincidence. I was talking to a professor here at the college."

"Oh, yes?" Daintly's eyes watched me over the rim of his glass.

"Imagine my surprise: He was from my home town! Small world, isn't it?"

This cliché didn't reassure Daintly. "And he knew me?"

"Only indirectly. He mentioned another Michaelmas alumnus in the area. Someone he'd read about in the local paper. There was some land development plan, wasn't there?"

Daintly nodded. "What's his name?"

"Thorston, I think. A Dr. Thorston."

"Huh. I don't remember him. A young man?"

"Your age, maybe. Dark, round face. Wears glasses." As I spoke, a car engine turned over some little distance away.

"Yeah?" said Daintly, suddenly uninterested. "I can't place the name. He probably wasn't in my class."

"Probably not."

"Well, I guess that's all I can tell you."

We shook hands on my way out. Daintly smelled of whisky, and there was something else, a faint psychic odor, familiar to me now after a hundred investigations: Wilson Daintly was afraid of something.

66

The waterside cottage was set far back from the road, and by the time I reached my car, there was no sign of the other visitor's vehicle. The highway remained deserted all the way to St. Andrews, and, near town, some slatey clouds finally blackened a sky still pink and yellow at close to midnight. I had been asked to leave the Rover at a house near the harbor. Putting the keys under the seat and locking it as Sutherland's associate had requested, I set out for the hotel along The Scores, a sea-front street lined with tall university buildings and fine two- and three-story sandstone townhouses. Trees and shrubs hung over the garden walls, casting nebulous shadows on the pavement, and I stopped twice, thinking I heard steps behind me. The streets were empty, though, the resort's night life apparently consisting only of the conviviality available at a few central pubs.

Halfway along to the R and A, The Scores was pierced by a wide alley running between the walled and gated quadrangle of the old university and the blank sides of large classroom buildings. The gathering clouds had not succeeded in dimming the twilight, and as I hurried down the dark pathway toward the lights of North Street, I sensed movement behind me. I glanced back without breaking stride, and a shape moved in a doorway. But the utter peacefulness of the surroundings, the chapel clock tolling the midnight hour, and the lone car passing on the main road assured me that this was only some late tippler making his way home. I was a step away from the brilliantly lit sidewalk of the cross street, when someone moved behind me. This time instinct set off all the alarms. I stepped aside, turning to see who was there, and that slight movement saved me. Something long and heavy connected with my arm and shoulder instead of my head. I fell back against the rough stones of the wall, flung out my arm, and yelled. There was a blurred motion, then the sound of feet at the head of the alley, and my assailant turned and fled, leaving me with only the impression of a large dark form that darted into one of the university entrances and disappeared.

7

"AND YOU SAY YOU'RE HERE FOR TWO WEEKS on a holiday?" the policeman asked.

"That's right. With my husband. He's been commissioned to do some paintings of the Open."

"That right? Has he got a favorite?" the officer asked, glancing up from the form he was completing.

"Harry says Peter Bryce is looking awfully good."

The officer nodded sagely. "My money stays on Player, but I've heard the same from a number of quarters." He also liked the chances of Faldo and conceded Nicklaus was his sentimental pick. The policeman was quite an aficionado, and his analysis of the practice rounds further postponed my departure from the station. That was fine. There had been a few bad moments right after a frightened teenager had summoned him to the alley. The officer, smarting under the insult of an assault committed within a block of the station house, had looked earnest enough to make a case out of it. While the youth prodded my shoulder, the policeman found the mark on the wall where my attacker's weapon had struck.

"It isna broken," the boy said. He was a student on his way home from a late party.

"No, I'll be all right. I can move my arm."

"Lucky, that," the officer remarked, his flashlight revealing a powdery white patch on the sandstone wall. "This was a blow of some force. Fortunate you were near the wall."

"I heard someone. Just an automatic thing. I jumped aside."

"Better get some X rays taken."

"I'll be all right. Thanks. I only have to go to the Centre Hotel."

"Oh, I'll need to take down a few particulars, Miss. The station's across the way."

His "few particulars" had occupied the better part of an hour, but at last, he seemed to have conceded there was no more to be wrung from the odd case of an unprovoked attack on a visiting American.

He pulled his form from the machine and pushed it across for me to sign. "Pity you didn't get a better look at him."

I was thinking the same. The suddenness of the attack, the darkness of the alley, and the speed of my assailant's retreat had left me with only a man's silhouette against the lights from The Scores. I shook my head. "It happened so fast," I said.

"Oh, aye. Usual reaction. But should you remember anything more, you'll contact us, first thing?"

I assured him I would.

"With the Open and all the holiday makers, you're bound to find a few toughs. After your purse, no doubt, but we don't like to take chances."

No indeed. He had reason to be alarmed. Not too many purse snatchings begin with a clubbing. This one might have been a lot worse: My shoulder was intact but sore enough, and only very good luck had kept me out of the nearest emergency ward. "I understand," I said, "especially at a resort."

The officer smiled. "That's it. And sometimes people bring their troubles after them." He smiled again, and I was glad that

Inspector Stewart and Sergeant Barnes were off duty. They could have asked some awkward questions—the kind Harry asked the next morning.

* * *

"What'd you do to your shoulder?"

"I told you, I got pushed into a wall. Kids running about late at night."

I pulled my sweater on, but not quite quickly enough.

"My bride is a transparent liar. Look at this." He turned me around, so that I could see the bruised line across my back and shoulder. I didn't need to see it: I could barely raise my arm.

"I went to the police," I said, on the defensive.

"And told them all about the R and A business and the charming alumni of Michaelmas College."

"A business like this is always confidential."

"Even when the police are involved?"

"Especially when they are involved."

"You know who did it."

"Wrong. I have a candidate, but I honestly didn't see the man. Just that he was big and wearing something dark." The only person whom I could imagine hitting me over the head in an alley in Fife was Wulf, but my memory of the incident did not confirm that supposition. I had seen Wulf and Thorston several times, and somehow I couldn't be sure. Something didn't fit.

"Maybe the police were right. The town is jammed."

"Could be. I'm going back to see Dr. Thorston this morning anyway. I'm guessing he's not a particularly good liar."

Harry compressed his lips and looked annoyed.

"Standard operating procedure. Besides, look at this place. What could be safer?"

"Staying out of the whole thing and letting the local police in on what you're doing for Sutherland."

"I don't tell you how to do your illustrations, you know." I was neither at my best that morning nor in the mood to take advice—good, bad, or indifferent.

"Pigheaded as usual," Harry said. I selected a few of his own faults for comment, but our argument ended with a concession: I promised to call him after my interview with the professor, an agreement that turned out to be fortuitous.

I caught Dr. Thorston immediately after class. He was fiddling with the lock on his bicycle as I approached, and he straightened up with a start when I spoke to him, looking flushed and rumpled as if he had spent the night in his clothes.

"I'd like to talk to you," I said.

"Not now, Miss Peters." He deposited his chain and lock in the basket. "I've been up since the wee hours." He ran his hand through his untidy hair. "Scottish historians' conference up in Aberdeen. Some of our seminar participants decided to make a night of it. I was lucky to manage class."

"I'm sorry, but this is important. It won't take long."

He shook his head. "No border ballads this morning. My head's splitting and today we did Hugh McDairmid. A figure I find unsympathetic. Powerful, no doubt, but with a certain dissonance. My sympathies don't lie with the moderns, anyway."

"Today, I'm concerned with my profession, not yours, Dr. Thorston. Perhaps you remember," I added and taking out one of my cards, handed it over.

His reaction surprised me. "So you lied to me," he said violently, his face turning a shade redder. "You've been after me all the time."

"I assure you—" I began.

"Sneaking about my class! An interest in Scottish poetry! Ha! So who is it? That damn London dealer? I got the Gibbon edition fair and square."

He was beginning to attract attention, which, I suspected,

was the point of his outburst. "Dr. Thorston," I said, "something serious has happened since your class. I have no interest in your business affairs at all."

"Well, what's it about, then? I'm not accustomed to dealing with—whatever you are—a private detective?"

"I'd rather not talk on the street."

"I suppose I'll have to invite you to my apartment."

"Unless you'd prefer my hotel room."

He did not. He pivoted his bike and set off, wheeling it toward the cathedral. Evidently the condition of his head ruled out idle chat, for he said nothing more until he had unlocked the side door of a house near The Scores. "I have the top floor," he remarked.

His apartment was reached via a curving stone stair, dark and solid in the favored Scottish style. At the top, he unlocked a small and very low door, which gave access to a remarkable series of rooms. From what I could see from the threshold, the entire apartment was lined with books from floor to ceiling. There were paperbacks and hardbacks, tiny yellow-backed French novels and massive folios. There were books with fine linen-covered boards and others with crumbling leather spines, and magnificent examples of the bookbinder's art shared shelf space with tattered academic wrecks. There was a daybed, which obviously functioned for both sitting and sleeping, and a trestle table with a typewriter and piles of papers. This was accompanied by a straight chair. The rest of the room was occupied by bookshelves and by bulging cartons whose literary contents exuded the dusty odor of aging paper. It took me a moment to encompass this bibliophile's treasure, but once I had stepped inside, I saw something else of interest: The living room window gave a narrow view of the waterfront street. If Thorston had not indeed been drinking in Aberdeen, he could easily have spotted me walking alone the previous night.

"Did you cycle back and forth to the train?" I asked.

"The bike is purely a poverty measure with me," he said.

"Normally, I take a cab. But I'm sure that's not what you wanted to ask me."

"May I sit down?"

He gestured toward the straight chair, then, discarding his jacket and loosening his tie, flopped on the daybed opposite me. The flush had left his face, to be replaced by a yellow-tinged pallor. "I'd appreciate it if you'd come straight to the point," he said, beginning to fiddle with a medallion he wore on a thin gold chain around his neck.

"I believe you attended Michaelmas College in Hartford?"

"What does that have to do with anything?" He dropped the medal and glared.

"I'm interested in obtaining some information about another Michaelmas graduate, Peter Bryce, the golfer." I explained my interest as I had to Daintly, using the excuse of an athletic company seeking an endorsement. Thorston did not interrupt again, but from the first mention of Bryce's name I had the feeling that the professor's attention was focused elsewhere. "Could you tell me anything about him—about what sort of man he might be?"

"This is hardly vital and essential, is it, Miss Peters? I was in school almost ten years ago. How could my opinion—if I had, in fact, known him—be at all revelant? This is a waste of my time. Write the college if you want information."

"Ordinarily, that's what I would do. But something strange happened last night."

Thorston became noticeably quieter, and he waited with what might have been apprehension.

"Last night, I paid a visit to another Michaelmas graduate, Wilson Daintly, the builder. He was interested in developing some land near the golf courses—perhaps you've read about him in the paper?"

Thorston nodded, without comment, and began to nibble absently on his medal.

"We had a curious conversation. I had apparently interrupted a visit, and I had the feeling he was anxious about something—although that may not be important. Anyway, I drove back to town and returned the car I'd borrowed to a driveway along The Scores. Very near here."

There was still no reaction from the professor, but there was no doubt that I had secured his interest, however silent he remained. I went to the window. "I walked along that street toward my hotel and cut through an alley running beside the quad. Do you know the one?" I asked, turning to look at him.

"Certainly."

"Within sight of the main street, I was attacked by a lone man who apparently had been hidden in or behind one of the college buildings. Attacked with a stick or a club heavy enough to have killed me if I had not been close to the wall so that the blow was deflected."

The remaining color left Thorston's face, and he sat upright. "Are you all right? You weren't hurt?"

"A few bruises," I said, flexing my painful shoulder. "Nonetheless, it was a closer call than I cared for."

Thorston rose nervously and moved aimlessly around the room. He seemed genuinely, and more deeply, disturbed than the situation really merited. "Almost inconceivable in a town like this. But then violence is never really expected, is it? Always a mystery."

"I will agree with you in this case. The police suggested some vacationing tough."

"You went to the police?" His voice was agitated.

"I would have preferred to handle it myself, but they were summoned. After all, an inch back or forth, and they could have had a homicide."

"Of course, that was inevitable. I'm very sorry, Miss Peters."

"They put it down to a purse snatching."

To my surprise, Thorston shook his head vigorously.

"You don't think so?"

"Be careful, Miss Peters."

74

"About what?"

He shrugged his large shoulders. "You doubtless know your own business," he said hastily. "I'm sorry I can't help beyond good advice: Be careful. One never knows today. I sometimes think the world—"

"When I picked myself up in the alley, do you know what my first thought was?"

He stopped midway into his dissertation.

"My first thought was Wulf."

"What is wrong with you?" he demanded loudly. "Why don't you leave me alone? Wulf! What do you mean? Did you mention him to the police?"

"I preferred to talk to you first."

"It's a very good thing. I'd have had you up for slander— false accusations. I didn't trust you from the first. A casual meeting in the Laundromat! Fortunately, I knew where you were from right away."

"I'm not so sure you'd have had a case, Dr. Thorston. Let *me* advise you this time. Wulf is not a normal resident of a modern community. He is armed. He is suspicious. He is hostile."

Thorston broke in loudly, but I continued. "I told you the other day that I didn't appreciate your playacting. He very nearly hit me with that club he carries."

"This is goddamn ridiculous—"

"What else was I to think, when someone later tried to bash me over the head?"

"Wulf is a mere linguistic experiment—"

"Get rid of him, professor. Forget your experiment, it's gotten—"

"A mere imaginative construction—not the sort of thing a detective would understand, but a new way of looking at the world, of dealing with phenomena, with the violence, with—"

This time, he broke off of his own accord, looking angry and uneasy as if he had been indiscreet.

"On the contrary," I said. "Investigations require a considerable degree of imagination, especially in the matter of motivation. Right now, mine is at work on two separate but potentially related phenomena, the mugging and my recent meetings with three Michaelmas College graduates. Not the best of times for them."

Thorston had regained control of his temper, and putting his hands in his pockets, he went to stare out the window. Despite his haughty, irritable outbursts, he struck me as being almost unbearably oppressed by some worry or trouble stimulated by my presence. Perhaps Wulf had felt that, too, and I wondered why.

"Why did you say that?" he asked after a moment.

"Well, you have Wulf to deal with, Wilson Daintly seems to have had a business setback of some proportion, and Peter Bryce—"

"What could possibly happen to Peter?"

"So you did know him."

"You lied to me," Thorston announced loudly. "This has nothing to do with a sporting goods company. Get out of my house." He stepped away from the window, and in the low, book-crammed room he took up a great deal of space. In retrospect, I can see that I had misjudged him, led astray, as most people were, by his theatrical manner and dramatic gifts. In spite of his imagination and his acting, the professor was, at bottom, a man for whom truth was extremely important.

I stepped behind the table and ostentatiously settled myself in the chair. "You know, Dr. Thorston, had I mentioned Wulf to the police, I am sure you would have had an awkward interview with them. You're a resident alien here, and you have to watch your step."

He gripped the edge of the table with both hands, and I had the nasty thought that he was going to tip the heavy top, typewriter, and papers onto me. "I can prove I was in Aberdeen last night. Not that I have to prove it to you."

"I'm glad to hear that," I said. "But for your sake—and the university's—it would be better if the matter never arose."

He shifted his weight and straightened up. "What do you want?"

"I told you before: some information about Peter Bryce. Is he the sort of man who makes enemies?"

Thorston's expression darkened, and looking away he said, "Wilson Daintly could have told you that."

"Daintly said he'd never met you."

"That's a laugh."

"Why should he lie, Dr. Thorston?"

"Why should you? Why do you want to know about Peter?"

I folded my hands on the table. "Because someone's threatened to kill him. And I've been hired to protect him."

"You?" Thorston broke into a loud, harsh laugh.

I shrugged. "My methods have been known to work."

He leaned belligerently over the table again. "I can imagine," he said sarcastically.

"Perhaps your linguistic experiment should have been with a character from the modern era," I remarked pleasantly.

"Get out of my house," Thorston roared, and this time, he lifted the front of the table. I jumped up and he dropped it back onto its trestle, spilling books and papers and rattling the typewriter. He flung open the door, but I delayed.

"You still haven't answered my question. Would Peter Bryce have any enemies? Or do I stop by the police station?"

For a moment, Thorston stared at me without answering, a blank, hostile, unreflecting stare like Wulf's. "Only his friends," he said finally. "Only someone who knew him well." And with this pronouncement, he raised the medallion to his teeth again. I had thought it a religious medal, a St. Christopher, perhaps, but it was a small antique coin. Thorston noticed my look and dropped the medallion back under the collar of his shirt. "Don't come again, Miss Peters," he said and shoved me

77

roughly out of the apartment. "Wulf is right," he added violently; then he slammed the door in my face.

I was halfway down the stair after this humiliating exit, when I heard the door open. There was a step in the hall, then the door thundered shut again. For a man with a bad hangover, Dr. Thorston certainly wasn't overly sensitive to noise. I looked up at his windows when I reached the street, but there was no sign of him, and since there were little spits of rain and the cloudy harbingers of a downpour, I did not loiter. Ordinarily, I would have returned to the hotel, but I was still irked with Harry, and more than a little unsettled by my interview with Thorston. I crossed the street to a phone booth and dialed the Centre Hotel.

"Harry Radford, please, in room fourteen."

"Anna! Good thing you called."

"Just to report I'm safe and sound."

"You'd better come here right away. That Wilson Daintly called and asked to talk to you, and a Detective Inspector Stewart and a Sergeant Barnes stopped by."

"Oh?"

"They're waiting in the lobby. I said you'd be right back."

"What do they want?"

"Routine, apparently. They just found out about your accident last night."

"Un-huh. Did Daintly leave a number?"

"He expected to be at home. You can call him when you get back. I have his number."

"Better let me have it now."

"The police are waiting," he reminded me after he had read off the figures.

"Be a sweetheart and don't mention I called."

"Anna," he warned.

"They don't need to know until I've talked to Daintly. Otherwise, they'll keep me all afternoon filling out their stupid forms. I'll call you in a little while and that will be time enough to give me their message."

Before Harry could protest this plan, I hung up and immediately called Daintly's cottage, where the phone rang a long time unanswered. I didn't like that. Next, I contacted all three local cab companies, posing as a university secretary trying to locate a book the absent-minded Dr. Thorston might have left in a cab that morning. Several tuppences later, I had the information that Dr. Thorston had indeed been in one of the MacIntosh taxis, but the evening before, when he'd been met in Dundee off the II:I5 P.M. from Aberdeen: Melvin Thorston was not only an obvious liar, but an exceptionally clumsy one.

Daintly's number still gave no answer, and carefully skirting the streets near the police station and the hotel, I made my way to one of the garages that rented cars; they were closed for the noon hour. Cursing the quaint manners of civilized life, I went to the bus depot and caught one of the leisurely buses that run between St. Andrews and Dundee. Forty minutes later, I was in Tayport, and with the rain beginning to come down steadily, I picked my way over the cobblestones to the harbor and from there along the soaking fields to Daintly's cottage. The rain and mist had almost obliterated the fine view of the river, and set by itself in the fields, the cottage today wore a bleak and generally unappetizing aspect. I rang the bell, then rapped on the door. No one appeared, although there was a white BMW in the single car garage. I walked to the rear of the house and tried again. The only sign of life was the large yellow cat, which was sheltering from the rain under a bush, shifting its wet paws disconsolately. I found the back door unlocked. The cat darted inside, and I stood for a moment in the kitchen, listening to the rain on the tile roof and wondering what had become of its owner. "Mr. Daintly?" I called. "Anyone home?"

Silence. I checked the living room, where a half-finished cocktail was sweating a wet ring into a mahogany tabletop, and examined the bedrooms upstairs, while the cat crept about under the furniture. Then, selecting a large umbrella from the stand near the front door, I ventured outside. There were keys

79

in the BMW and a briefcase on the seat, as though Daintly had been ready to drive off somewhere when he had changed his mind or was prevented from going. The garden shed at the rear of the lawn was less informative, just the usual clutter of rakes and hoes and edgers alongside a neat stack of clay pots. Despite his expressed interest in roses, I didn't imagine Daintly spent much time there. Beyond the outbuildings was the thick hedge where last night's shy visitor had hidden, and behind it, a narrow path. I could see the mast of a sailboat and, remembering Daintly's reputation as a yachtsman, I headed for the water. The boat was tethered to a small dock, and there was something floating beside it under the gray rain. An old tire or a jacket, I thought, but I broke into a run, sliding down on the stones and mud to the water's edge. The tide was in, the green waters of the estuary sloshing high over the rocks and kelp with a soft, sucking sound. The tweed hacking jacket, black with water, waved in the current, but the man inside hovered motionless above the barnacles, the water now revealing, now concealing, his dark brown hair.

I threw down the umbrella and splashed into the river, the frigid water numbing my feet and ankles. The body was only out to waist depth, prevented from drifting further by the angle between the dock and the boat. Seizing the back of his jacket, I towed the man to shore, then, flopping onto the rocks, hauled him up the bank. Out of the water, he seemed immensely heavy and slippery, and it was several minutes before I could draw him completely from the river. Turning him on his back, I felt for his pulse and heartbeat and was about to attempt resuscitation, when I noticed the mess and dent on the side of his head. Wilson Daintly had been less fortunate than I had been. The full force of some large and heavy weapon had crushed the side of his skull.

I sat back on my heels under the downpour and contemplated this discovery. The shock of the cold water had set me shivering uncontrollably, and the wind off the river lashed gusts of rain over me and over Daintly's white face, where little pools of water were already collecting under his glazed eyes. When I got my shaking hands under control, I touched his pockets: a pack of sodden cigarettes, an expensive lighter, his wallet with numerous credit cards and fifty pounds in assorted bank notes. His killer had not wanted money. There was a small bottle of aspirins in his pants pocket and a large cotton handkerchief tucked into his vest. I was replacing the latter item, when I noticed that there was a tear in the fabric as if something had been ripped through one of the button holes. Daintly, I remembered, had worn a most ornate pocketwatch with an antique fob: a coin, in fact, rather like the one Professor Thorston had kept putting nervously to his lips during our interview. I had seen that this morning without making the connection, and, curious about Daintly's watch, I hastily patted his vest pockets again. No watch, no chain, no fob. When I was sure it was not on the body, I got up and searched the bank, then, gritting my teeth to keep them from chattering, I stepped into the river near the dock. The water was clear enough, but I could find nothing glittering against the kelp, and, finally, my hands white to the knuckles, I waded back onto the shore, picked up the umbrella, and returned to the house. I left my flooded shoes at the door and discarded the rest of my sodden clothes in the back entry-way, before wrapping myself in a tartan rug. I realize that I should, at this point, have gone straight to the phone and contacted the constabulary, but I figured another fifteen minutes in the rain would hardly matter one way or the other to Wilson Daintly. Instead of telephoning, I retrieved a thin pair of leather driving gloves from my coat pocket, started the electric fire for my wet clothes and for the miserable cat, and began to search the cottage.

8

"JAMES SUTHERLAND, PLEASE. No, it's urgent. Anna
Peters. P. P–E–T–E–R–S. Thank you."

"I was in a meeting," Sutherland said when he finally came
on the line.

"Never mind. This is more important. I'm at Wilson
Daintly's house. He is definitely not your boy."

"You've thought that all along, but I don't suppose you can
prove it."

Sutherland's problem was that he couldn't stand contradic-
tory subordinates. Opposition brought out a snippy manner
that made me sympathetic to the old duffers on his committee.

"Someone else has proved it," I said. "He's dead."

"Dead? You mean a heart attack or what?"

"No, I mean dead as in killed. Probably murdered. I fished
him out of the Tay twenty minutes ago. His head was bashed
in."

"You don't need to be graphic."

"I wanted you to get the picture."

"You're in his house. What are you doing there?"

"Telephoning you for a start and having a look around."

"This is a police matter, Miss Peters, and I'd suggest—"

"That's why I'm calling you. Would you call Inspector Stewart, say, in ten minutes? That'll give me a chance to finish going through Daintly's things."

"I really don't think—"

"Thinking's what you hired me for," I said and hung up the phone. Squeamy clients are almost as bad as their opposite. Worse, if you're standing half-naked and freezing in a victim's seaside cottage, especially a cottage without secrets. There didn't seem to be much of interest except for a fine collection of cashmere sweaters, one of which I immediately commandeered. Daintly's desk, his bureau, his bookshelves revealed nothing unusual—and no sign of a murderer's hasty search, either. I wondered if the killer had been frightened off or if Daintly's elimination had been his sole concern. There was not the slightest sign of any disturbance, and it wasn't until I searched a small chest of drawers in the back bedroom that I came upon a thin leather envelope, stuffed carelessly with a jumble of correspondence. The name of the Gruen Foundation caught my eye, and I leafed through the papers, mostly photocopies of letters between the foundation's secretary in New York and Dr. Melvin Thorston, describing the project with Wulf and the various negotiations for cash in hand. Thorston's letters were extraordinary documents, full of high-flown academic jargon, servile appeals for cash, and frankly ominous suggestions that he would go over the secretary's head to his friend, foundation bigwig, Wilson Daintly. The imminent arrival of members of the Fife Constabulary prevented me from reading these long and interesting missives with any degree of care, but one thing was clear: In the best possible academic way, Melvin Thorston had been on the take for some time. If Wilson Daintly scarcely knew him, it was peculiar that the foundation should have devoted so much time and effort to furthering the professor's eccentric schemes. And interesting, too, that a large hand had scribbled comments on the copies: "undesirable" to a suggestion that Thorston reside for a term in Cambridge, Massachusetts, and "encourage this" to his suggestion that Wulf be created in Nuremberg or Heidelberg. I had the feeling that Daintly had been unpleasantly surprised when Thorston showed up on his doorstep in Fife, and for the first time, I wondered if Wulf's flamboyant appearance was not part of some inordinately whimsical blackmail scheme.

I was contemplating this intriguing idea when police cars rolled down the drive with a great scrape and rattle of gravel, and hastily replacing the correspondence under a stock of tennis clothes, I went downstairs to greet my guests. They were not particularly pleased to see me, Detective Inspector Stewart going so far as to question my unexpected absence from St. Andrews that afternoon; he had, unfortunately, asked the operator at the hotel if Mr. Radford had had any calls during the morning.

"Daintly's down by the dock," I replied and shrugged.

"You'd better show us where you found him," the inspector said, and out we trooped under a file of black umbrellas like so many poisonous mushrooms: Stewart and his factotum, Sergeant Barnes, myself, and three other officers, two of whom carried a stretcher. The examination of the site and corpse and the removal of the body occupied a good half-hour, most of which I spent in a state of advanced chill on the edge of the dock. Then we marched back to the house, and Stewart, evidently thinking I had served penance enough, dispatched a constable to fetch me some dry clothes and suggested a talk. I wrung out the soaking ends of Daintly's ill-used rug and agreed we had interests in common. While his colleagues began a minute search of the house and occupied themselves with phone calls back and forth to their headquarters at Dysart, Stewart and I sat in the spare bedroom upstairs and got down, as he put it, to "brass tacks."

"Your presence here is somewhat irregular," was the way he began.

84

I disagreed. "Mr. Daintly had phoned me. I returned his call, couldn't get an answer, and decided to take the bus to Tayport."

Stewart raised his eyebrows, gently incredulous. "Not the speediest means of conveyance."

"The car rental was closed for lunch," I said.

"Well, no doubt the ticket collector will remember you."

"She should. We had quite a discussion about which stop was nearest the harbor."

"Fortunate for you—if she can place the time."

I agreed this seemed to be a point in my favor. "Along with my efforts for Mr. Daintly. I did not realize at first that he'd been murdered."

"That has not been established."

"No, of course not. A fall resulting in a wound to the back and side of his head and some magical means of transportation to where I found him—face down in the Tay—that's all that's needed."

"I'm not looking for humor, Miss Peters."

"No, and I think we'd get on better if you told me what you are looking for, inspector. I anticipate pneumonia at any minute."

"First, let me tell you what I have to offer. As a material witness, you could conceivably be tied up here for quite some time. More or less time, as you can imagine."

"I can indeed."

"Good. Now, Miss Peters, had you been seriously involved, I don't suppose you would have inconvenienced yourself to the extent of retrieving the body and telephoning us."

"Thank you."

"On the other hand, I doubt that someone totally disinterested in Mr. Daintly's affairs would have delayed some"—here he stopped and consulted the notes he had taken during our first discussion by the water—"fifteen or twenty minutes before calling for assistance."

"Well," I said as airily as possible, "it was a shock. And the river is terrifically cold."

"The cold, I believe. The shock, I am more dubious about. When you did not reappear this afternoon, I took the liberty of making an inquiry about you. Wonderful things these new computers. The line on you, as my American colleagues would say, is that you are an investigator of considerable talent, running a respectable business. Confidentially, they say you can be unscrupulous."

"Idle flattery."

"Nonetheless, I imagine you will be anxious to rejoin your business—and your new husband. A nice chap, that."

"Harry is completely scrupulous."

"So I can believe. Now, Miss Peters, I think we have a common ground for discussion."

"Providing it doesn't compromise my clients' interests."

"Quite."

"Then how can I help you, inspector?"

"Why had you visited Daintly?"

"A number of reasons. Some confidential. I can tell you, though, that he and Bryce are both alumni of Michaelmas College—a small institution in Hartford, Connecticut. Because of the threats, I wanted to know what sort of man Bryce is."

"And also people on the R and A committee thought Daintly was trying to cause trouble for them?"

"I never believed that."

"That's as may be."

I smiled. Inspector Stewart did not smile back.

"You don't search a dead man's house to find out the character of one of his acquaintances."

"Is that an observation—or an attempt at entrapment?"

"I want to know if you found anything, Miss Peters, and why you were looking."

"Your men are searching the house now. As you can see," I gestured toward Daintly's baggy cashmere sweater and the plaid rug, "I'm hardly concealing any evidence."

"Nonetheless."

"I don't want to be detained unnecessarily."

Stewart nodded. "I'll do my best."

I produced the correspondence. "For reasons quite unconnected with the R and A business, I checked into the background of one of the local eccentrics here, Dr. Melvin Thorston, alias Wulf. The guy with the cape and the stick. Do you know him?"

"That I do."

"His academic 'research' is being supported by an obscure American philanthropic foundation, the Gruen. I had already come across it, when I was getting a file on Daintly. The late Mr. Wilson Daintly was a trustee and probably the main financial support."

Stewart ruffled through the papers without comment.

"Strangely enough, neither Daintly nor Peter Bryce admits ever knowing Thorston, although he seems well informed about them."

"What are you suggesting?"

"I find it odd that three alumni of a small New England college turn up here at the same time. I find it odder that one is threatened, one is loony, and now one is dead. Almost as odd as the fact that someone has conceived a grudge against a famous golf course and that an American professor is spending the summer trying to turn himself into a fourteenth-century Scottish swineherd."

"I'm not sure this Yank invasion is desirable," the inspector said.

"The Open would lose a certain luster without us."

"The sweet with the bitter." He stood up. "Obviously Mr. Bryce will have to have some protection until we get this sorted out."

"And Professor Thorston? He may be in the same boat."

"We'll have a talk with him. Daintly's secretary will be along to the morgue to identify him officially, but it wouldn't hurt to ask Thorston to have a go as well."

"A good idea."

"This has rather put your little mishap of the other night in the shade," he remarked as we started downstairs.

"I never took it too seriously."

"But as you say, it's odd, isn't it? You talked to Bryce, visited Daintly, then were attacked."

"The same way as Daintly was killed—if I'm any judge."

"It makes you wonder," agreed the inspector, who went to the phone and dialed the police station in St. Andrews, while I joined the yellow cat in front of the electric fire. I was just beginning to welcome the first signs of a thaw when his call was returned.

"It's for you, sir. The station."

"Thanks. Stewart, here. Oh, you've found him. What? When did this happen? You're sure of that? I see." He looked at his watch. "Have someone go over there right away and stay with him. And call Mr. Irving at the R and A. I think they should be informed if they don't already know. Right. Thanks." He hung up the phone, his face troubled. "I don't like this at all," he said.

"Something serious?" I asked.

"Something odd," he replied. "Professor Thorston has been involved in a road accident."

* * *

The gray sheets of rain hid the hills, and the mist pruned the tops of the trees, turning the country into a flat, sodden plain. Stewart's small white car smelled of fog and cigar smoke, and his windshield wipers made a soft, monotonous squeal. The policeman was thoughtful. When I spoke, he seemed surprised, as though he had been far away from the gentle asphalt serpentine connecting Tayport and St. Andrews.

"What happened?"

"There was a collision between the professor's bicycle and a

88

delivery van on Golf Place. That's the street behind the R and A. It sounds as if he's broken his arm. Maybe a head injury, too."

"Do they have the driver?"

"Yes, one of the caterers. It's a local firm, not a mark on the driver's record. There doesn't seem to be any doubt it was an accident."

"Still—"

"Exactly. We're going to the local hospital. Since the surgeon was on duty, they kept him there." The inspector sighed. "What do you know about this man Thorston?"

"He's very talented and very peculiar. A bit unstable, I'd say."

"An actor?"

"I can't decide."

"You may soon have a chance," Stewart replied sourly.

"Why's that?"

"He's insisting he's Wulf. Barnes says they can't understand half of what he's saying."

*   *   *

The hospital faced the massive buff walls of the cathedral precinct. It was an angular, gabled, three-story building with a new wood-and-stone addition at the back. Dr. Thorston was in the men's wing of the old part, sitting up in bed while two ancient gentlemen huddled near the windows and watched him and the constable with a mixture of fascination and anxiety. I stopped at the door.

"I think I'd better wait here."

"What's wrong?" There was a shade of suspicion in Stewart's voice.

"Wulf's taken a dislike to me. If the shock has really done something to Dr. Thorston, I think I'll be better out of the way."

"All right. The waiting room's down the hall."

I nodded and left, but returned to linger directly outside the door, where Wulf's loud gutteral voice resounded clearly, but incomprehensibly. Inspector Stewart patiently examined the details of the accident, asking his questions slowly and clearly, while Wulf alternately maintained an obstinate silence or responded with a torrent of dialect, much of which, as far as I could tell, concerned being trampled by an immense, bewitched horse. After a while, one of the old men was enlisted as a sort of interpreter, and lengthy discussions followed on the precise meaning of some of Wulf's more archaic phrases. The interview was maddening and farcical, and if Thorston were indeed in his right mind he was certainly pulling off a great performance. At length the doctor returned after reading the x-ray plates. The break was in the wrist and fairly bad: Thorston would have to be moved down to the operating theater to have it set.

Inspector Stewart came out to the hallway to consult with the surgeon. "What's your opinion?" he asked. "About the personality change? The speech? Is he faking?"

"I'm not a psychiatrist," the surgeon said, "but he's in quite a bit of pain. I doubt he could exhibit the total conscious control necessary if this were a performance. He will have to be examined by a specialist. I would suggest moving him to Dundee or to Edinburgh if this personality shift continues. Of course, it's not inconsistent with a severe shock."

"But this was not a terribly serious accident, was it?" I asked. "As accidents go."

"No. We would have to assume Dr. Thorston is a highly unstable personality. The accident could have been enough to trigger this manifestation."

"The shock of it," Stewart repeated.

"That's right."

"Or a fright?" I asked. "Would that have done it?"

"Yes, certainly. From the accident."

"Or before," I said.

Stewart looked at me. "He practically turned into the van," he told the doctor.

"Well, circumstance and motivation are your problems," said the surgeon briskly. "I've got to see about his arm. He'll be awake later tonight, but I wouldn't recommend too much pressure on him."

"Thank you, doctor," Stewart said. He stuck his hands in his pockets and started down the hall, looking genuinely baffled. "A complicated human being," he remarked.

"Rather delicately balanced."

"Why did you ask about a fright before the accident?"

"I saw Thorston this morning. He seemed nervous and upset."

"Any idea why?"

"He claimed he'd had a hard night at a historian's conference."

"That's possible. Oh, here's Paul," he said as Constable Barnes approached down the hallway. "Well, anything?"

"Same kind of machine."

Inspector Stewart raised his eyebrows. "You took a sample?"

Barnes showed us a piece of paper with a few lines typed on it.

"We'll have this checked. You were right, Miss Peters, about the typewriter. It was a Royal Standard that typed the note to Bryce."

"Who owns the other machine?" I asked.

"The professor does," Stewart replied, and collecting his overcoat from the lobby, he left the hospital.

* * *

Around ten-thirty that night, the rain stopped, leaving pink-tinged clouds that spotted the evening sky like carnival balloons. I put on my jacket.

"Where are you going?" Harry asked.

"I thought I'd go out for a walk."

"A bit late, isn't it? After what happened on your last evening stroll."

"Come with me, then. I'm not going far. How about a twilight sketch for *Sports Illustrated*?"

"According to the art director, I've turned in enough 'atmosphere' already."

I'd rather been ignoring Harry's project. "He liked them, though, didn't he?"

"Nice of you to ask," he replied with a touch of malice. "But, yes, he did. I need a few more action drawings. Starting Wednesday, I've got to be on the course all day."

"Oh, that's right. The Open begins day after tomorrow."

"You really are following this event closely."

"Sutherland's 'little job' has taken on increased dimensions," I said. "Shall we go? We could stop for a drink somewhere."

"All right. What about that pub by the course?"

"No good. I've an errand down at the other end of town."

"I thought as much," Harry replied.

"Damn artistic instinct," I said.

At the end of the main street, we entered the roofless cathedral gatehouse, then followed the high medieval walls that curve toward the harbor. I wondered if Wulf had spent much time along that walk and what he had been doing cycling behind the golf course. And running into a caterer's van.

"What's this?" Harry asked.

"The local hospital."

"You're too late to visit."

"Thorston should be out of the anesthesia now. The police will recognize me. I think I'll get in."

"Why the guard?"

"The connection to Daintly and Bryce, mostly. They're arranging protection for Bryce as well."

"He won't like that."

"No?"

"Naw. He's a real macho type. And temperamental."

"I thought he had a reputation for being very cool under pressure."

"Oh, yes, but he prefers everything his own way. Everything has to be just so or he raises hell. He doesn't lose his head, though."

"I'm glad to hear that."

We entered the reception area and spoke to the night nurse. She was dubious, but fortunately, the policeman on duty remembered me.

"Just a thought," I said. "I'll only be a minute. If he's still a bit groggy, perhaps the American voice might bring out Dr. Thorston. But if it's a bother—"

"I think it will be all right. The inspector looked in earlier. And the doctor's set the wrist."

Thorston had been moved to a small room by himself. The curtains were open, and the large, high windows let in the lavender night. He was sitting up with a small lamp lit by his bed, but he did not move when I came in and his eyes remained blank and cloudy.

"How are you feeling, professor?"

The man on the bed made no response.

There was a drawer in the bedside table, and I reached over to open it. Inside was his wallet, a ring, a nail clipper—and the medallion. I lifted the chain. The medal was an old coin mounted in a ring. On one side was a head with dolphins and on the other, a chariot drawn by four horses. The edges were nicked and irregular with age, but the figures were beautifully carved. I raised the coin and Thorston's eyes followed it, but he never said a word. The curtains at the window moved slightly in the cool night air, and from the harbor a gull cried in a harsh, empty voice. I stared at Thorston for a moment, and then, when the silence in the room felt right and the voices of the nurses down the corridor faded and the murmurs of the old men in the next room dwindled, I shook the chain slightly and asked, "Does Peter Bryce have one of these?"

Without hesitation, Professor Thorston whispered, "Yes."

9

I DIDN'T MANAGE to get any more out of the professor, further questions being met with Wulf's blank stare and cryptic response. A single word was scarcely a conversation, so it was quite unfair of Inspector Stewart to accuse me of withholding information. But he discovered this only later, and the following day was notable chiefly for the famous golf incident, which, in the gossip-hungry atmosphere of pre-Open St. Andrews, created something of a sensation.

I got a firsthand version from Harry at a restaurant that evening.

"Have a good day?" he asked as he slid the knapsack with his sketches and equipment under the table.

"An interesting day—how about yours?"

"I sure picked the right threesome."

"Oh yeah? Who was that?"

"Faldo, Aioki, and Bryce. Emphasis on the last."

"A hot round on the links for Golden Boy?"

"In more ways than one. What are you having?"

"The plaice, I think."

He ordered and, when the waitress left, added, "I'm surprised you hadn't already heard."

"I've been busy." I, too, had been concerned with Mr. Bryce, but from a different perspective.

"It was a funny thing. I joined them as they went off at 11:30. Bryce was late, in fact, although that didn't seem to bother him. He was joking with everyone. He can be quite a charmer."

"So I've heard." But not seen. Bryce's charisma had not been on exhibit during our meetings so far.

"He had a new driver with him—or, I should say, an old one. A lucky club from his college days."

"Un-huh," I murmured without real interest. The eccentricities of golfers and their clubs was one thing I'd observed in my week at the Home of Golf.

"He showed it to all of us. Said he'd carried the club for luck for years, but hadn't used it in some time. In honor of the Open, he'd cleaned the driver and intended to use it for the round."

I said I was sure this fascinating tidbit would be on the national news.

"This is the preliminary," Harry said. "You're spoiling my story."

"Sorry. Go on."

"His game went well for a couple of holes, then he began to have trouble with his drives. He was in and out of the rough, and from what I heard later, he really lost his temper. At the time, I was sketching Aioki and not paying much attention to Bryce."

"So what happened?"

"We got to the fourteenth, which is a par five that runs beside the Eden Course. Bryce had bad luck with his drive—as he'd been having right along—and wound up in the rough next to the wall separating the two courses. It's low, but solid, and the rough is pretty high. Anyway, he said something colorful when he saw where the ball had landed and slammed the driver into the wall."

"I thought the caddie carried the clubs."

"He does, but Bryce had been so annoyed when the shot went off course that he marched right off the tee with the driver in his hand. I happened to notice him carrying it."

"I just wondered."

"Well, when he saw where the ball landed, he got madder than ever and cracked it again. He's got some arm. The shaft bent and the club face split. It was like something out of that Laurel and Hardy movie. Do you remember the one?"

"Where they wreck the bushes and the car?"

"Yes, and there's a Scotsman in the picture, come to think of it. The business on the course was like that—funny, but sort of embarrassing, too."

"I suppose he can afford another driver."

"That's not the point," Harry replied. "It just isn't done. The writers descended like vultures. Temper tantrum on the Old Course! Even the caddies seemed flabbergasted."

That put things in a different light. "You said Bryce has a reputation for being cool under fire."

"He does. They call him Peter Ice. That's one reason the press is making so much of the incident."

"And what did he do with the club? He didn't just leave it lying in the rough, did he?"

"No. He apologized for losing his temper, picked up the driver, and handed it to his caddie. Bryce told him to chuck it out; he didn't want to see the thing again."

Harry was right. This did sound peculiar. "Does he travel with his own caddie?" I asked. "Or is he using some local fellow?"

"One of the locals. A nice older man. We had a chat the day I sketched Bryce. He's been around a long time."

"Do you remember his name?"

"Jack something."

"Ask when you're over there tomorrow, O.K.?"

"Sure. Why are you interested?"

"Just a general concern with Mr. Bryce. You're sure clubs aren't busted up fairly often? You see those comic post cards—"

"Not at this level. And not someone like Bryce. We'll buy an evening paper and you'll see," he said, and pleased to be the proprietor of this piece of gossip, Harry went downstairs to the newsstand and returned with the *Evening Telegraph.*

"AMERICAN SUPERSTAR FEELING THE PRESSURE?" asked the headline, and the destruction of the "lucky college driver" was detailed with a sense of drama that would not have discredited a major disaster. "Bryce needs to pull himself together if he's to have a shot at the Open," the writer concluded, finishing his speculations with the suggestion that the American's temperament was "suspect for a course as treacherous as the renowned links at St. Andrews." Possession of a "suspect temperament" was almost enough to make me sympathetic to Bryce. I wondered if the golfer's bad manners had been triggered by the arrangements the police and the R and A had made for his protection. I had been at their meeting, routed out of bed early in order to lend, as the discoverer of Daintly's corpse, a certain authenticity to the athlete's supposed danger.

We gathered in a private office at the Old Course Hotel: Irving, Greene, and Sutherland, Inspector Stewart, Bryce, and I. Stewart outlined the steps that could be taken with the constabulary's overextended manpower, while the rest of us joined forces to urge compliance with his suggestions. At first, Bryce was having none of it.

"Has there been a single bit of trouble? Barring that bogey yesterday at the eleventh—not a bit. I don't want people following me around." About the latter, he was particularly insistent.

"There'll be no one 'following you around,' Mr. Bryce," Irving soothed. "If you'll just have your meals in the hotel and not go out alone, that's all we're asking. During the actual play, there'll be a man with a walkie-talkie assigned to your threesome. No one will notice anything different. He'll be no more

97

distracting than the media personnel or the course marshals."

"I prepare for a tournament in my own way," Bryce insisted. "I happen to like being by myself. And that doesn't mean being shut up in a damn hotel room or being nursemaided around by a supernumerary traffic warden. Especially over anything as trivial as these ridiculous threats."

"Mr. Daintly's murder adds a certain substance," I said, "and although you may not be aware of it, another Michaelmas graduate was injured the same day." Wishing to make as strong a case as possible, I omitted to add that this was pure happenstance.

"Oh?" said Bryce, suddenly interested. "Who's that?"

"Professor Thorston. I think I mentioned him to you the other night."

The golfer's expression went blank. "You may have. No one I know. What happened?"

"He was struck by a van while riding his bike near the course."

"Too bad," Bryce replied with perfunctory sympathy. "Was he badly hurt?"

"Busted wrist. Possible concussion."

A shrewd, sharp expression slid into Bryce's light eyes and then took its leave just as smoothly. "That will lay him up for a while." He paused a fraction of a second. "Where's he now?"

"He's in the local hospital," Inspector Stewart said, "but I wouldn't count on visiting him there. He may have to go to Edinburgh for treatment."

"Bad break, huh?" Bryce said.

"It looks like it," the inspector replied, tactfully glossing over the professor's psychiatric symptoms. "The point is, Mr. Bryce, that Daintly's death and the professor's accident have made us more inclined to take the threats against you seriously. It would also help if we could determine if there is something you have in common with Daintly and Thorston—besides all being Michaelmas graduates."

"I don't suppose there's a plot to wipe out the alumni," Bryce said in a jocular manner, but he made an effort to be helpful and ended by accepting Stewart's arrangements more meekly than we had dared anticipate. In fact he was as gracious as possible and seemed happy to cooperate—although he may have taken his irritation out on the unfortunate driver later. If so, I was partly responsible, because I followed him out of the room when the meeting ended. "Mr. Bryce, could I speak to you for a moment?"

He stopped on the stair, not very pleased. "What about?"

"In private, if you don't mind."

He hesitated, no doubt seeking the most final refusal, when a band of lurking journalists approached, mikes and note pads at the ready; he was then still the darling of the press.

"Please," he said to their volley of questions and appeals, "I've got to get ready for my practice round. No, nothing's wrong. Oh, the meeting? A little trouble with a parking ticket."

This brought a laugh, but no cessation of the questions. Bryce chose the lesser evil and grabbed my arm. "I have some private business with this charming lady," he said with that false jollity that in certain men conceals both a suggestion and a contempt. The reporters made way for us, however, and we hurried upstairs. As Bryce unlocked the door of his room, he said, "I hope this will be quick—I have to change."

I stepped inside before I answered. "That depends entirely on you, Mr. Bryce."

He didn't answer right away. I walked to the glass door fronting a balcony overlooking the tee for the famous Road Hole. "Marvelous view."

"If you're playing well."

"And you are."

"So far."

"And fair?"

"What's that supposed to mean?"

"My job is to help see that nothing unfortunate occurs at the

Open. I was called in because of certain incidents, and my employment was, so to speak, confirmed by the threat against you. I have a vested interest in your safety."

Bryce inclined his head. "How flattering."

"Under the circumstances, I would think that it would be in your interest to cooperate with me."

"In any way I can."

"That's what I would have expected. What I believed, in fact. But now I find you haven't been completely candid with me— or with the police and the committee."

Bryce's eyes narrowed. He walked over to the bureau and picked up a pack of cigarettes. He shook one out and asked, "Who says?"

"I say. Why have you pretended you never met Professor Thorston, for example?"

Bryce let out the smoke he'd inhaled with a sigh of exasperation and stared at the ceiling like a martyred man. "That idiot."

"It is true, though, that you know him?"

"Of course I know him. How that has any bearing, I can't imagine."

"Neither can I. But then it might have. He knew Daintly well, didn't he?"

"Yes, he knew Daintly well. He'd been living off him for the last couple of years."

"Why was that?"

"Oh, you know the type," Bryce said, suddenly confidential. "Old college pal gets into financial difficulties and begins to show up on his friends' doorsteps. Wilson was a soft touch— and what the hell—he's made a bundle the last few years. What did it cost him to throw a little to the professor? What a brain! You wouldn't believe it to see him now, but we were all a bit in awe of Thorston. He could have been anything—outside of sports, that is."

"What happened to him?"

"The war got him. That's what I heard, anyway. I never saw him again after college. He became peculiar."

"Peculiar in what way?"

"I'm a golfer, not a psychologist." Bryce reached into the armoire for a pair of golf shoes and another of his vivid sweaters. "What I'd heard," he added, "was a persecution complex —with outbreaks of rage. I don't know if that's true."

"You might have mentioned that to the police."

"Why should I make trouble for the guy? He's got enough already."

"Under the circumstances—"

"He's got nothing against me as far as I know "

Below the balcony, the undulating course was touched with the rust and lavender of heather and wild grasses, and the immense double greens were polished and satiny. Bryce sounded like a good guy trying to keep his old college ties in repair, but it passed through my mind that he might be sowing doubts about my informant, Thorston.

"And Daintly?"

Bryce followed me to the door, buttoning his sweater. "You think old Mel killed him?" He seemed to find the idea laughable.

"I was thinking more that Thorston was blackmailing him. How does that sound?"

The change in Bryce's face surprised me. He'd swallowed a bludgeoning death and a traffic accident quite cheerfully. Blackmail touched a sore spot. His expression turned hard around the edges of his mouth, and his light eyes assumed a metallic sheen. "I wouldn't suggest things like that."

"You mentioned yourself that Daintly was Thorston's main source of support. You put it down to philanthropy. I've always found information in hand paid better."

"You're in a cynical profession," he replied, then shrugged. Bryce had obviously played the easygoing jock for a long time, and it fit him pretty well. "Whatever it was, was strictly between Wilson and Mel."

I stepped into the wind on the balcony. "Yet I'm told you and Wilson were good friends," I said. "I'm surprised you have no ideas about his relationship with Thorston—or why he was killed."

Bryce moved suddenly behind me, and I automatically shied away: My experience in the alley had left its mark.

"Careful, Miss Peters," he said, grabbing my arm. "That's a low rail. You could take a nasty fall from here." His eyes were less solicitous. The nonverbal communications people should have studied Peter Bryce. He was uncommonly good at expressing his feelings through the tritest platitudes. What he was giving off now was pure hostility.

I forced a smile and edged back toward the door. "We can't have that," I said. "Another accident would be too much of a coincidence. I wouldn't want to put you in an awkward position, Mr. Bryce."

"Keep it in mind," he replied. "And that I'm the victim of threats and harassment. You're—"

The phone by his bed purred, and he broke off to answer it. Bryce seemed an odd choice of victim to me, and if Thorston were trying to get something out of him, I could only wish the professor luck.

"Yeah. Two minutes. All right." From the subsequent conversation it appeared that some question about his starting time had arisen, and as he talked, I paced around the hotel room. There was a *Herald-Tribune* on the desk, folded to a story about the Open. I lifted it to read the lead and noticed a set of keys beneath. There was a car key and one for a trunk or a suitcase, but the interesting thing was that they were linked to a fine antique coin. It was not exactly like the professor's but it looked of similar vintage.

"Eleven-thirty? I'll barely make it. That woman from the committee is still here."

Bryce was hardly going to be driving anywhere if he had to be on the links at eleven-thirty, and as his clothes were hung neatly in the armoire, he wouldn't miss his keys for a while. I laid the newspaper down as casually as possible and glanced over my shoulder.

"No, that's not suitable," the golfer was saying, his back to me. "Well, have it changed. Listen, they're getting me out there today—it's the same old crap. Yeah, tell them that. Okay, I'll be right down."

I palmed the keys under cover of smoothing out his paper and had them safely in my jacket pocket before Bryce hung up the phone.

"You'll have to go," he said shortly. "They've moved up my starting time."

Nothing suited me better. "Sorry for the inconvenience," I said. "And once again, good luck with the tournament."

"As a matter of fact," Bryce said easily, "I'm feeling lucky today."

"I'm glad to hear it." I headed for the door. My feeling was that his luck had just changed.

In town, I made straight for the hardware store. "I'd like a small pair of pliers," I told the clerk.

He produced several.

"No, I need something lighter. It's to close up a link on a bracelet."

He rummaged about for a time, then produced a pair with thin pincers. "These do, do you think?"

"Yes, and I'll take a small screwdriver and a hammer as well."

He folded these up in a paper for me, and I returned to the hotel, where I spread a towel on the desk, unwrapped my tools, and had a good look at Bryce's key chain. The design resembled Dr. Thorston's: a pair of horses galloped across one side, but mounted rather than harnessed. The reverse carried a man on a dolphin, and like Thorston's medallion, this coin had worn and irregular edges and a patina suggesting great age. For a few minutes, I stared over the roofs and chimney pots of the town and tried to remember the exact design of Daintly's watch chain and fob. When only an impression of ancient silver came to me, I turned to the task of the moment. I wrapped the coin in a piece of handkerchief to protect it, then holding it with the pliers, I used the point of the screwdriver to pry open the last link of the chain. After several tries and a near impalement, I opened the link and released the ring that bound the coin. After making sure the operation had not caused any damage, I left the keys and tools in the bottom of my suitcase and went downstairs and around the corner to a jeweler's shop.

"I need some advice," I told the woman. "I found this near the beach."

She took the coin and held it to the light. "Looks old."

"I thought it was just plastic until I felt the weight."

"Oh, it's metal, all right. Probably real silver." She rubbed the surface. "Feels like it. This could have come off a bracelet or a necklace. We'll have Mr. Craig take a look if you don't mind waiting. He's working in the back right now."

I said this was fine, and a few minutes later, a bald man with a thin nose and hooded eyes examined the coin through a jeweler's glass.

"I'd suggest you turn this in at the police station," he said. "Someone will be missing it."

"It's valuable?"

"As these things go. This is a silver coin, Greek, around 300 B.C. or a trifle later. Good state of preservation, beautiful design, well executed. Not desperately rare, but of fine quality. You say you found it on the beach?"

"Near the rocks."

"It's not been in the water." He turned it over and examined the surface again. "Probably just recently lost. Yes, I'd take it to the police."

I thanked him and returned to the hotel room, where I

selected a thin sheet of drawing paper and, using one of Harry's soft pencils, made as precise a rubbing as I could of the coin's size and design. Then I reattached the chain with the keys and walked down toward the course and Bryce's hotel. I was in a very thoughtful mood, and I practically bumped into Irving, who was puffing along the crowded street between the R and A and the hotel.

"Oh, Mr. Irving. I'm afraid I was daydreaming."

"Pondering our case, I hope."

"As a matter of fact, I was."

We exchanged reflections on the latest developments, agreed that all had been proceeding smoothly, and hoped, in Irving's words, that our prankster had "gone to ground."

"Are you on your way to the hotel?" I asked.

"No, but I could go over. Have you some little errand?"

"I found these in the parking lot earlier," I said, producing the keys, "and I just realized I'd forgotten to turn them in."

"Huh," said Irving, "sort of thing Greene's very up on. Early Greek, I'd say—or perhaps from Syracuse. Genuine, is it?"

"I wouldn't know."

"Looks old. Car keys on it, too. Someone will be after this. I'll leave it at the desk."

"Fine. If you'd—you just found it in the parking lot. All right?"

"Fleeing the limelight, Miss Peters?"

"You could put it that way." We shook hands, and I returned to the hotel in plenty of time for another long transatlantic conversation with Harriet.

* * *

"You want some dessert?" Harry asked.

"What?"

"Dessert—tarts, cream cakes, the assorted indulgences of the country. Do you want some?"

"Oh, yes, sorry. I was far away."

105

"So I'd noticed."

"Your golf anecdote started a train of thought."

"Anything to do with the tool kit I found in your case?"

"You've been doing some investigating of your own."

"Looking for extra socks."

"Yes, it might. I'm not sure. The three of them are dubious in one way or another. The two, I should say. Daintly's out of contention. I came across something interesting—"

We were interrupted by the waitress. "There's a telephone call for Anna Peters. It's from America."

"That'll be Harriet. Order me pie, and coffee, too, please," I told Harry and flew upstairs. I returned feeling at once satisfied and sober. A hunch looked as if it were going to pay off, but proving it correct was going to be awkward.

"Bad news?" Harry asked, seeing my face.

"Good and bad. I'm making headway, but I'm afraid I'm going to have to fly home."

10

"DO YOU WANT ME TO CALL YOUR MOM?" I asked
Harry as I stuffed a couple of shirts and a pair of slacks into
my case.

"I'm not sure that's a good idea. Do you want these pliers
and things?"

"No, I'm done with them. I just thought she'd like to hear
how you were, now that you've been definitely committed to my
custody."

"You know, dear, you don't really have a good grasp of the
conventions. You're actually supposed to finish your honeymoon instead of flying home without a moment's notice."

"I'm sorry," I said, "but I can't see any other way. And when
Harriet told me what she'd come across—"

"I know that," Harry said. "It's not as though we've just met,
is it? But mothers don't understand these things. You're supposed to be blindly devoted to me and unwilling to leave me for
an instant."

"I always imagined your mom was very clear-headed about
me," I said, folding up my blazer. "I didn't think she had any
of these illusions."

"She doesn't, but I'd rather she could pretend she did."

"Okay. No calls to momma."

"Sensible." He didn't seem too happy.

"On some things momma may be right," I said. "This is a bit grim, isn't it?"

"A fitting climax to a wedding trip devoted to golfers."

"I didn't mind that."

"I know you didn't," he replied, ruffling my hair affectionately. "That's one of the things I like about you."

"It's a good thing we're basically two of a kind, although I don't think you've ever pulled anything quite this awful." I shrugged. "The question is, is Thorston guilty? If he isn't, then he, Bryce, and the course are all still in jeopardy."

"Thorston's the choice at the moment?"

"Looks like it."

"I can see why. From what you've said, he had opportunity and motive, plus the complication of creeping lunacy. He sounds like a menace."

"He gives a good lecture," I argued in the professor's defense.

Harry made a face. "You want to work it out yourself," he observed, "as if the current explanation weren't perfectly good enough."

"No, that's not true. If Thorston were extorting money from Daintly, he would hardly have murdered him. That doesn't make sense—especially if we also assume he was threatening Bryce in order to get something out of him."

"Do we know that?"

"According to Stewart, the note wasn't typed on Thorston's machine, but on one of the machines in the history department."

"That doesn't sound good for the prof."

"Not at all. What bothers me is that he had to have information damaging to Daintly—possibly to Bryce as well. But no one's got any ideas what that might be."

"I suppose there are always lurid possibilities."

108

"I'm interested in one from 'sixty-eight."

"Why 'sixty-eight?"

I sat down cross-legged on the bed. "Thanks to *Sports Illustrated* and the invaluable Harriet, I've had a look at the biographies of Daintly, Bryce, and Thorston. They have only two things in common: attendance at Michaelmas College and an unexpected hiatus in their careers, followed, in the cases of Daintly and Bryce, by wealth and professional success."

"Thorston's a different matter," Harry reminded me.

"I thought so, too, at first. Now I'm not so sure. Thorston went from college into the army—not an expected move. He was a brilliant student. He could have gotten deferred. And money can't have been a problem. He had all sorts of scholarships after the service."

"Maybe he's just the sort who joins up. It was the thing to do for a few of us." Including Harry.

"Not so many by 'sixty-eight. Anyway, Thorston's two years in the army coincide with the two years Daintly spent doing who knows what before he arrived in Houston and entered the development business. Bryce finished college, then did the same thing. A couple of years doing odd jobs, then wham, onto the tour and into the big time."

"I'm not convinced there's anything very sinister in that."

"None at all. Now here's an interesting thing. Thorston follows suit—until the last couple of years. I looked him up—he's considered a leading educator in his field, an associate professor at Duke, grants, and a list of publications as long as your arm. Then what? He goes on leave to accept the Gruen fellowship, which is small potatoes compared to his regular salary and the big foundation awards, and comes here. It doesn't make sense. St. Andrews University is old and beautiful, but it's an undergrad institution. Thorston's a high-powered scholar and researcher."

"You're forgetting Wulf."

"Oh, he no doubt had something to do with it."

"Yeah—he's crazy as a fruitcake. There's your explanation."

"But Daintly kept pouring money his way—and, if I read the correspondence between them right—trying to keep Thorston out of the States. I find that interesting."

"I don't know if I'd break off a vacation over it."

"Me neither. Bryce clinched it."

"Bryce?"

"Yeah. He was willing to tell me all Thorston's symptoms—to discredit him, I'm sure, but he hadn't mentioned his relationship with the professor to the cops. 'Didn't want to make trouble for an old college acquaintance.' Does that sound like our hard-nosed golfer?"

"It keeps everything out of the press."

"Sure it does. But he even pretended he didn't know Thorston—or Daintly. He's going to very great lengths to disassociate himself from them—and he's putting up with the nuisance of police protection rather than saying, 'There's this nutty fellow who writes me threatening notes but who's quite harmless. I don't want any fuss.' The police could have had a talk with Thorston—perhaps the prof takes a holiday for the duration of the Open, and everything is handled quietly."

"You think he's really afraid of the professor?"

"He's contemptuous of him, but Thorston knows something, and I'm sure whatever it is explains the trouble at the course as well as Daintly's murder." That was my theory. It had sounded so far-fetched to Harriet that she'd predicted we wouldn't find anything. But she had; a very long shot, but one that felt right. In Hartford tomorrow, I was sure I'd get what I needed. "I'll be back for the final round," I promised, feeling guilty. "Maybe the day before."

"You know where I'll be," Harry said. "I'm beginning to feel I live on the course. Got everything?"

"I think so."

He closed the case and set it on the floor in the corner. "I'm afraid this hasn't been much of a holiday for you either."

110

"You have to make these little sacrifices when you marry a man in the public eye."

"You're exaggerating my potential fame."

"Not at all. Your pictures are going to be very successful, and then we can continue taking romantic holidays enlivened with interesting criminals."

"I had more conventional recreations in mind—moonlight walks, leisurely dinners, picnics in the sun."

"There's not been an awful lot of sun lately," I said, "but it's not too late for Old World romance. Let's go stroll in the ruins, neck in the twilight, wander in the gloaming—whatever seems suitable."

Harry looked out the window without much enthusiasm. "It seems to be drizzling again."

"So get your umbrella. You're awfully conventional for an artist," I said. "I'm afraid sometimes that's going to hold you back."

* * *

Bradley Field lay in a smothering embrace of heat and smog that floated a steamy blue haze over the tobacco fields and shimmered the air currents above the runways into iridescent curtains. The doors of the plane opened, and we stepped out into smoke-colored air. The trees and fields beyond the airfield were hidden in haze, and the terminal squatted, blunt and ugly, at the end of the vast acres of concrete and asphalt. Welcome back. It struck me as odd that, while I had managed to avoid my native city for over ten years, I should have returned almost as soon as I was married. Remarried, make that. I'd left my first husband in Hartford, and I could honestly credit my somewhat violent exit from his life for much of my subsequent career. I had not thought of that in years.

"Excuse me, ma'am," the stewardess said.

"Sorry." I moved on down the ramp and into the terminal, where Harriet was waiting for me, wearing a vivid pink suit that

111

made no concessions to her size. On the floor was more luggage than I had taken for two weeks in Scotland, and she was burdened, additionally, by an immense handbag and a suitcase-sized tote filled with papers and memos. Her greeting echoed through the terminal. "Anna! How are you!"

"I'm fine. Is everything in order, Harriet?"

"Don't worry about a thing. You look tired. I hope marriage is suiting you."

"Marriage is fine. Air travel is something else again."

"Isn't this ghastly! I was delayed an hour and a half. And I was annoyed, too, because I wanted to stop and see Ralph first."

Ralph was Harriet's oldest boy, a dutiful youth who was pursuing dentistry with the sort of passion most men reserve for women or fast cars. "I'm sure you'll manage a visit," I said.

"I'm certainly not very happy with the college," she continued. "Not with this business."

"Ralph's only here on a summer program."

"Investigation's an eye opener. You just don't imagine Michaelmas students involved in anything—"

"No proof yet."

"It's changed my whole idea of the atmosphere of the place," Harriet persisted. "Ralph would have stayed in Washington if I'd known what I know now. You can't be too careful with your children."

I agreed to this and resigned myself to a discourse on maternal rights, privileges, and duties. This one lasted until we reached our rented car.

"Oh, shall I drive? You look tired. It is a long trip, isn't it?"

"No, no, that's all right." Harriet's driving is a terrifying caricature of her great virtues, attention to detail and flexibility of response. Transported from her natural habitat of files and forms to the open road, these traits produced a myopic hesitancy, alternating with alarming shifts in speed and direction. I took the wheel.

"You can direct me," I said.

Harriet unfolded a road map. "Mr. Morton lives in West Hartford."

"Fine."

"Off Asylum Avenue. Do you know where that is?"

"It's been a while, but I'll find it."

"He sounds like a nice man," she said with a smile of approval. Harriet has managed to negotiate nearly fifty years with only two human classifications, "nice" and "not nice." This does not leave much room for the subtleties of human behavior, but then I don't employ Harriet for her psychological insights.

"How's Harry?" she asked.

"Good. Very busy."

"I almost said on the phone, 'Don't come; I'll handle it.' He can't be happy about this."

"Harry's known me for a long time."

"Still, I'll give you a piece of advice." Another perennial. I was tired of traveling, and I began to wonder if, after all, Baby, my other assistant, wouldn't have been easier to take. It does seem too bad that useful skills are so often accompanied by irritating habits.

"I've always felt my family took first place," Harriet continued. "Pete and I agreed on that."

"Un-huh."

She elaborated for a while, but the sound of her voice was lost against the roar of rush hour traffic along I–91. A hot, moist wind blew through the open windows of the car like the stale breath of summers past, and the pavement wobbled white and stifling in the July heat. I had left on just such an afternoon: a sudden violent argument, a blow, a girl hastily throwing her clothes into a cheap cardboard case. He had sat up and rubbed his head, and I had slammed the door in terror and run down the stair. I understood he ran a cleaners now, and I shook my head in disbelief. To the west, the sun hung in the haze like a garish ornament, punctuating the tedious day, and the glare began to make my head ache. When we swung around the city toward the suburbs, I asked Harriet about the man we were going to meet.

She interrupted her monologue, changed to the large, lavender-rimmed reading glasses that tormented her weak eyes, and produced a folder with notes, clippings and memos. " 'James T. Morton, sixty,' " she read. " 'Former Hartford Chief of Detectives, now an insurance investigator, working for Aetna.' He does a lot of training programs," she explained. "He doesn't do too many actual cases."

"How'd you find him?"

"I did as you suggested. I contacted the large insurance companies in Hartford to see if they had had a claim on a coin collection loss in the late sixties. The people at Aetna were quite helpful and gave me Mr. Morton's number. He knew a case right away. Apparently something locally famous."

"Any Greek coins missing?"

"Yes. It was an interesting collection—coins with horses, principally, and there were a number of rare and interesting pieces. But he said he'd have to see a full description to make sure."

"When did this robbery occur?"

"April 21, 1968. I have photocopies of the main news stories."

"Would that be the Brainwithe robbery?"

"You remembered."

"Home town tragedy," I said.

"Terrible thing."

I agreed. The case had been front page stuff for days. It had all the ingredients of horror and irrationality combined with the ingenious, almost fateful, touches that seem essential to capture the public imagination: the "unbreakable" safe, the Brainwithes' obsession with security, the absence of viable suspects. Add the fact the victims were old Hartford Brahmins, and the crime took on classic dimensions, yet it was simple in essence: The robbers had figured out how to crack the rich lock manufacturer's personal safe, and gaining access to the house, had

114

opened the device and taken a large amount of cash, securities, and valuables. But what began as a caper turned into a slaughter, when Caroline Brainwithe and Robert Langley, her escort, returned unexpectedly early from an evening party. They surprised the thieves—perhaps recognizing them, the police theorized—and after a short, violent struggle were murdered. Langley was stabbed with a paper knife, Miss Brainwithe battered about the head. The sound of the struggle woke Nora Reilly, the elderly housekeeper, who imprudently investigated. She died of a head injury at the foot of the main stairs. The carnage was not discovered until the following morning, when the cook found her colleague's body after she arrived for work. I remembered Thorston's cryptic comment on the brevity of violence; the murders at the Brainwithes had been a matter of minutes.

"Imagine keeping so much money in your house!" Harriet remarked.

"He had faith in his locks."

"Yes. Mr. Morton said the Brainwithes had been locksmiths for generations."

"That's right. And, if I remember, Brainwithe had some new safe that needed an electronic genius to open."

"You'd think someone with those abilities would have had better things to do."

"Maybe it was the challenge," I suggested.

"Peculiar kind of challenge."

"Peculiar case. Where do we turn off?"

Harriet had another consultation with the map and shortly pointed out a block of frame houses facing a large open field. "Here we are."

I parked the car and skimmed her notes and the photocopies to refresh my memory, pausing only a moment over the news photos: the victims in life, the house, and the shambles inside, with white outlines chalked on the floors like surreal ghosts from a murder staged by Cocteau. The New York papers had printed rather more ghoulish shots. I didn't need to study them.

115

I had recently seen a fatal head injury at close range, and the chilly waters of the Tay had not improved the effect. It was better to concentrate on the financial details, covered with scope and imagination in consideration of New England monetary obsessions. Had the safe held one hundred thousand dollars—or two—or, as the press and locals had speculated at the time, was it nearer a million? The Brainwithes' spokesman had maintained it was simply a "substantial amount" and branded the published reports "wild exaggerations." In addition to the cash, negotiable securities and part of a coin collection had been stolen, but nothing else in the house was missing, and fine jade figures had been left behind as too bulky to carry. Untouched, too, had been some exceptionally rare medals; the thieves had not been greedy. Then there was the safe. Brainwithe and other experts maintained it could have been opened only by someone who had studied the device at first hand; yet everyone on the staff, in the plant, and in the Brainwithe circle had alibis. The coins never appeared on the market. Unexplained wealth did not suddenly emerge in Hartford. There were no real clues, and the crime fit neither the pattern of a professional job nor of an amateur's crime of opportunity, but shared characteristics of both. Its details made it unique, its success, flukish; but it was not an isolated incident. On a tiny scale, it was like the urban riots of the period, marking an end of certain assumptions, codes, and privileges. With the sixties, Hartford had lost its dignified old prewar atmosphere without gaining very much in compensation. It traded in stuffiness for flash and only gradually realized that the shiny, new, big-money boys didn't have any answers either. The Brainwithe case was just another little footnote in the general decline of urban civilization.

"Okay," I said to Harriet. "Is he expecting us this early?"

"I said before seven."

We rang the bell, and a well-dressed matron with snow-white hair ushered us into a wide and comfortable living room with shag carpeting and a grand piano buried beneath photographs of young relatives. Morton was waiting for us in the den beyond. He was short and rather stout, but neatly turned out, and every inch the important insurance executive. He didn't look much like an old cop in his fine gray suit, with the light hair above his ruddy, smiling face bleached from rounds and rounds of country club golf. His manner, though, must have proved an asset in both his professions: an easy, gently probing affability that elicits information without apparent effort. "Miss Peters and Mrs. Edgar," he said, advancing to shake our hands. "We met on the phone," he added to Harriet with a smile.

"That's right."

"Can I offer you ladies a drink?"

I declined, but Harriet accepted a Manhattan, and Morton poured himself a gin and tonic, before settling down to study us. "It's not every day I meet charming ladies with information about one of my old cases," he commented.

I find this vein of bantering condescension tiresome and time consuming, but Harriet searched politely for a topic and settled on Ralph. "I was shocked," she said, "to think this might be connected with the college. My son is attending Michaelmas for the summer."

"I hardly think he's in imminent danger," Morton replied gravely.

"Ralph will survive," I said, seizing the opportunity to suggest she call her son. "You can take the car, if you like. I can get back to the hotel myself."

"Oh, that would be good," Harriet said. "I'll leave my papers."

"Fine. The phone's through here," Morton directed; and when she had left to make her call, we settled down to business.

"So you worked on the Brainwithe case?" I asked.

"One of my last."

"A tough one to end on."

"I never closed it."

"I'm glad to hear that. Harriet will have explained our interest."

"And you're representing?" he asked casually.

"An organization in Scotland. I'm sorry, but I can't be more specific. It is quite a delicate matter."

"I see."

"I was originally hired—that's hardly the word: it began as a favor for a former client—to find out a little about Wilson Daintly, a developer with some land in Fife. Since I was on vacation, I had to do that through my office. Harriet looked everything up for me."

"Daintly?" Morton said with interest. "He's American?"

"And a Michaelmas College graduate."

Morton nodded. "I questioned him."

"In the Brainwithe case?"

"He was a friend of the Brainwithes' nephew. He'd been in the house dozens of times and had expressed curiosity about the workings of the new safe."

"Promising."

"But no case. He had an ironclad alibi for the evening of the robbery, and the one thing everyone seemed to agree on was that he hadn't the brain for the job. Mechanically hopeless. But he seemed bright enough to me, otherwise."

"Wilson Daintly was murdered this week at his home outside Dundee."

"That puts a different complexion on a number of things."

"It does." I explained the presence of the other Michaelmas alumni in the immediate area and concluded with a description of the coins each man possessed.

Morton studied the rubbing I'd made. "Too bad you only managed to copy this one design."

"And that I didn't examine Daintly's at close range. The fact that it was removed from the body was what made me conscious of the coins. Otherwise I'd never have given them a second thought."

"No." He rose for a stack of papers on his desk. "Even if both coins appeared in the collection, there is no proof that they came from the Brainwithe safe—or that these men stole them."

"Agreed, but combined with certain details of their biographies—and the fact that Professor Thorston appears to have engaged in a little genteel blackmail—it seemed worth a check."

Morton opened a notebook. "I made a record of the missing coins. They're an interest of mine although I can't indulge on the Brainwithes' scale." He ran down the entries, then selected a reference book on coins from his bookshelf. "This one appeared in the collection," he said. "A silver didrachm from Tatentum. Around 281–272 B.C. A nice coin. The other one we can't be sure about, because your description is not as exact as a numismatist would desire. Possibly this silver tetradrachm?" He found a picture of the coin and passed the book to me.

"This looks very much like the professor's medal. He wears it all the time."

"And this other belongs to Peter Bryce?"

"That's right."

Morton's face grew serious and reflective. "I really thought you were on a wild goose chase," he said, "but I must admit this is suggestive."

"Yes, it seems too much of a coincidence."

"If you'd been able to examine Daintly's—what was it?"

"Watch fob."

"That would have been more significant."

"It's significant that someone removed it from his body."

Morton nodded and absently began to fill a pipe. "Neither Bryce nor this Dr. Thorston was ever questioned. I made very complete records, and I kept copies, as a matter of fact. You're right—I hated to concede on my last case. Daintly, now—"

Morton said and paused. "He was a visitor, he had expressed an interest in the safe, and had been given the opportunity to study its workings."

"The minimum requirements."

"He was a hard boy to get anything out of. I would like to have leaned on him a little, but there wasn't a shred of evidence."

"And he had an alibi?"

"Home all evening. His landlord played poker with him that evening. Since we could fix the time of the robbery accurately, Daintly was covered."

"Why were you interested in him—I mean, beyond the routine?"

"Instinct. He was one of the few people in the Brainwithes' group, or in the plant, who—how can I put it?—who seemed capable. Who took the whole affair coldly. The staff, the workers at the plant, most of the friends were genuinely shocked." Morton sighed. "By and large, the Brainwithe circle were sheltered people, in the sense that they could confidently expect never to be touched by violent crime. Ironic, of course, that the Brainwithes were in the security business. And very private people. The extent of their wealth was not generally realized until the robbery, and certainly the amount of cash they had on hand was a well-kept secret."

I nodded. Something in Morton's tone made me think he was not entirely sympathetic: a reaction, I suppose, to years of working among the largely unsheltered residents of the city.

"For the family and their friends—even, I may say, their staff and the employees at the plant—the robbery and the murder came as a profound surprise."

"But not to Daintly."

"That was my impression," Morton said.

"Not just youthful bravado?"

"No, a real absence of surprise that I found worth questioning."

120

"Possibly just a matter of temperament."

"Possibly, and he lacked the skill needed for the job."

"How many people were involved, do you think?"

"At least two, we figured. Probably not more than four."

"As I remember the story, the safe worked on some electronic system."

"Yes, it was quite complicated. We had experts down from MIT to explain the process. It worked on a voice command—Mr. Brainwithe's. They feel it was opened by an electronic device that produced tones of the same frequency."

"Necessitating a recording of Brainwithe's voice."

"Yes. Therefore our interest in their friends, staff—people who came into frequent contact with him. They were all covered. And a knowledge of electronics and of the technical aspects of human speech—they're a rare combination."

"Yes," I said. I turned over the reports and papers for a moment. "You never talked to Daintly's friend, Melvin Thorston, you said."

"Nope. Should we have?"

"He is a linguist," I said, "and people tell me he's brilliant."

"That's only half the equation," Morton replied. "Languages wouldn't have been enough."

"He was an electronics specialist in the army."

Morton considered this momentarily, then held out his hand for the file. "Here's Daintly's statement," he said. " 'On the night of April 21, 1968, I was playing poker with Louie La Fleur and several other residents of'—let's see, here it is: 'Question: Who else was in this game? Answer: Louie and I and Margaret, Louie's wife, and I think Mel was there. Margaret wasn't there all the time, though. Question: Who is Mel? Answer: Another student. Melvin Thorston.' " Morton looked up. "What do you think of that?"

"I think perhaps you questioned the wrong student."

"Not if you're right in thinking Thorston was blackmailing Daintly."

121

"He didn't mention Peter Bryce?"

"No. Presumably, being younger, Bryce lived on campus."

"I'd like to know where he was that night."

"So would I, Miss Peters," Morton said. "I'm afraid we didn't cast our net quite far enough."

11

THE NEXT MORNING, Harriet dropped me at the gates of the college. Ralph was to be at the medical center for a lecture-demonstration and had invited his mother to attend. "I'll be back just after noon," she said.

"That'll be fine."

"Are you sure you won't need me?"

"Not until then, I don't think."

Harriet smiled with relief. She doesn't like actually meeting the subjects of her researches, which is perhaps just as well, for her compulsion to put people at ease limits the incisiveness of a personal interview.

"Give Ralph my best," I called, then I passed into the shadow of a heavy Gothic archway and entered the quad.

Michaelmas College was built with the best Hartford money of its time, and the staunch Episcopalian businessmen had looked across the Atlantic for its prototype. Handsome dark stone buildings with Gothic roofs and turrets embraced three sides of a long quadrangle that had been left open on the east to provide a panoramic view of the city. There were trees and ivy, Civil War cannons, and several green-tinged statues of Michaelmas notables, forever raising bronze swords to encourage phantom regiments. It was only ten o'clock, but already a bluish smog sprawled over the city, and even the pampered lawns of the college were turning worn and brown in the prolonged heat. A few girls with cascading hair and minuscule shorts sat studying under the trees, while two of their male colleagues lethargically tossed a Frisbee along one of the paths. I found the sign for the president's office and went upstairs.

"Oh, yes, Miss Peters. You called earlier," the secretary said.

"Short notice, I'm afraid, but I have to return to Scotland tomorrow or the next day."

"That's all right. I explained to Mr. Brewster. He'll see you now."

Brewster was holed up in an office with paneled walls and a splendid view. Beyond the spires of the chapel and the green trees of the city, I could see the river curling in a liquid glitter. "Miss Peters," she whispered, and shut the door behind me. The man in the swivel chair rotated slowly from a survey of his domain, rose, and shook hands. He was handsome in a tweedy sort of way, with an angular face covered with very fine, nearly unlined, pink skin. He had light eyes and beautiful clothes, and he exuded an impression of immense, if slightly stuffy, cleanliness, as though he had spent his days in a very refined and isolated atmosphere.

"How do you do?" President Brewster said. "I always like to have news of Michaelmas alumni, but in this case, I'd rather have been spared the information."

"Yes, I'm sure. I'm sorry."

"I hadn't heard about Wilson until your call. Quite a shock. Mrs. Brewster and I have just returned from the Bahamas. Once a year, I like to get away completely. I don't even read the papers. A nice boy, Wilson. In student government here."

I nodded.

124

"He was so generous with the college. When we needed a new shell for the lights a couple of years ago, Wilson came through for us. And just recently there was a gift for the women's lacrosse team. We'll miss him," the Prexy declared, with a regret, which, while monetarily based, was nonetheless sincere.

"I'm sure he'll be remembered," I said.

"He will be indeed." President Brewster smiled, folded his hands and leaned forward slightly. "Now, Miss Peters, the business of the morning."

"There's little doubt," I replied, "that Wilson Daintly was murdered."

Brewster shook his head with sad distaste.

"I'm concerned at the moment with two other Michaelmas graduates, both in the Fife area, who may also be in danger: Peter Bryce, the golfer, now at the British Open, and a linguistics professor, Melvin Thorston. Could you tell me something about either one? Almost anything might turn out to be helpful."

"In danger," Brewster repeated. "In what way?"

"I'll tell you, strictly confidentially, please, that Bryce has been threatened. That was how I became involved. Wilson Daintly's murder may have been a coincidence, but the three men knew each other—evidently from their college days."

Brewster nodded rapidly. "Yes, yes, Bryce and Daintly were good friends. He's made a great success, hasn't he? We're proud of him, of course, although I'm sorry to say he's not the sort who remembers the college. Not a serious offense, I suppose, but in these days of shrinking endowments—"

"I understand."

"Well," Brewster added more genially, "one makes excuses for the illustrious."

"And for ability of all sorts?"

"Meaning?"

"I was thinking of Dr. Thorston."

Brewster's expression became vague. "Thorston? Thorston?"

He reached for the bookcase beside his desk. "What year was Thorston?"

"'Sixty-eight. The same as Daintly."

President Brewster selected one of the yearbooks and flipped through the pages. "Oh, Thorston. I do remember," he said without any particular satisfaction. "An amateur actor. He appeared in *The Importance of Being Earnest* that year. Talented, I'm told."

"He seems to have extraordinary abilities in languages."

"You might see Duclos about him. Yes, he was one of Duclos's protégés, as I recall. Not really the Michaelmas type, Thorston. A bit Bohemian, you might say. Not that we're against the arts here at Michaelmas, but the well-rounded student is still our aim. A liberal education in the best sense of the term," he added in smooth, rounded tones, as though I were a stop on his fund-raising circuit. He was probably good with funds: He gave an impression of culture without eccentricity and of education without scholarship.

"Duclos?" I asked.

"Dr. Duclos in our foreign language department." He pushed his intercom button. "Rose, is Al on campus this summer?"

"He's in class until eleven today."

"Thank you, Rose. Have a talk with him, Miss Peters. He'll have some information, I'm sure. You might see the athletic director about Bryce, but the rest of that department is off for the summer."

"I'll start with Dr. Duclos," I said. "I appreciate your help."

"Not at all," the president replied, "but the less said about the college connections—the better." He sighed, wearied with the eternal vigilance of public relations. "We'll have to do something for Daintly. A plaque or something. Perhaps on the boathouse. I'll contact Bryce. They say he's in a good position for a shot at the Open. Perhaps under the circumstances—"

"Yes," I said. "That sounds like a good idea."

"The Daintly Boathouse—" Brewster shook hands with me and opened the door. "The women's lacrosse program gives less scope," he added. "I think it must be the boathouse. Rose, come take a letter. Good morning, Miss Peters."

Following the secretary's directions, I crossed the quad to one of the modern buildings hidden behind the medieval inspiration of the original college. Professor Duclos was in an office on the third floor, behind a desk covered with books and papers. When I entered, he stared with a baleful expression, as though his stint at rounding off the boys and girls of Michaelmas was beginning to discourage him.

"No conferences now," he said. "Conference hours are posted. I'm having lunch." A strong odor of salami and pickles rose from behind the academic debris.

"I'm sorry to bother you," I replied, "but this is quite urgent. I've just been to see President Brewster. He suggested you might be able to tell me something about Melvin Thorston, a student of yours ten years ago."

"I know when I taught Melvin," the professor replied. "I haven't had another *student* since. Why do you want to know about him?"

I moved several dictionaries and a stack of exams from one of the chairs and sat down. "Another Michaelmas graduate, Wilson Daintly, was murdered this week," I began, and sketched the situation that had brought me to Hartford. Duclos listened in silence, occasionally taking a bite of his odoriferous lunch. When I concluded, he wore an expression of deep sorrow. "Ahhh," he said in a disgusted tone.

"From what President Brewster said," I resumed, "you knew Thorston and were fond of him. I might as well tell you that he is in serious trouble. Perhaps you know something that might help him."

"What would that be?" Duclos asked. "Melvin was a linguist of near genius, a boy with all the intellectual requirements but without the personality. There it is."

"What do you mean, 'without the personality'?"

"Even the scholar's life requires a certain nerve, a certain confidence—perhaps more than you might credit. Melvin lacked—not courage, exactly—but the inner confidence necessary to shape a life's work. It accounted for Peter Bryce, too."

"Bryce?"

"His relationship with Peter was not wholesome. I don't mean anything perverted, but his fascination was unwise."

"Bryce pretends he scarcely knew Dr. Thorston."

"There may be some truth in that, although not in the way he means. Peter Bryce was a golden boy. The darling of the campus. Athletic hero. A young man of great charm and great coldness. He was born to be idolized."

"And Thorston admired him?"

"Excessively," Duclos said shortly. "The attraction of opposites, one might say. Peter had the social polish, the athletic skills, the confidence."

"What did Thorston have?"

"Great talent, a first-rate intellect."

"Did Bryce appreciate that?"

Duclos raised his hands and shrugged expressively before pouring himself a cup of coffee from his thermos. "Peter struck me as the complete pragmatist. If he liked Mel, it was for what Mel could do for him."

"Were they in class together?"

"Peter was rarely in class at all. The glamor of having a leading amateur golfer sufficed for a surprising number of teachers," Duclos said sourly.

"So presumably, Bryce was not simply concerned with getting a little help with the books?"

"No. Academically, Peter had his own resources."

"I see. Or rather, I don't. What about Wilson Daintly? Did you know him?"

"The third member of the triumvirate. I use the word advisedly. It was a trio with many strains."

128

"Why was that?"

Duclos twisted his mouth in thought, then said, "Adolescent politics. These were three unusual people—in their own areas, you understand. There was a certain rivalry. A spirit of emulation is perhaps more exact. And then I've always felt that three is an inherently unstable grouping. There is always a tendency of trios to resolve themselves into duos."

"In this case with Peter as the pivotal figure?"

"That would have been my guess. He had the least need for friendship and so was indispensable to the other two."

"Wilson as much as Mel?"

"Oh, yes. Wilson needed an audience—a clientele, if you would. You smile, but all the human passions are observable at every stage, in every group. Wilson was the archetypal politician."

"And Peter, an attractive supporter?"

"He represented the athletic bloc."

"But am I right in thinking Wilson lived in the same building with Mel?"

"That's right. Upperclassmen had the option of living off campus. There used to be quite a few boarding houses and apartments that rented to the students. They've gone out of business since the new dorms."

"Did you know the owner of the one Daintly and Thorston were in? A Louie La Fleur?"

"Not personally. He was a French Canadian, though, because I remember Mel used to mimic his accent. He had a great knack for dialects. La Fleur was something of a character, I believe. He was the local bookie for years."

"Is he still around?"

"I don't know if he's even alive. If he is, he's probably still down on Zion Street. He didn't sound like the sort of man who moves around a lot."

"I'll check into that."

"It's been a long time," Duclos said reflectively.

"Yes, but Daintly and Thorston kept in touch."

"Oh?"

"The Gruen Foundation was supporting Mel's latest research."

"A waste of time and talent," Duclos said shortly.

"Daintly, as far as I can determine, supplied the Gruen Foundation's money."

"Wilson never had much appetite for the scholarly life."

"Mel must have found the means to change his mind."

"Persuasion was hardly his forte," Duclos said skeptically.

"Nonetheless, the money came in regularly. Any idea why?"

The professor's glum expression darkened still further, as though he were contemplating something unpleasant or only half clear. After a moment, he said, "Your best idea would be to visit Louie."

"Yes, I'll see if I can locate him." I rose to go, and as I was replacing the professor's disorderly books and papers, Duclos emerged from behind his desk. "I was afraid they'd ruin him," he remarked abruptly.

I stopped, some of his folders still in my hand. "In what way? What do you mean?"

"There was a—tension between the three of them." He shook his head. "Not good for a personality like Mel's. He took everything to heart and kept things too much to himself."

"You're sure there was no sexual relationship?"

"No, no, nothing like that. Bryce was girl crazy and Mel, too, I think—he just had less luck."

"I see."

"I never did find out what happened," Duclos continued reflectively. "There was something. I think that's why Mel enlisted in the army. A combination escape—and atonement, maybe. There was something on his mind, anyway. After the service, he wasn't the same. He went at a bad time, you see, to a bad place. They put him on search and destroy, looking for mines or traps, some such thing. It damaged him: Look at this

130

latest craziness of his. I wouldn't be surprised at anything."

"Not even Daintly's death?"

"That I was surprised about."

"Yes?"

"Wilson was a smart boy. I didn't think he was the sort to get himself murdered."

"I'd heard he wasn't much of a student."

"Scholarship isn't everything, is it? They were three bright boys. Each in his own way. I'd remember that, if I were you." Duclos crushed the wax papers from his lunch and replaced the top on his thermos.

"Just one more thing," I said. "When he was in the army, Thorston worked with electronic equipment, rather than languages. Did he have any interest in electronics in college?"

"Yes," Duclos said shortly, continuing to tidy up his desk.

"An unusual combination of interests?" I suggested.

"Not at all. He was fascinated by the way speech sounds could be reproduced electronically. He had some ingenious ideas, which, if carried through, might have led to an improved artificial larynx. I had hoped his work would move in that direction," Duclos said, "instead of obsolete dialects and idiotic psychological experiments. But," he added with scarcely disguised resentment, "he wouldn't take advice from me. Not after the Brainwithe girl died."

"Would that be Caroline Brainwithe? The woman who was murdered?"

"Yes. A sad case."

"What did she have to do with Mel?"

"Speech pathology was her field. She worked in the lab here."

I had known that. It had been mentioned in the news stories: a mere coincidental detail. "But Michaelmas wasn't coed, then."

"No, but she was here as a special student. Graduate level, naturally. The family was an old Michaelmas contributor."

In Duclos's stuffy office, the stale odor of the luncheon meat

131

began combining disagreeably with the smog. "And Mel and Caroline Brainwithe were friends?" That had not come up in the investigation, I knew.

" 'Friends' would be going too far. On her side at least. She was already a young lady of a certain sophistication. But not a bad student. Not in Mel's class, of course, but she didn't need to be. He was much taken with her, in his own way. He stopped work in the lab the day after she died."

Duclos looked away thoughtfully for a moment, then opened the door abruptly. "I've no more time to talk," he said.

I gathered my things and started to thank him.

"A waste of time," he said, his face dark.

I considered some platitude, rejected it, and nodded. As I started down the corridor, the door shut and the lock clicked.

* * *

Harriet was waiting at the college gates, full of her visit with Ralph. I managed to ignore this recital until she declared, "So there's a good chance Ralph will be accepted."

"Uh-huh?"

"Accepted," Harriet repeated expectantly, "for the dental school?"

"What?"

She sighed. "Something wrong?" she asked.

"Sorry. My mind was on other things."

"I got that feeling. Find out anything?"

"I'm not too sure." An apparently straightforward black-mail-extortion scheme was taking on some complicated accompaniments, the oddest being Peter Bryce's position. Daintly's friend and Thorston's folly, he seemed to be the connecting link between two increasingly dubious characters. I didn't care for the way things were shaping up at all.

"This way," Harriet said. "The car's over here. Are you ready for lunch?"

"Later. There's a man I want to see on Zion Street. It's close."

132

"Should I come—or would you rather go alone?"

"Doesn't matter, but perhaps you should come. An old bookie might find you reassuring."

"You have the oddest ways of doing things," Harriet said. "I've never met a bookie."

"Then you can complete your education. What house number did Morton give us for that Louie La Fleur?"

Harriet opened her notebook, and I glanced over her shoulder. "Just down the street."

We pulled out of the tree-shaded lot and bumped down the steep road from the college to the shabby area below. Despite the grandeur of its Biblical name, Zion Street is unprepossessing, a row of aging brick and wood tenements interspersed with a few dreary shops and a dark, unsavory bar. The address was for one of the tenements, now divided, it appeared, into a three-family house. There was a peeling label next to the ground floor doorbell reading "LA FLEUR."

"We're in luck," I commented, pushing the button.

A truck heaved itself into low gear and tackled the slope, and two women arguing in Spanish passed on the sidewalk. I pushed the bell again; then Harriet and I stood on the sweltering porch and waited.

"I don't think anyone's home," Harriet said with ill-disguised relief.

Unwilling to give up, I hammered on the door.

"Who you looking for?" someone called from the upper story.

"Does Louie La Fleur still live here?"

"Ask Margaret. She's 'round back."

A narrow alley, lined with broken glass, crushed cans, and burdocks, led to the rear of the building, where there was a storage space, covered with a wooden lattice, and three porches, one above the other. Wash was strung between their rails and a half-dead elm, in whose meager shade a large German shepherd lay, dispirited by the heat. It growled softly as we emerged into the white sunlight, and for a few seconds there was no other sound. Then I heard the soft, rhythmic squeak of a rocker on the lowest porch. A woman holding a bottle of beer was sitting far back in the shadows. The rails and the gingerbread trim of the porch interrupted the glaring noontime, casting deep greenish black shadows on the worn floorboards, the old wicker furniture, and the clapboards on the wall. Several fluffy gray and spotted kittens staggered about on soft, unsteady legs, and as we climbed the steps to the veranda, we were engulfed by a smell of beer and cats. The rocker stopped squeaking. Its inhabitant was sixty—or more likely, prematurely decrepit. Her gray hair straggled unkempt, and despite the heat, she wore a long black blouse with the sleeves rolled up to reveal patched and purpled arms. Her face was worn and puffy, and a good deal of alcohol had gone into its expression of slack bewilderment.

"We're looking for Mr. La Fleur," Harriet said. "We'd like to speak with him."

"No chance of that," the woman replied and took another sip of her drink.

"Why not?" I asked.

"Louie's been dead a year. A year next month."

"Oh, dear," Harriet exclaimed. "Are you Mrs. La Fleur?"

"Far as I was concerned."

"I'm very sorry," Harriet said in a kindly way. There was no response. "I'm Harriet Edgar," she continued, "and this is Anna Peters, my employer. My, it's hot! Worse than in Washington."

"You ladies from Washington?" Mrs. La Fleur asked. Her voice was at once dreamy and nervous, as though behind that somnolent presence was an alert, high-strung personality, temporarily tranquilized by drink.

"That's right," Harriet said. In her best Washington hostess manner, she attempted small talk, an effort rewarded by an invitation to sit down. We each took a greasy wicker chair and

134

moved it back from the glare. There was a temporary lull.

"What'd you want to see Louie about?" Mrs. La Fleur asked. "Not many people have asked about him," she added.

"I'm sure it must have been a great sorrow," Harriet said. Louie's virtues were discussed for a few moments: Unlikely as it seemed, we were evidently being cast as visitors on a condolence call. Harriet made all the appropriate noises, and when Mrs. La Fleur began to sniffle, politely handed her a Kleenex. My assistant had virtues I'd overlooked.

"We came to ask your husband about one of his old lodgers," I said finally.

"Who was that?"

"Wilson Daintly. Do you remember him?"

"I knew Wilson," she said. "Lived here—must be ten years ago."

"That's right. And there was another student, too. Melvin Thorston. Do you recall him?"

"We had a lot of students," she said reflectively. "Louie liked students."

"Was he fond of Wilson Daintly?"

"Everyone liked him. We used to play cards together sometimes."

"Who were his friends?"

"That boy who's the golfer used to come by a lot." She laughed a little. "And the actor. My, he could imitate Louie. He could fool me if I was in the other room and couldn't see who was talking. I'd have sworn it was Louie."

"That would have been Melvin Thorston."

"Well, you forget the names."

"I'm sure."

She shook her head. "Mel? Was that his name?"

"I think so. He's an amateur actor with some talent."

"Dorston, did you say?"

"Thorston. With a *T*."

"I didn't think that was his name. I know who you mean, all

right, though. I always liked him myself. A funny kid. But Louie and him never got on."

"Oh?" I said, trying to conceal my interest.

"Like cat and dog. Argue. Couldn't even agree on the time of day."

"Awkward."

"Much as I liked the boy, I was glad to see him go. Mel, that's right. That was his name."

"Yes."

Mrs. La Fleur heaved a heavy sigh. "Long time since we've had students. Them new dorms. Now they expect a whole apartment if they're going to rent. It's not worth the trouble.

"'Course if we'd had students, Louie would be alive today."

"Oh? Why's that?"

"Louie was alone in the house. Somebody walked in and that was that. I come home and there he is on the floor. Hit from behind was what the police said."

"With what?"

"Anna!" Harriet exclaimed, adding, "How awful for you, Mrs. La Fleur."

Mrs. La Fleur wiped her eyes and reached for her beer. "Lived with that man twenty years," she said.

"Did the police find out who'd done it?" I asked after a moment.

"You kidding me? In this neighborhood? Nobody sees nothing anymore. They didn't care about Louie. Someone walked in off the street, they said. They said people would have known he had money. But that wasn't true."

"That Louie had money?"

She nodded.

"He used to place a few bets, though, didn't he?"

"That never did anyone any harm. Besides, Louie'd retired. Everyone knew that. 'Course you get some of these people on drugs. They'd try to rob anyone."

"Louie was killed in a robbery, then."

136

"Naw. That's what I'm explaining," Mrs. La Fleur said. "I'd like another beer." She pointed to a carton in the corner. "You ladies like one?"

I got her a bottle, but declined her offer. She opened the beer and lit a cigarette.

"That's what the police thought." She shook her head and added craftily, "But there wasn't nothing taken. Nothing but my Louie." She wiped her eyes on the back of her hand, and Harriet, good scout, patted her on the shoulder consolingly.

"Why you so interested, anyway?" Mrs. La Fleur asked, suspicious. She sat up with sudden energy, her eyes momentarily alert.

"Wilson Daintly's been murdered. His friend, the golfer Peter Bryce, has been threatened. Another friend was recently injured. Louie was one of Daintly's friends, too."

Mrs. La Fleur slumped back into her chair, her eyes searching my face restlessly. "What has that got to do with it?"

"I'm not sure. It just doesn't seem healthy to have known Wilson Daintly, does it?"

She looked away, as if to evade this conclusion. The rocker started to squeak again, a monotonous rhythm of boredom and misery. One of the kittens made a mess on the floor, but its owner took no notice of it nor of the other odors issuing from the domestic livestock.

"It must have been difficult for you and Louie when the new dorms went up."

"Difficult for a lot of us. Oh, things haven't been the same. But they never are. Won't be again. The students were better off with us. But there you are."

"Of course from the parents' point of view," Harriet began, but I glared at her for silence.

"Did Louie get another job—or expand the bookmaking?"

"I told you, Louie retired."

"When was that?"

" 'Seventy or 'seventy-one. He said it was time."

"Just like that?"

"It's what I said, isn't it?"

I considered my next question carefully. "Did Louie receive money from someone? Did he have money coming in regularly?"

"What are you? From the Internal Revenue?" She set down her bottle angrily, and then, as if frightened by her own hostility, shrank further back into the rocker.

"I gave you my card," I said. Mrs. La Fleur consulted this again. Out in the yard, the shepherd rose to its feet, turned around, and flopped down in the narrow shade of the elm. A little dust stirred in the yard, and the sickening heat was all embracing. "You would like to know who killed Louie, wouldn't you, Mrs. La Fleur?"

"Wouldn't bring him back," she said sensibly, but the rocker creaked again, in a little nervous obbligato.

"Did Louie have money you didn't know about?" I asked softly.

After a long silence, she nodded. "He said one of his old friends would take care of him."

"How long ago was this?"

"When he retired."

"He never elaborated?"

She shook her head. "Louie was always very close-mouthed. Part of his business. Louie was a real pro," she added, "in a small way, but a real pro." She sniffled, and Harriet agreed with her effusively until I tapped her ankle with my foot. Unexpectedly, Mrs. La Fleur had more to say.

"Last year, Louie said things would be looking up. That's how he put it. 'Looking up.' He said there'd be a change in our 'financial picture.' Louie could be quite a card."

"How long was that before he died?"

"He was killed in August, the nineteenth of August. It was a day like this, stinking hot. When I found him, I mean. He'd talked about the money in the spring. We were at dinner one

138

night and he put down the paper—Louie always bought the evening paper for the results. A habit after all those years. He dropped the newspaper and said, 'Margaret, things are going to look up.' Just like that."

"Could it have been something he saw in the paper?" I asked.

"He didn't say." She set the beer bottle aside. "Another dead soldier," she remarked.

"One other thing. You said you used to play cards with Wilson Daintly."

"Yeah. Me and Louie and some of the boys would play. Low stakes. Nothing important."

"But one of those games was important, wasn't it?"

"None of our games was important. I told you. Low stakes. We played for fun. Not that some of those boys couldn't have afforded it. We used to run a fine boarding house. It's not what it used to be." This time she got up herself, quite unsteadily, and moved the remains of the carton closer.

"I'm thinking of the game on the night of April 21, 1968."

"That's a long time to remember a friendly hand of poker," Mrs. La Fleur replied. She ran her hand through her witch's mane of gray hair.

"That was the night the Brainwithe house was robbed. Do you remember that case? Their daughter, the housekeeper, and a friend were murdered."

She shrugged. "I never followed the papers much. Louie did, for his business, but not me. Not much worth reading." She seemed about to go off on another tangent, but this was halted by her attempts to open the beer.

"You would remember that young Daintly was one of the people questioned, surely. The police talked to all the Brainwithes' friends. To everyone who'd had access to the house."

"Yeah," she said, a trifle bitter. "That was one of the important murders. Who'd they question when my Louie was killed?"

"They seem to have exerted themselves," I agreed. "And presumably, people without an account of their movements for the night of the twenty-first were questioned more closely. Do you know where Daintly was?"

"How would I know?"

"He said he played cards with Louie, you, and some of the other tenants here."

Mrs. La Fleur poured herself a long drink and shoved away a kitten that was attempting to clamber over her slipper. Then she pushed back her hair with a nervous gesture, and the rocker began to squeak again. "What night was that?" she asked.

"The twenty-first of April. A Sunday."

There was a subtle change in her expression.

"Is something wrong?"

"It's possible we played poker," she said, "but Louie was always an orderly man. He liked to keep his accounts up to date. He always did his books on Sunday nights."

12

"NOT MUCH HERE," I remarked to Detective Paloucci, who slammed one of the big green file drawers shut and returned to sit tipped back in his chair with his feet up on the desk. I'd contacted Paloucci a few years earlier during some work for one of the local insurance firms and had found him a clever detective and an honest straightforward guy. Since then, we'd had occasions for cooperation, and he'd made no problems about filling me in on the La Fleur murder.

Now he lit a smelly brown cigarette and ran a weary hand over his brilliant black eyes. "What can I say? No witnesses, no clues, no cooperation."

"No cooperation?"

"Naw. The woman—what's her name?"

"Margaret? Mrs. La Fleur."

"Yeah, only it's Margaret Something Else. Common law."

"Oh, yes, I see. Margaret Soucey."

"Right. Nothing from her. To hear her tell it, she and Louie lived on manna from heaven instead of on the NFL point spread and sore-legged nags at Aqueduct."

"She claims he'd retired."

"Maybe, maybe not."

"She does seem to have been pretty broken up by his death."

"By that and old rotgut. She's a lush—we couldn't get anything useful out of her. Louie had no enemies, no friends—you've heard the line."

"Un-huh. Now she feels the police should have done a more thorough job."

Paloucci shrugged and threw up his hands. "A year ago, she just wanted him for the funeral and the quicker the better."

"What did she and Louie do for money?"

"Well, they weren't on welfare."

"Think he had some money stashed?"

"Probably. But it wasn't robbery. We went over the place pretty good, and there were no prints, nothing suspicious."

"It sounds like someone he knew."

Paloucci tipped the ash off his cigarette. "That was my theory, but as I say, no cooperation. We never got a motive, we never got any indication of a stranger in the neighborhood. Nobody was telling us anything."

"Mrs. La Fleur seemed more inclined to talk today."

"Yeah. After the fact."

"Do you know what she's living on? It can't be much from the look of the place."

"I can find out for you."

"Please."

While Paloucci dialed a contact in the welfare office, I read the sparse account of the killing of Louis La Fleur, white male, aged sixty-seven. He had been struck from behind sometime between 10:00 A.M. and noon on the morning of August 19. The body had been discovered in the kitchen of the ground floor of the La Fleurs' three-family home on Zion Street at around 3:00 P.M. by his common law wife, Margaret Soucey, who had been away overnight visiting friends in Plainville. None of the neighbors had heard any suspicious noises; both doors were found locked. There were no fingerprints, nor any sign of a search, and nothing was missing from the La Fleur home. Testimony supported Margaret Soucey's claim that Louie had retired from his bookmaking business. No motive was ever established for the crime. Various leads had been followed; all had proved abortive. The closest thing to a clue was the second floor tenant's testimony that she'd "maybe heard a doorbell ring. It was not her bell, and she couldn't be sure, because the children had the TV on." She estimated this was shortly before ten. At that time, the killer had apparently gained access to the La Fleur apartment, either because he was known to the victim or through guile, and murdered the ex-bookie. Who or why had proved impossible to establish.

"She's living on welfare. They're trying to get her some kind of widow's benefit off Louie's Social Security," Paloucci said, putting down the receiver.

"That's worth knowing. Thanks a lot."

"You find anything?" he asked when I returned the file.

"I'm afraid you're right. There's not much to go on."

"Naw. Odd case. I knew the fellow assigned to it. Funny thing," Paloucci remarked as he rolled open the file drawer, "he gets assigned to this case involving a dead bookie, see, and the next afternoon doesn't he win the office pool for the tournament. He said that was all his luck shot—never did anything with the case." Paloucci laughed and I joined him.

"What tournament was that?"

"The Sammy Davis. The old ICO renamed. Hartford's premier sporting event."

"The big golf tournament?"

"Sure, all the names come—in the press releases. What's the matter with you—never read the sports pages?"

"I stick with the police news," I said, and after more banter of this feeble sort, I thanked him and hurried downstairs to where Harriet was waiting, wearing a reflective, melancholy expression.

"That poor woman," she said as we climbed into our stifling car.

"What poor woman?"

"Mrs. La Fleur, of course." Harriet's tone hinted disapproval.

"Yes, sad case," I said. I was thinking that golf tournaments were unhealthy events for Daintly and his friends. I'd have to call Inspector Stewart.

"Did they do anything for her or just not care?"

"Do what?"

"The police? What did they do about her husband? It's an awful thing."

"The police have a different line," I said. "The widow La Fleur, whose legal name is Soucey, by the way, had very little to say to them. The word at headquarters is *uncooperative*."

"I don't believe it. They're just covering up."

"Maybe. I'm inclined to see it the other way."

"You're getting a bit hard, Anna. That poor woman was in tears."

"Oh, she was fond of him, all right. That doesn't mean she'd necessarily cooperate with the cops."

"That doesn't make sense."

"Doesn't it? The police weren't going to bring him back from the dead. And their asking too many questions might have disturbed Mrs. La Fleur's livelihood."

"What do you mean?"

"Somebody was paying Louie money. Money that kept the La Fleurs off welfare. When Louie died, the money stopped. Mrs. La Fleur is now broke."

"They owned the house."

"Probably it had to be sold. Mrs. La Fleur looks like a woman who's lived pretty close to the margin."

"I still don't see why there wasn't a more thorough investigation," Harriet said primly.

"They couldn't afford it. Noble sentiments like justice and

retribution cost money. Dig out my notes, would you?"

Harriet went through my bag until she found them.

"The meeting with Bryce, the first one. See if there was a reference to the Sammy Davis Open."

While I maneuvered the car through the midday traffic on the concrete Mixmaster around central Hartford, Harriet consulted the notebook. "Your writing's hard to read."

"Yeah, neatness counts. What's it say."

" 'Said he'd had threats before.' That it?"

"What comes next?"

" 'Asked when? At the Sammy Davis Open in Hartford.' "

"I thought so. Harriet, see if you can find out where Thorston and Daintly were last August nineteenth. It'll probably be easier to do back at the hotel."

"All right."

"You can get a bus from here," I said, slowing at the corner of Broad Street.

"Where are you going?" Ahead of us lay the tangle of superhighway, overpasses, and monolithic offices that encircle the ornate Victorian capitol and the diminished greens of Bushnell Park.

"Local paper. I've got to see a man about a golf tournament."

"Oh."

I pulled over to the curb and stopped. Harriet unloaded her totebag and purse, then stood for a moment in the wilting sun.

"What's wrong?"

"It's discouraging," she said.

"What is?"

"This whole thing. They all seem to be guilty of something, don't they?" she replied.

*   *   *

I considered that possibility on my way up to the paper's library, where none of the various permutations of guilt was eliminated by the stories from the previous year's Sammy Davis

Open. Peter Bryce had gone into the third round at eleven under and, tied for second, had teed off at one-thirty. That was the day Louie La Fleur's mysterious assailant had entered his Zion Street residence at approximately 10:00 A.M. and dispatched him with a blow to the back of the head. The paper for the next morning carried the story, a narrow column of type on the front page, "CITY MAN FOUND SLAIN," which added nothing to my knowledge. The sports pages, however, were lavish in their treatment of my other interest. It appeared that Bryce had had one of his rare bad days on the links. He had bogied half a dozen holes and seen his fine score plummet. " 'A touch of stomach virus,' " he claimed, "but," the news story continued, "he wasn't making any excuses." The interview made him sound like a reasonable, charming man, which caused me to wonder if there aren't personalities born to be filtered through newsprint, just as certain faces are fated for enhancement by the camera lens. The next day, he partially redeemed himself, picked up three strokes, and finished fourth at eight under. Perhaps they didn't call him Peter Ice for nothing.

I made a note of Bryce's starting times for all four days of the tournament, recorded the fact that the competitors were mostly housed at the Sheraton-Hartford, and then began a careful perusal of the papers from March on. Two hours later, my eyes were aching, the under-air-conditioned library felt like a sauna, and I was convinced that there were no references to either Thorston or Daintly in the local paper. What was much in evidence, though, was the meteoric rise of Bryce's career. There were any number of references to him, his score appeared in the results of most of the important tournaments that spring, and there were two pictures of him. In one, he was driving off the seventeenth tee in the Greater Greensboro Open; in the other, he was acknowledging the plaudits of the gallery after winning the Milwaukee Classic. "Sometime in the spring," Mrs. La Fleur had said, and Louie always read the sporting news. He could hardly have missed Bryce's move into the big

146

time, and for a man with slender savings, a drinking wife—and if I was correct—a little blackmail habit, Bryce's winnings must have looked very tempting. It certainly wasn't beyond belief that Louie, who had provided Daintly with his alibi, had been collecting from the wealthy developer for years. That struck me as Daintly's style, too. He'd been quietly supporting Thorston, less, I suspected, out of compassion or any interest in obsolete Anglo-Saxon dialects, than to keep the professor out of the way. With one "old friend" on the payroll, he'd hardly have murdered to avoid a second. No, Daintly would have been Louie's "friend," who sent him a little now and again and whose real wealth would have exceeded Louie's grasp or reckoning, anyway.

Bryce was another matter. The golfer's earnings were public knowledge, and the sports world was Louie's own milieu. The bookie might well have decided to secure his retirement by putting the bite on Bryce. And Bryce, being no fool, had realized his own vulnerability and taken drastic steps to remove the threat to his career and his earnings. It was all very plausible, but far from provable, especially when an alternate reading might just as easily produce Dr. Thorston's name. He was a flake at best, a nut at worst, and he might not have needed elaborate or logical justifications for doing away with an old and disliked acquaintance. It seemed, in fact, as if Harriet had been quite correct, and the only remaining question was whether one or two or all of the Michaelmas triumvirate had been implicated in the Brainwithe case. I was tempted, but I could not decide. I had flown over three thousand miles because I thought they were; the difficulty was the messiness of the conclusion. After sitting stewing at the desk for a few more moments, I got up and asked the librarian for the file of clips on the case. Along with them were some photos that the good New England paper had decided were not for public consumption. Except for their revelations of the brutality of the act, they were meaningless: Neither Caroline Brainwithe nor Mrs.

O'Reilly was recognizable, and Langley's features had suffered a permanent and horrific distortion. The news cuttings proper carried three blurred, noncommittal photographs of the victims in life: Ms. Brainwithe, blonde with a long, homely, honest face; the housekeeper, small and dumpy with her hair tucked under a net; and Langley, a dozen years too young, caught by some yearbook camera. That these sudden and violent transformations had occurred at the hands of three exceptionally clever students did not seem likely. Yet, the thieves could not have foreseen the conclusion of their adventure: The denouement had probably taken them as much by surprise as it had the victims. Thorston's dissertation on violence had omitted mention of the smallness of its steps, the almost invisible nature of the increments that edge the personality toward devastation. I knew about that. Had I been a trifle stronger—or weaker—that long ago summer afternoon when I departed Hartford, my subsequent career might have been very different—or nonexistent. I had not, after all, considered murdering my former husband, when I stood at the stove putting bacon and eggs into the heavy cast-iron skillet, which twenty minutes later I hurled at his head. When they—or he, or she, or whoever—deciphered the secret of Brainwithe's safe, the mess of blood and bone on the marble floor had not been anticipated. That was the surprise events had kept in store. I refolded the clippings and returned the soft, yellowing papers to the file, along with the photos, protected by their thin Manila cases. As I gathered my belongings, I thought that the killings at the Brainwithes must have had long reverberations even for the people who had been lucky enough to get away with murder.

The newspaper's library was at one end of a twisting corridor lined with chopped-up offices consisting of beaverboard and glass partitions. Farther along was a small glass-walled room where teletype machines hammered away, spewing out buff and yellow streamers imprinted with baseball scores and stock reports, murder trials and exotic disasters. The building then opened into two large bays. Beyond the low barriers on each side of the corridor were masses of gray-topped desks, each with an immense typewriter, untidy hanks of teletype copy, an overflowing ashtray and pots of paste and pencils. The sun bored through the smog to give a rust-tinged glare to the western windows, and there was a smell of ink and newsprint and the stale, smoky odor of overworked air conditioning. The sports section was empty except for one stout, graying man flipping through his mail. When I approached, he said, "We're not taking golf scores yet."

"Doesn't look as if the staff is in," I commented.

"Four o'clock. Phones go in at six."

"I can't imagine playing anything in this heat," I remarked.

"They manage," he said. He sorted out a few remaining envelopes, dispersing them in the writers' mailboxes. "Can I help you?" he asked when he was finished.

"I want to ask a couple of questions about the setup of golf tournaments. I was in the library looking up some information —for an insurance claim from last summer." I handed him my card. "Boring stuff—I started reading the tournament reports. The paper did a very attractive job on it. Some really nice layouts."

"Thank you."

"Rather a belated reader response."

"So long's it's good."

"I'm interested because my husband's doing some illustrations over at the British Open."

This caught his attention, and we discussed golf and sports magazines and the art of sports illustration for several minutes. "I've got a bet on Peter Bryce," I said finally. "What do you think the chances are of his blowing up again this year the way he did in the Sammy Davis?"

"Let's see how he's doing," my informant said. "It's time I got this stuff anyway." He went into the teletype room to return with a banner-sized string of copy that he folded accordian fashion and laid on the desk. "Well, your bet looks good at the moment. He's in the clubhouse with five under. He's got to be in contention with that. He's lying third at the moment."

"Maybe last year was just a fluke."

"Odd tournament. Everyone had fantastic scores until the last day—except Bryce. He played badly the third day—got his bogies in a round early. But that's not characteristic. He's a pretty sound golfer." The writer shrugged. "A prima donna, though, about details. Claimed he'd gotten some stomach upset from the lunch tent—as if the rest of us hadn't eaten there and survived. Well, if we were making that kind of money—"

"We could indulge ourselves, too."

"Right." He sat down at one of the large desks to lay out the evening's work, and I thanked him and left. I was beginning to think I'd put my money on the right horse until I got back to the hotel.

"What did you find out?" I asked Harriet.

"I've had quite a time," she said. "Some of those people are beginning to wonder why all the calls about a job application." She looked unhappy. The more creative aspects of lying do not attract Harriet, who fibs badly.

"All for a good cause, remember."

"I'll try. Wilson Daintly was in Houston, then in the U.K. handling details on that property he wanted to develop. He was away most of July and all of August."

"That lets him out."

"Yes. That's almost a relief."

"Un-huh. Now for Thorston."

"Well, he finished up his term at Duke and flew to Germany in late May. I talked to someone in his department, and she remembered."

"And he was away all summer and then moved on to St. Andrews?"

"That's what I'd assumed, but he was back."

"When?" I asked, suddenly alert.

"For two weeks in August. Through the tournament."

"May have been a coincidence. Where was he?"

"He was at a conference on Middle English."

"That certainly sounds harmless. Where was it?"

"It was at Yale, and Dr. Thorston delivered a paper on August eighteenth."

I let out my breath. "Presumably leaving him free to roam around Connecticut on the morning of the nineteenth."

"I'm afraid so." She looked positively distressed.

"What do you mean?"

"Well, I called Yale to double check about the conference. Dr. Thorston left a rather bad impression."

"Why?"

"He gave a very good paper, but he never showed up for the seminar on it scheduled for the next morning."

"Great," I said. "Get me a flight to either Preswick or London, tonight, would you?"

"You're not going to turn around and go right back!"

"You were the one who was worrying about my leaving Harry all alone. And get me on that connecting flight to JFK."

Harriet looked at her watch. "You'll have to leave now to catch the Hartford–New York plane. I'll make your other arrangements while you're on your way."

"All right. I'll call you here when I get in."

"Yes." Harriet smiled. She loves complicated arrangements, intricate connections, elaborate forays through red tape and schedules. "That will work out fine."

13

CONTRARY TO HARRIET'S OPTIMISTIC ASSERTION, things did not work out fine. True, I was on a flight to London that night. And true, I was in contact with the CID of the Fife Constabulary. That was the good news. The bad news was that the London plane had developed a hitch in its electrical system, delaying our departure until well after midnight, and that Detective Inspector Stewart was off duty when I called. I left a message. When I arrived in London the next afternoon, I tried again. This time, the inspector was in, but he was not in any mood to exchange confidences with an overseas colleague.

"Well, it's not much to go on, is it, Miss Peters?" he commented when I had finished a rundown of my efforts in Hartford. "This is all circumstance and speculation."

"I couldn't agree more," I said, scarcely able to keep the exasperation out of my voice, and pushed more coins into the phone, which was beginning a shrill demand for money. "But it is suggestive. Especially since either of them could have murdered Daintly."

"Bryce has no motive," Stewart replied, his voice at once bored and irritated.

"If the three of them were involved in a major robbery in the States, he had as much motive as Thorston, maybe more. He's the one who stands to lose money. Thorston was dependent on Daintly, he's no reason—"

"Murders don't always need important reasons."

"Sure," I said, "but if you're wrong, Thorston is in real danger. I don't see why you can't keep an eye on Bryce as well as on him. I think it would be worth—"

"Peter Bryce is still five under for the Open this afternoon," Stewart replied in a frosty voice. "I hardly think a man in his position is a very plausible potential murderer. And he's been very decent about Professor Thorston. He's refused to press charges about that threat, and he went to the hospital to see the professor, too."

"He would," I said sourly. "And did he have anything interesting to say to Thorston?"

"I wouldn't know," the policeman said. "Professor Thorston climbed out a window at the hospital last night. Neither Peter Bryce nor anyone else has seen him since."

This news put me in much the same mood as Stewart. Worse, in fact. I was finishing up twelve plus hours in airports and aircraft. Several unfortunate things were said on both sides, and as I remember both the integrity of the Scottish police and the desirability of women investigators were called into question. This time when the telephone began squeaking loudly for change, I slung the receiver onto the hook and stamped out for my connecting flight.

I'd rented a car at the Edinburgh airport, but even so, it was dinner time before I pulled into St. Andrews. Over the sea, the sky was a dark blue-purple, but the sun shone golden on the town, the Open tents, and the green courses. Harry was still toiling at the studio, and our room at the hotel was littered with sketches and clothes. Propped up on the desk was a note: He loved me and would be back after nine. I scribbled a line in return, then, too restless for a proper meal, bought a paper of fish and chips and puzzled over Professor Thorston's flight. Had guilt, fear, or Wulf determined his departure? I hesitated to choose among such pregnant alternatives, but in any case, I decided it was a mistake for Stewart to look for Melvin Thorston. From what I had absorbed of the professor's theories, I figured that Wulf was the personality of choice for a time of violence and turmoil. Having come to this conclusion, I dispatched the remains of the fish supper and headed down the row of houses alongside the cathedral precinct.

Thorston's apartment was in the upper floor of a substantial house of stone construction. Like most of the older property in town, it was larger than it appeared, extending far back from the modest façade on the street and ending in a garden. Thorston had had his own entrance off a pend, a covered alley, at the side, but tonight I rang the front bell. Almost immediately, there was a great clomping from within, and a tall, thin woman with a mass of disheveled red hair jerked open the door.

"Mrs. Gilchrist?"

"Yes."

I handed her one of my cards. "Are you Dr. Thorston's landlady?"

"Yes, but I'm really not prepared to discuss Melvin. The police have already been here."

She started to shut the door, but I put my hand on it and took a chance. "If you want to help Dr. Thorston, you'd better talk to me. He's in very serious trouble. I know. I've just come back from Hartford, Connecticut."

I don't know what she knew, but Hartford was the magic word. She hesitated only a second, then stepped aside.

"We can sit in here," she said.

The Gilchrists' living room had a fine old fireplace, equipped with an electric fire, a great clutter of bookshelves and glass-fronted cupboards crammed with academic paraphernalia, several large, much-worn velvet easy chairs, and a baggy couch nearly lost under newspapers, baby toys, and a crocheted afghan. A few potted plants stood near the large window, but the rest of the room was spartan academic, its bare floor providing a convenient place for a plump blond baby with beautiful eyes and a belligerent expression who was alternately hammering the boards with a rattle and chewing energetically on the handle. It stared at me with an expression of alert malevolence, threw down the toy, and immediately started to howl.

Mrs. Gilchrist gave an embarrassed sigh. "He's always that way with strangers. Here, Ian." She knelt down and picked up the toy to distract the infant, who allowed himself to be rather quickly pacified. I sat down in the more resilient of the two chairs and waited until Mrs. Gilchrist had deposited her offspring in a swing affair suspended from the doorway to the inner rooms of the apartment. The child was balky and energetic, and I had plenty of time to take in the piles of history volumes, the old framed prints, the assortment of artifacts on the mantel, and the peculiar costume of my hostess. Like a number of faculty wives I've encountered, Mrs. Gilchrist affected the ethnic style: peasant clogs, a droopy skirt of Near Eastern drabness, a thin, dark cotton T-shirt, and a shawl. I half wondered if this collegiate refugee ensemble was not designed as much as a reproach to the meager salaries of academic life as to colorful materialism.

"Sorry," she said. "He does act up."

"He looks like a fine healthy baby."

"Oh, yes." She gave the child a solicitous, nervous glance, and thus encouraged, the baby began to sniffle.

"I came to see you," I began hastily, "because Dr. Thorston's left the hospital."

"I know. As I said, the police have been here."

"The police think he's implicated in the killing of Wilson Daintly, the developer who was found dead in Tayport earlier this week."

She nodded rapidly. "I knew about that, too. It was such a shock to Melvin." Mrs. Gilchrist had a careful, refined voice, more English than Scottish, but the restraint in her speech was deceptive. She pulled nervously on the fringes of the afghan and kept glancing at the baby, who bounced up and down, fat, happy, and dictatorial. "He'd known Wilson since their college days."

"Daintly was the main financial support for the Gruen Foundation, which supported Melvin's work. Did you know that?"

"We never discussed—" she began, but couldn't muster quite enough conviction to finish the sentence.

"Well," I said, "I don't find it plausible that Melvin would have murdered his main benefactor, do you?"

"Oh, Mel would never have hurt anyone," she replied with passionate conviction. "He's the kindest man." She twisted another loose strand of the afghan, threatening to dismember one of the lacy yellow squares.

I nodded.

"Not everyone sees that. How kind he is, I mean."

"No," I agreed. "Frankly, he struck me as a man with a violent temper."

"That's just his manner," she said quickly. "It means nothing. He should have been a man of the theater." She gave a faint smile after this declaration. "Melvin has so many talents. You'd understand that once you got to know him."

"Yes?"

"I didn't think so at first. He has a—a rather awkward exterior."

That was it precisely, but at the moment, it was his interior that concerned me more.

"Since Douglas has been away so much—"

"Douglas?"

"My husband. He's on leave from the university. He's a specialist in pre-Roman and Roman Britain." This seemed a source of discontent, because Mrs. Gilchrist's long, thin face lengthened further. She was younger than I'd thought, and she looked almost overwhelmed by her husband's excursions, her

156

demanding baby, and her purportedly homicidal lodger.

"Is he doing field work somewhere?"

"Yes, they're excavating a large fort along Hadrian's Wall. He's been gone most of the summer."

I made a sympathetic sound and nodded as a number of scenarios passed through my mind.

"That's why I'm certain Mel couldn't have killed anyone," she continued. "He's been so kind while Douglas was away. Of course, we're both interested in poetry."

I remembered Thorston's beautiful reading voice.

"He even read to Ian," she said.

"Very helpful." Even the tritest of triangles have their unexpected subtleties.

"Yes. And Ian is good for Melvin."

"He likes children?"

"Oh, yes. He's very natural with children. He relaxes with them."

"Dr. Thorston did strike me as a rather tense person."

"He's had his troubles," she said with a sigh. Poor Thorston. Perhaps his misfortunes had become an attraction. It happens.

"He needs company," she continued. "A family setting."

I agreed, but as I read Mrs. Gilchrist, she was one of those women burdened with the caretaking impulse yet lacking in practical abilities. The house was a wreck, and the baby, now leaping in its bouncing swing and screaming, seemed destined to gain the upper hand. Thorston with his dramatic impulses, suspicions, and shifting moods would have fit right in.

I waited until she had released Ian and set him on the floor again with some toys. "Then there's the question of Wulf," I remarked.

"Wulf was a brilliant idea." She gave me a half suspicious, half resentful look. "You have to appreciate his imagination. Melvin is very brilliant."

"Undoubtedly. And an actor of some talent. Still, I don't imagine that everyone appreciates his efforts."

"Douglas—" she began, then stopped and shook her head. "Not everyone understands Melvin. He takes a lot of understanding," she added with disarming candor and fervor. I began to fear that her assessment of her friend was highly colored with emotion and wishful thinking.

"Certainly someone with an appreciation of languages," I began.

"Yes, that's what I tried to tell my husband. And a sense of the theater. Melvin has a very strong sense of the theater."

"The police," I said, "are deficient in that respect."

She raised her head sharply.

"They are talking about a deliberate attempt to build an insanity defense."

"That's preposterous. Melvin's done nothing. Nothing." She sighed again, in exasperation. "It's his personality, I know. People aren't ready for someone as sensitive as he is."

There might be some truth in that. It was hard to say. "Still," I said, "we have to face up to one question at the moment: Was Melvin completely in control of the part he was playing."

"It wasn't a *part,*" she exclaimed indignantly. "It was a spiritual experiment."

"Yet didn't it ever cross your mind that Wulf might have taken a dangerous hold on his personality?"

She waved aside this question. "He was the kindest man. Really. You had to understand him."

"But you know that after his accident, the police were unable to obtain a coherent statement from him."

"He'd taken a bad fall, that's all. A concussion, probably."

"Even allowing for the effects of shock, Mrs. Gilchrist, he showed very bizarre behavior. Behavior explainable only by great anxiety or great fear, perhaps. Was there any reason?"

She shrugged and looked away, her fingers, shredding the strands of the afghan, betrayed her. "He was often unhappy."

"Did he say what about?"

"No."

158

"Something long past?"

"Oh, I think so. He always seemed happy here with us."

"Until lately?"

"Well—"

"I think we must ask ourselves if he is acting in his own best interests. Whatever has motivated him, the police are convinced he has something to hide."

"That's so stupid," she said.

"Not from the police point of view, I assure you." There was an awkward pause. "I presume they came to ask you where you thought he might be."

"I told them that I didn't know," she said quickly, as if I suspected her of some indiscretion. "He has some friends up north—I mentioned them."

"Those are Dr. Thorston's friends. Melvin might go there. Wulf certainly would not. The police choose to look for Dr. Thorston; I am more interested in his alter ego."

She did not reply.

"Where would Wulf be apt to hide, Mrs. Gilchrist?"

She balked at this, which made me think she had come to the same conclusion. Perhaps I was not off on the wrong track after all. "You haven't told me why you're interested. I don't know what right you have to be asking all these questions." With this belated concern for caution and propriety, she straightened up and fixed me with a very serious look. I revised her age downward again, settling on twenty-two or -three.

"I was hired as part of the security for the Open. While engaged in my duties, I discovered Wilson Daintly's body."

"Oh, how awful for you!"

I agreed and dilated on this horror for a moment. Mrs. Gilchrist was sensitive and liked to be thought sympathetic. At the moment, it suited me to indulge her.

"I don't know what to do," she said at last. "Melvin trusts me. I'm really the only one. And I don't know you." She found my card on the couch and ran a nervous finger over it like a palmist seeking the clues to my character in its lines.

"If Melvin did not kill Daintly," I said firmly, "he is jeopardizing his case. Returning here would strengthen the presumption of innocence—if nothing else. And there's another thing."

She caught the seriousness in my voice. "What?"

"He knew Daintly, went to school with him. Suppose Melvin is also in danger?"

"Oh, that's impossible. Who'd want to hurt Melvin? No, it's impossible."

"Nothing's impossible. I was hired specifically because there had been threats against the golfer, Peter Bryce. He was a college friend of both Daintly's and Melvin's."

"He didn't mention that," she said quickly. "He didn't say anything about that at all."

"Who didn't?" Apprehension ran ahead to suggest the answer.

"Mr. Bryce. He's come twice. To ask about Melvin when he was in the hospital and again this morning. He came in just before his round. 'As a fellow alumnus,' he said. That's all."

"When did his round begin?"

"Late. One-thirty, I think. He's with the leaders." Sensing my alarm, she added, "It did seem all right to tell him. It was, wasn't it?"

"I'm sure, but under the circumstances, I think you'd better tell me, too. There's been a good deal of anxiety since—"

"Yes, that's right. Of course, he may not be there. It's only an idea. I'm sure the police would have laughed—"

"I'm not even smiling."

"No. You make me nervous, Miss Peters. I just hope nothing has happened to Mel. We're all so fond of him." She fiddled with the afghan, then began. "Well, there's a derelict farm cottage to the south and west of here. It's very old. Mel met the farmer somehow, and he used to stay there when he was studying Wulf. When he was trying to create the character."

"How do I get there?"

Mrs. Gilchrist was set to hesitate again. Bryce, I imagined, with his handsome face and star qualities had probably had an easier time, an idea that made me like him even less. I glanced at my watch. Even allowing for interviews after the round, he was going to have a head start on me.

Again she detected my anxiety. "You take the road toward Crail," she began and outlined some complicated directions.

"And another left at the wood?" I asked, writing down the last of her instructions.

"Yes. It's just a track. I wouldn't recommend taking your car any farther than the wood. It's not far from there to the cottage. You'll not miss it—nothing else around but potatoes and sheep."

"I'll find it. Thank you, Mrs. Gilchrist." I rose and prepared to leave. "By the way, how did Melvin manage the trip? It sounds fairly far."

"He cycled usually. I ran him out in the car once or twice."

"That looked like his bike at the side of the house."

"He never came back for it. He may not be there at all, not with his bad arm."

The baby started to howl, and on this cue, I said good-by.

"He's such a nice man," Mrs. Gilchrist repeated as I reached the door. "He couldn't possibly have hurt anyone. You must believe that." She looked perfectly miserable.

"I'm betting on it," I said. "Otherwise I wouldn't be going after him, would I?"

*   *   *

Following Mrs. Gilchrist's instructions, I drove down the coast toward Anstruther. Clouds hung over the sea to the east, heavy, wet, and dark, with a curious pinkish underlining that ran between their swollen masses and the thin line of the cliffs and the deep green and gold fields. Below the worn cliff faces were narrow strips of beach—occasionally sand but more usually rock outcrops or desolate strands strewn with boulders. Harry and I had walked that way. In the sunlight, the coast was of rare beauty, but its deserted stretches now reminded me of the melancholy shores painted by Harry's great idol, Edvard Munch. It was impossible to understand those pictures without a knowledge of the northern beaches, strewn with gray and buff rocks touched green and black with sea wrack, their mysterious skies reflected in still, frigid bays. It struck me how appropriate a certain gravity of aspect was in such landscapes, which seemed to demand a cast of mind different from the biases and expectations of warmer, more stable climates. The north perceives beauty and warmth as an effect of light, a glory vanishing in an instant, and so contemplates even its greatest magnificence with a melancholy pessimism. I saw that very clearly, although how these reflections were to help me in the present circumstances, I couldn't imagine, and, setting aside idle speculations, I turned off the coast road and headed inland.

The land grew hilly away from the sea, and the rolling farmland was dotted here and there with small dark woodlots. The one I wanted was a dark patch of pines opposite a swath of barley. I spotted the slate roof of a large stone farmhouse perhaps a mile away; otherwise, the only inhabitants were the black-faced sheep and a noisy flock of rooks. At the edge of the wood was a farm track. I pulled onto this and managed several hundred yards before I spotted the cottage from the top of a rise. Preferring to make my visit a surprise, I reversed the car along the track to an opening in the wood. There was room for my car, and once parked, it was not easily visible from either the road or the track to the cottage. I listened for a moment, but no other cars passed, and, after making sure there was no one else on the way to the cottage, either, I went to look for Wulf.

14

THE COTTAGE SAT IN PALE BUFF GRAIN FIELDS with the slate-colored east behind it. To the west, where the sky shimmered lemon and gold, a small dark cloud passed before the sun, throwing its shadow upon the fields like the shade of a great scimitar, its progress swift and irrevocable. In the warm light, the abandoned cottage glowed in tones of sienna and biscuit; the sudden darkness revealed the gaping windows, the battered roof, the squalor, making Professor Thorston's residence there an eccentricity in bad taste. Then the light returned, and against the dark sky, the cottage again became a picturesque accent in a pastoral landscape.

There were trees at the back of the house and a rampant hedgerow that ran in tangles of raspberry bushes and hawthorn to the wood. The front yard was choked with a mess of stinging nettles and leathery, aggressive docks with shriveled blossoms and unnaturally vigorous foliage. I stopped and listened: A ring-necked dove flew away from the top of the house, and in the trees, wood pigeons made soft noises; the cottage itself was silent, the open doorway revealing a tarpaulin rigged like a tent and a ground sheet spread on the floor. The fireplace of the cottage had been cleaned out, and there were signs of a fire. Despite the gaping roof and the open doorways and windows, the interior was clean and not uncomfortable as a camp shelter. Thorston had preferred not to live in true swineherd misery, and for the first time, I began to give Stewart's theory of a deliberate insanity defense some credence.

There was no sign of the professor in the main room of the cottage, nor, aside from a cupboard with camping supplies, any trace of him in the adjoining room, an even more dilapidated area virtually open to the sky. I returned through the connecting door. The rising wind whistled in the grass and weeds, but I noticed that Thorston had not relied on such bucolic sounds for entertainment: He'd left a small transistor set to Radio Two, and I wondered if the professor had been using it to follow the tournament.

Outside, at the back of the cottage, I found another small yard overgrown with untidy bushes and flowering weeds as high as my head. In the midst of this miniature jungle were the remains of a garden shed and of a stone wall, perhaps seven feet high and broken down at the ends, which might once have formed part of a barn. Pushing aside the weeds and branches, I made my way to this barrier and with one hand on the wall, I leaned around to see what might be concealed behind it. I was met by a long and very sharp piece of steel, which came out of a tangle of bushes and took up residence under my jaw. On the other end of it was Professor Thorston.

He did not speak at first, but stood there looking surprised and disheveled. His bushy hair stood up in tufts all over his large, round head, his clothes and the sling in which he carried his injured wrist were filthy, and behind his thick glasses, his eyes moved restlessly between my face and the fields beyond. He emanated a sense of great uncertainty, and I was unpleasantly aware that if I had bet on the wrong man, I had placed myself in a very dangerous situation. I put my hand gently against the wall and eased a step backward.

"Don't," he said sharply.

I stopped.

"You lied to me," he said, furious now, with one of those disconcerting shifts of mood. "You've been following me all the time."

"You're wrong there," I began, but Thorston swung the javelin so close to my face that I jumped. The point scraped against the stones of the wall.

"Don't move," he said. "And don't put your hand in your pocket. Stand right against the wall. And drop the bag."

I did as I was told, and he flicked open the flap with the point of the javelin.

"And your jacket. Take it off for a moment." He poked at it with the spear and then tapped the sides of my legs with the weapon. "You're not armed."

"What did you expect?"

He looked momentarily chagrined and moved the javelin away. "But you've been following me, bothering me. I didn't trust you from the start."

"Nonetheless, I've come a very long way to talk to you. Over three thousand miles in the last day and a half."

At this, he said nothing, but watched me, alert and anxious, while I wondered how best to begin. The matter needed careful handling and speed, too. The final rounds for the day had surely been completed, and unless Peter Bryce preferred to wait until dark, he could confidently be expected at any minute. Mindful of this, I glanced toward the road and the wood, and Thorston noticed.

"Who are you looking for? Who knows you came here?" he demanded. "What did you tell those idiot police?"

"The police are looking for you elsewhere as far as I know. But you have concerned friends."

"What do you mean?" His friends' solicitude caused alarm, for he lost another shade of color. "I don't know anyone here."

"What about Peter Bryce? I understand he tried to see you at the hospital. He seems suddenly very interested in you."

"He doesn't know where I am," Thorston said quickly.

"You're wrong. I expected to find him already here. The police may find Professor Thorston's habits a mystery, but people acquainted with Wulf—"

"Have you been to see Pamela? You'd no right to do that. You'd no right to bother her." The point of the javelin descended again in my general direction, and I tried to slide away from the wall. Thorston was having none of that, however, and this time, the javelin scratched my neck. About Pamela Gilchrist, he wasn't fooling.

"I'm not the only one," I said.

"Peter?"

"Yes. Another alumnus of Michaelmas College, concerned about a fellow American."

"When was this? When did he see her?" he demanded in a panic.

"Today—and once before. She was anxious about—"

"Yes, of course. She would have talked to him." He tightened his grip on the javelin. "I hadn't expected it, but that's just what he'd have done. Been sympathetic, amusing. He has a way," Thorston said. The javelin trembled in his hand.

"I pointed out to Mrs. Gilchrist that under the circumstances, someone else should know where you were."

"She's been kind," he said.

"She's worried. It would be better for you—and for her—if you came back to town with me now."

"I don't need advice, Miss Peters."

"Suit yourself, but as I said, I've come a long way to talk to you. From Hartford."

Thorston reacted to shock in a curious way: He grew very still and quiet.

"You told me you were protecting Peter," he said after a minute.

166

"I was and I am. But motivation, professor. Motivation. Why would someone threaten Bryce and murder Daintly?"

A light film of sweat formed on his forehead. "And where did you go in Hartford?" he asked with a pretense of calm.

"I visited a couple of old acquaintances of yours, Dr. Duclos and Louie La Fleur's widow."

"Widow?"

"Margaret."

"Louie's dead?"

"He was murdered nearly a year ago, in August."

"I didn't know."

"Yet you were in the area then."

"I didn't read the papers."

"I've just spent a good deal of time reading them."

"A waste of your time."

"You lack imagination, professor. I don't think you realize how serious this could be for you."

"Oh, don't I? I'm running around here in the sticks for fun?"

"The police, you know, are convinced you've killed a man."

"They're right," he said. "In a moral sense, the police are perfectly correct."

"Fortunately for you, only the legal sense counts."

"For me it makes very little difference, but with the accident—"

"Wilson Daintly was murdered before your accident," I reminded him.

"I never planned to kill Wilson. Perhaps he deserved—but no, he was not so much to blame," Thorston said heavily. "And he paid his debts."

"Through Wulf?"

"That's right." He gave a weak smile. "Wulf and other things. It's too bad Wilson did not have literary interests. He lacked an appreciation of dramatic irony."

"Which you supply?"

"Oh yes."

"I've asked myself several times why Daintly was so generous with your projects."

"Generous? He wasn't generous! The bare minimum, my dear Miss Peters. Nothing more. From his largesse my little stipend was nothing. A trifle. He'd had so much."

"Had?"

"I think he was losing his touch." And Thorston gave another slight smile and a little dry, coughing laugh.

The conversation I'd overhead at Daintly's cottage drifted in and out of memory. "Financial trouble?"

"He said."

"And Bryce?"

"Peter?"

"Yes, where did he fit in?"

A nervous shudder made a muscle jump near Thorston's mouth. "He ruined my life. He lied to me. As you did." And with this he swung the javelin again, forcing me back against the wall. "I intended to kill him. That's what you wanted to know, isn't it? Isn't it?"

"It simplifies my job."

Thorston's small, dark eyes were flat and cold as he rested the point of the javelin against the hollow of my shoulder. I tried to remember where the big veins were and swallowed the lump of fright that rose unbidden from the back of my throat. Then he let up slightly and remarked, "I like some things about you."

"I'm relieved to hear it."

"You put on a good show. I can appreciate that."

"Speaking of shows, was it you who damaged the Course?"

"The Course?"

"The recent vandalism: sand on the greens, a Jolly Roger on the eighteenth, that exploding device. That was the tip-off, incidentally."

"An early warning," he said. "Peter's always had things so easy. There never were consequences for Peter. Just events.

There were no connections," he continued reflectively, "no repercussions. Peter is a free man." His anger shaded off to bitterness. "People will put up with a surprising amount for his sake."

"Well, they were hardly going to prevent him from playing —all that was petty mischief."

"Wulf was a different matter; he didn't have my second thoughts," Thorston continued. "He was free, like Peter." The professor's voice dropped and coarsened. It really was a most remarkable instrument, more rich and supple than its possessor, the voice took on Wulf's sound and quality unbidden. I saw for the first time that this was the wreckage of a remarkable personality, and it no longer seemed strange that he wished to destroy the man responsible for his collapse. "Wulf lacked moral scruples."

"And the means?"

"I am surprisingly accurate with this," he replied, moving the javelin slightly. "Collapsible." He swung the weapon up, tapping the butt smartly on the ground. The spear telescoped with a click. He snapped his wrist and the weapon resumed its former length.

"Very ingenious, but then you're an expert with mechanical devices, aren't you?"

Instantly he resumed his loud, hectoring tone and threatening stance. "Duclos told you that, didn't he?"

"Yes."

"What else did Duclos say?"

"That you were his best student."

"What else? Did he say I lacked the right temperament? That I lacked nerve? That was his diagnosis. He was different. I could tell you stories about Duclos. Did he tell you that?"

"He felt you'd undergone some type of crisis."

"What did he say about that?"

"He blamed Daintly and Bryce."

"He doesn't know."

"I'd say rather that he isn't sure."

Thorston stared at me for a moment. I could hear his breathing. "And you, Miss Peters? What's your conclusion?" he asked softly.

I picked my words carefully. "You were not entirely to blame," I said. "You did not foresee the consequences. I don't think you would have—" I hesitated, for this was dangerous ground if I'd figured him wrong, or maybe even if I'd figured right. He'd been guilty for years, and he had, perhaps, become so used to the burden that a little more wouldn't matter.

Thorston did not speak. His face was the color of clay and his eyes sank into the flat remoteness of his alter ego. "You've followed me all the way," he said. "I knew it from the first, from the moment I heard you speak. Your voice," he began, but whatever he intended to say was lost. He stopped in mid phrase. I heard it, too: a car approaching slowly along the main road. "Back here," he commanded. "No, walk close to the wall. We'll soon know if you are correct. But don't make any sound. If it is Peter, I'd be at a disadvantage. You understand that?" The spear was close to my throat and I nodded. "You mean nothing to me." I nodded again, for fear made him dangerous. "I'd recommend you stay out of Peter's way; he'll be no help to you. He's lethal, I assure you." Then he gestured for me to precede him around the corner of the wall and into the thorns and nettles growing between it and the shelter of the hedgerow. "We'll go right to the trees," he said, "but don't try to run."

This caution was unnecessary. Thorston had picked our escape route with an eye to his limitations. The bushes and weeds were so dense that our progress was slow, and it was no effort for him to keep me well within the range of his weapon. He called a halt at the hedgerow, pushing me through a narrow opening in the hawthorns. "We'll wait here."

An insect began ticking off the time in the grass, and large horse flies buzzed over our heads and got into our hair. My arms and legs were beginning to burn from the stinging nettles, and we passed several uncomfortable minutes before a figure appeared along the track from the wood. It was a man, wearing a dull camel-colored sweater. I doubted it was Bryce, but Thorston nodded. The figure passed out of sight behind a rise, then reappeared. It was the golfer all right, and he was walking swiftly and decisively, like a man on an important errand. He did not hesitate as I had but approached the cottage, calling, "Mel? You there, Mel?" in a low, hard voice.

Thorston went very white.

"Where the hell are you, Mel?" Bryce's handsome head emerged from one of the rear windows. "I want to talk to you, old buddy."

Thorston remained silent. Bryce swore and disappeared inside the cottage. "Straight ahead," the professor whispered.

"Don't you want to talk to him?"

"Hurry up," he said, his voice revealing fear, either of Bryce or of his own wayward impulses, and he pointed down a cowpath running along the hedge. Behind us, we could hear the golfer. "There's nothing to be afraid of," he called at one point, and Thorston's mouth twitched.

As we neared the trees, we had the bad luck to frighten a group of rooks, which flew up in a noisy mob.

"He'll have seen them," Thorston said. "Damn it, hurry up."

"Where are we going?"

"Do you see his car?"

"There's something parked on the road."

"And yours?"

"I left it in the wood."

"Automatic?"

"Transmission? Yes."

"I knew it. Women prefer automatics. Put down your bag." He tipped the contents out, picked up the keys, and slipping his cast from the sling, took them in his injured hand. Then he stood without saying anything, as if listening for the sound of a man pushing through the branches of the hedgerow. It was already twilight under the shade of the high trees, and the fine leaves over our head formed a green canopy interspersed with round pink and gold spots of light. "Perhaps Duclos was right," Thorston said, "but I'd be at a disadvantage. This isn't the time."

He tapped the butt end of the javelin on the ground, collapsing it into a neat walking stick. "Unnecessary now," he said. "You can pick up your bag. All I need is the car." He stepped back a pace. "Sorry to leave you, but I didn't ask you to come. It won't be my fault. 'Not entirely,' as you've said so judiciously." He shrugged and turned slightly; foolishly, I reached down to pick up the wallet, passport, and credit cards scattered about the grass. But if Thorston lacked real viciousness, he was not without resources, and I paid for my stupidity. As I bent down, he swung the javelin like a club. The weapon cracked across the side of my head and shoulder. The grass flared red and orange before turning black with purple edges, while the drone of flies and midges became a roar. I found myself on my hands and knees, and as I raised my head, Thorston moved toward my car in a dizzying elliptical orbit. I tried to get up, sat back down, and heard the car start. Then there was nothing. Lost minutes. I shook my head and felt the ache. The car was gone, and I was sprawled on the grass with the javelin near my hand. A yellow patch of sun wavered through the branches and in it, a cloud of midges hovered like flecks of gold dust. But the rooks were silent, and there was another sound, amplified by the stillness: someone breathing hard, as if he had been running. I moved my protesting head a fraction and saw Peter Bryce. I had not heard him approach. He stood just within the grove of trees and watched me with a chilling intensity of expression. His face showed no sign of recognition, either because he believed I was still semiconscious or because the psychological mechanism that protected his self-interest had already switched on. I tried to say something but was unable to form the words; then I noticed the brick in his hand. Bryce flexed his fingers slightly, and my mind cleared. I realized that the golfer almost certainly had learned about my trip to the States and that he was shrewd enough to have perceived my destination. If I had guessed right about him, I was in very great danger. And should something happen to me, Melvin Thorston would conveniently take the blame.

Bryce remained several yards away. I had the feeling that as long as I kept still, he would hesitate, considering his options and planning his next move. I had few of my own to consider. The farmhouse was too far away, the cottage offered no protection, my car was gone, and Bryce was a professional athlete in the peak of condition. As I took a deep breath, I noticed the slight movement of his shoulders. He had decided something; I had to get up. As I struggled to rise, Bryce stepped forward, but my hand touched the javelin. Grabbing the shaft, I snapped my wrist and arm as hard as possible. I was not as adept as Thorston, but the sharp point emerged with a click, producing a spear perhaps three feet high. Bryce was momentarily distracted by its appearance, and leaning my weight on the shaft, I stood up unsteadily. It was clearly not a time for sincerity and confrontation.

"Am I glad to see you, Mr. Bryce!"

He didn't answer, and I adjusted the javelin to full length. "Formidable, wouldn't you say?"

"Huh," he said and some of the peculiar intensity of the moment drained away. "Mel's?"

"Yes. Left it with me as a souvenir."

A moment more, then Bryce shrugged and his face loosened a little. "Guess I don't need that," he said, chucking the brick into the weeds. "I wasn't sure what sort of crazy stunt Mel was up to." His smile was not particularly convincing, but I realized it was important to feign reassurance.

"Crazy is right," I said, rubbing my head.

"You all right? Perhaps you'd better sit down again. Here, let me have that," he said, reaching for the spear. I stepped quickly away. "No, no, it's okay. Better on my feet. This makes a pretty good cane. As long as you watch out for the point." I tipped it to show him, and he put his hand down. "Razor sharp," I said.

"Jesus Christ. He *is* crazy."

"Strong, too." I rubbed my tender head.

"Which way did he go? I heard a car. I thought it was mine."

"I don't know. I wasn't completely out, but I couldn't tell which direction. Not with the trees."

Bryce ran up to the road, and I followed slowly, leaning against the javelin. So long as I had it, I was fairly safe, whatever he had in mind. While there was little doubt that his greater size and strength gave him an immense advantage, he couldn't risk an injury. Not now. It wouldn't hurt to remind him of that. When I reached the car, I asked about his last round.

He was standing with his hand on the door, staring down the road as if trying to decide where Thorston would have gone and whether or not he should follow. He answered with a flickering smile, wistful and sardonic. "I'm tied for the lead with Watson and Oosterhuis," he said. "Biggest round of my life tomorrow," and his eyes darkened. I felt a moment's sympathy. Although he had an appreciation for dramatic irony, it wasn't making him very happy.

"A great honor. You'll be last to go off tomorrow, won't you?"

"Yes. And I can win it." He looked toward the clear, brilliant west and smiled. "Weather's gonna hold. The Old Course is no sweat when the wind's down. And I've got the nerves," he added.

"And the concentration?"

His eyes searched restlessly down the road before he opened the car door. "Right," he said heartily. "The hell with Mel. He can work out his own problems." He opened the trunk. "Just sling that pig sticker in here," he said.

174

I leaned against the javelin. "I think I'll keep it with me. I really feel worse now than I did a few minutes ago." To emphasize this, I started slowly and awkwardly toward the passenger's door, supporting myself with the shaft. The trunk of the car slammed shut.

"Damn dangerous thing," Bryce said.

"I'll knock it down." But I was careful to keep the sharp point out, and when I got into the car, I leaned the shaft against the dashboard. Bryce put the key in the ignition and looked at me as though sizing up his chances.

"You can put that in the back. No need to be uncomfortable."

He was half turned, one arm resting on the steering wheel, at once casual and alert, a subtle, dangerous man.

My excuses were running short. I glanced at the clutter of towels, windbreakers, and clubs on the back seat, and as if some psychic window opened, I felt the sudden chill of intuition. In that instant, I knew how Daintly had been killed, I knew who had killed him, and how the weapon had been concealed. "I don't want to scratch your clubs. Besides"—my mouth was dry, but I stretched for a light tone—"this cost me quite a bit. I don't want you claiming my souvenir. This is a unique trophy." I sounded ghastly and no doubt looked worse, but the point of Wulf's weapon was sharp, and as I spoke, I turned it toward Bryce. He could, if he made a fast move, do me a good deal of damage but not without getting his face cut up. We stared at each other for several seconds, deciding how far we ought to carry this particular charade and whether or not this was the decisive moment. Bryce made up his mind first, and I must confess he put a better face on it than I would have.

"Yeah," he said easily. "Old Mel's got the brains." He turned the key in the ignition.

The drive back to the coast proceeded in silence, Bryce occupied with his own thoughts and I with the general queasy feeling spreading downward from my aching head.

"Not much doubt, is there?" he said at last.

"About what?"

"Poor Wilson."

"Not in my mind." Bryce flicked his cool eyes from the road to my face and back again.

"Glad to hear that," he said. "My thought—and that's why I went to try to see Mel tonight—was that he's got to turn himself in, go for treatment. It's pretty obvious he's had a breakdown. I would think they'd be lenient. He had one before. Sad case."

"Yes."

"I'd be willing to help out. Financially. Get him a good lawyer. I don't want to be directly involved, but having friends to stand by him should help, too. Maybe you could handle the arrangements? A lawyer, contacts with the medical authorities—whatever is needed. It's awkward for me, but my business agent could handle all the bills—and your fee, of course."

"That's generous of you."

He looked at me again, quick, suspicious, and clever.

"But there's a problem with an insanity defense," I continued. "The police have already considered it. In fact, the main thing they have against Thorston is Wulf—they think he's faking and all that playacting is simply an attempt to establish an insanity claim. They seem to think your friend Mel is a killer capable of long-term planning and calculation."

"You don't sound convinced."

"He was more convincing this evening, I must say."

Another sharp glance from Bryce. "Why did you go to the States?" he asked. "As far as I knew you were supposed to be busy protecting me."

"In the short run, I thought you could take care of yourself."

He smiled ironically, "Thanks."

"And in the long run, I thought it would be good to learn something more about Mel Thorston."

176

"For the sake of my safety?" Bryce did not bother to keep the sarcasm out of his voice.

"Among other things. In some respects the police were correct. But not about Wilson Daintly's murder."

"No?"

"No. That's unsolved as far as I'm concerned."

"You prefer to wait and see."

"Exactly. But Thorston had other game."

"Yeah? Who?"

"You, Mr. Bryce."

"Old Mel?" He laughed, but not very heartily. It's unpleasant to be stalked, even by a fool. "And how was he going to do that?"

I touched the point of the javelin. "He wasn't going to do it. His alter ego was. Wulf, medieval Scottish swineherd and spearman. A nasty type, illiterate, violent, and accurate. With this, I mean."

Bryce didn't answer immediately, and I didn't offer further explanations. After we had reached the coast road back to St. Andrews, he spoke again. "He wouldn't have managed it.

"I'm not so sure. An athlete is vulnerable at an event like the Open. Wulf is a recognized character. The javelin telescopes into a harmless stick. And it's not too hard to kill someone if you are indifferent to the consequences."

"And is he?"

"Indifferent? It seems so. You would be a better judge of that than I."

"Me? I haven't seen him in years."

"I meant, you will know whether he has his reasons."

This time Bryce laughed out loud. "Mel's off his head," he said. "He doesn't need any reasons."

"Then you will need to be careful until he is apprehended," I said. "And we should stop at the next town to phone the police."

"I'd rather not get involved. The publicity—"

"You didn't tell the police you were going to see Mel?"

"No, I managed to get the car out without anyone noticing."

"They'll find out sooner or later."

"Better later."

"All right. I'll call. And say I hitched a ride. I'm no favorite with them at the moment, anyway."

He considered this for a few minutes. "Yeah," he said, "but not in town. One of those phones along the beach—or along the road. I don't want to spend the evening before the last round giving a statement to the police."

"Understandable," I said, and wished I'd kept my mouth shut.

We were fairly close to the town when Bryce spotted a pull-off. At the back was a track leading to a group of farm cottages and, on the edge of the parking area, a red phone kiosk. Bryce slammed on his brakes and pulled in sharply. There were trees behind the strip of asphalt and a curve of land partially screened the lot from the road. Nothing was stirring on the twilight farm landscape around us, when he stopped the car at the very back, near the kiosk. "You have any change?"

A truck passed, giving me a false sense of security.

"Yes, I think so." I got out and walked toward the phone, the javelin still in one hand. Bryce reached the door of the phone booth ahead of me and pushed it open. I hesitated. "Are you sure you'd rather not call? You'd get some wonderful press mileage."

"Last thing I want," he said, his hand resting on the door.

I didn't like it, but I either called the police or called his bluff, and I had no proof at the moment. Nor very much security, either. I stepped into the kiosk, and as I did so, he jerked the door shut, catching my arm and the javelin between my body and the side of the kiosk. He grabbed for the weapon and would have managed to wrench it away from me, had the butt end not caught under the sill of the kiosk. I leaned my weight on the javelin and tried to turn around.

"Whoops, wait a minute," he said, his voice quiet, but strained. "You've gotten stuck."

A sound in the parking lot explained his sudden solicitude. A white car had pulled in and both the woman driving and the man beside her were wearing the check-banded hats of the Fife Constabulary.

"I told you this was dangerous to carry around," Bryce continued. His eyes were still and expressionless, but I'd seen that look before, in the woodlot when he'd come looking for Thorston with the brick. What was frightening was that with him violence was accompanied by such calm, such calculation: His physical and temperamental perfections rested on an overwhelming coldness.

The male officer got out of the car and came hurrying over. "Mr. Bryce?" he asked.

"That's me, officer."

"Glad we found you, sir. Best radio back, Mavis," he said to the driver. "You shouldn't be out on your own. It makes our job more complicated, you understand."

"I needed to get away. Nothing but press and media and fans." His smile was tight, but a smile, nonetheless. I didn't feel up to such feats of dissimulation and rubbed the new bruises along my arms instead.

"Oh, you're going to be popular with the fans, all right. And after tomorrow—"

"We'll have to wait and see," Bryce said.

"My money's on you," the officer said genially. Behind him, the car radio crackled.

"How did you find—the car?" I asked.

"When Mr. Bryce and his car were not at the hotel, the word was spread. We were on the way back from a traffic accident when Mavis spotted it. Just to warn you, you understand, Mr. Bryce. Until this Dr. Thorston is found, no one wants to take chances with an Open leader."

"It was fortunate you came along," I said, and Bryce jumped in to agree.

"We had stopped to call the police. Thorston has stolen Miss Peters's car. By coincidence, I came along and gave her a lift."

"Did you? Where was this?"

"Out in the country. I was driving around, and there all of a sudden I recognized one of my protectors. Pretty far off duty." Bryce managed a laugh, and the two officers joined in. He smiled a wide expansive smile and clapped a hand on my shoulder. Heroism suited him and, even better, the consequent spotlights.

"What is your car's make and number?" the driver asked. "I'll need to inform headquarters. It's the best chance we've had of picking him up yet."

I gave her the information, while Bryce exchanged small talk with the other officer. "We're to follow them back to headquarters," he said when I was finished.

"Fine."

"And maybe I'd better take that, miss," the policeman said, holding his hand out for the javelin.

"I was using it as a walking stick," I said. "It belongs to the professor, I think."

"Just the same. Sharp, isn't it? We don't want anything like that near our current co-leader." Everyone joined in the laugh at this little joke, before Bryce and I returned to his car. He fixed one of his cold, bland looks on me. "I think it would be best if I handled the statement to the police," he said.

"As you like."

"You haven't managed this too well."

"There are some who'd agree with you."

"The point is, we can get old Mel off easy on Wilson's murder. I've been around enough lawyers to know that."

"It's possible."

Bryce started the car and pulled out after the police. In the back, the golf clubs rattled like bones. I did not look at them:

Unlike Bryce, I was not used to socializing with people who wanted me dead.

"It's desirable," he went on. "The committee at the R and A will agree with me, I'm sure. If we stick to the facts in the case, you'll wind up your job successfully, and I'll get a good night's sleep. You'll agree that's important."

"Either and both," I said, and his eyes flicked from the winding curve of the roadway to mine and back again. Ahead, the town sat at the bottom of a long incline, its medieval stone towers and walls outlined against the bay.

"They don't want to fool around with theories," Bryce said.

"Nor ancient history, I suppose."

"No. You go nosing around that Thorston intended to kill me and they'll nail him for Wilson's murder. He's got enough against him at the moment."

"Suppose he hasn't given up on his plans? Suppose when you tee off tomorrow he's waiting for you?"

"A chance I'm willing to take."

"True friendship."

"I was always fond of Old Mel," he said. "I'll take care of him, as I said. And there'll be something in it for you."

"The unfortunate Dr. Thorston," I said.

"You know how it is," Bryce said, "some guys just lack the winning personality."

15

IF THERE'S ONE THING men are vulnerable to, it's a woman who conforms to their expectations. Neither Bryce nor Stewart had shown much confidence in me, and I figured the safest attitude with both was a shaken silence. I tried to look dumbfounded by recent events and anxious about the fate of my car and the reaction of the committee. Neither proved difficult. Feeling the strains of life as a jet set detective, I was staying awake strictly on anxiety. And then Bryce was very helpful. I began to look forward to seeing him play, because he was Mr. Cool, all right. He elaborated on his concern for his old friend Mel, on the cleverness of his interview with Mrs. Gilchrist, and on the fortuitousness of my rescue from the wilds of rural Fife. He managed throughout to cast doubt on my part in the affair and to emphasize the obviousness of Thorston's role in Daintly's murder.

Meanwhile, Detective Inspector Stewart sat looking precise and skeptical. He took occasional idle puffs on his pipe, while a typist clattered away at his elbow, but any questioning of Bryce was strictly pro forma. When the golfer was finished

Stewart said a courteous good night, and several of his officers wished the Open contender luck on the way out.

"Can I give you a ride back to your hotel?" Bryce asked me.

"There are some forms for Miss Peters to fill in." Stewart answered for me. "Regarding the automobile."

"I could wait—"

"That's all right," I said. "I can walk, thanks."

He left and the typist rolled another sheet of paper into the machine. Stewart leaned back in his creaking wooden chair, relit his pipe, and said, "Why don't you get those stolen property forms, Alex? Miss Peters will be out to sign them in a minute."

When the typist left us alone there was a silence, made more awkward by the unpleasantness of our last conversation. I had spent the last half hour damning Stewart for a fool dazzled by a big time athlete. Now I wasn't so sure. He was smoking calmly and thoughtfully, but the toe of one foot inscribed little circles, as though he were indeed concentrating on a problem behind that neat emotionless facade and slowly approaching a solution. I had the feeling the evening's events had altered his perspective in some way, and wishing to take advantage of that mood, I broke the silence.

"Odd case," I remarked.

"Very. I trust this evening showed you another side of Dr. Thorston's character."

"Yes, indeed."

"But you're not totally convinced." He leaned forward and set his pipe down carefully in the ashtray. "Well, there is some more to it. Would you be surprised to learn that Wilson Daintly had been in some financial difficulties recently?"

"Not entirely. I've never been satisfied that his sudden prosperity had a solid footing."

"Exactly. He seems to have had what you Americans call a 'sudden cash-flow problem.' He must have resorted to some short-term loans."

"And a debt came due?"

"Conceivably. The success of the development scheme in St. Andrews was apparently more important than we'd at first realized."

"You think he was killed because he couldn't come up with the money?" Stewart nodded, and I considered the proposition. "The visitor he had the night before—I told you they seemed to be talking money. It's possible."

"Yes, it could be. That puts Dr. Thorston in a better light— or it would have, except for his activities of this evening."

"How did you find out—if I may ask? Originally Daintly's credit seemed excellent."

"Your assistant, Mrs. Harriet Edgar, was our source. She was attempting to reach you, failed, and decided to leave a message with me. We had a most enlightening talk."

Hence my reprieve. Harriet's good nature had its uses. "I see. You can be sure any information from Harriet will be reliable. She's very careful."

"We double-checked. He did have a pressing need for money."

"And no obvious vices?"

Stewart shook his head.

"It doesn't rule out my theory," I said. "Assuming he was banker for Bryce and Thorston, he would have laundered the money."

"They might have kept their share themselves—assuming for a moment you are correct."

"Hardly. Getting money into legitimate circulation is a skill in itself. Daintly's bar in Houston—ideal. And the payments to Thorston through the Gruen. It fits."

"It's ingenious, but all theoretical. What I need is evidence. Irrefutable and overwhelming, in the case of your theory."

"But circumstantial and merely plausible in the case of Dr. Thorston?"

I thought he'd be angry at this; instead he laughed, a crisp throaty rustle like papers being rubbed together. Then he became serious. "If the case is to be developed, the evidence will have to be sound. But to select one man as a suspect—"

I nodded. With the best will in the world, it would be hard to put too much pressure on Bryce the day before the final round. Against the glamor of the Open and the tension of the competition, his complicity looked preposterous. Without powerful evidence, it was safer to concentrate on Thorston, who, thanks to my stupidity, was at least guilty of assault and grand larceny. The evening had brought mixed blessings.

"What you need is the murder weapon," I said. "You haven't come up with that, have you?"

"We have some theories."

"So do I."

"Unfortunately, what we need is the item."

"That might be possible." I couldn't sound too confident; the chances of finding what I wanted were now painfully slim.

"You find something; we'll examine it." He tamped his pipe carefully. "Of course, we wouldn't want you to interfere with police matters. I will add for your benefit that the R and A Committee is not particularly happy."

"They think I've been wasting my time."

"And theirs."

"I can now tell them who damaged their course."

He looked up.

"Dr. Thorston."

"His own admission?"

"That's right."

"That doesn't help him."

"I suppose not. Yet a man who does such basically frivolous things—"

"You're talking about the Old Course," Stewart reminded me sternly.

185

"If you apprehend Thorston, the committee can be assured the course and Peter Bryce are safe for the rest of the tournament."

"And if not—"

"Then I suppose they won't be pleased with you, either, Inspector Stewart."

He gave a sour smile, but we parted on better terms. Neither of us was in a strong position, and if anything blew up, we were first in line to catch hell. As I admitted to Harry when I got back to the hotel, both Stewart and I had been out-maneuvered as far as public relations were concerned. The R and A Committee had insulated themselves by hiring me. If anything went wrong, they could blame me, and the public would blame the police.

Harry yawned and put his feet on the bed. He leafed through a pack of sketches and yawned again. I paced around the room until I began to make him nervous. "Sure you haven't bet on the wrong guy?" he asked.

"No way."

"What have you got against Bryce? This professor with the nice reading voice knocks you over the head, steals your car, and leaves you miles from nowhere—and you're convinced he's innocent. Bryce rides to the rescue like the White Knight, and you suspect him of murder."

"Thorston needed the car, and he has the use of only one arm: Hitting me made sense. It did not make sense for Bryce to stand with a brick in his hand figuring out whether I'd suit him better alive or dead."

"That's pure supposition," Harry said in exasperation.

"You don't believe me?"

"I believe you. I don't agree with you."

"You haven't figured out how it was done yet, have you?"

"How what was done?" He put down his illustrations.

"Daintly's murder. The weapon hasn't been found. And I know why. You told me yourself."

"I did?"

"The golf club. Bryce's 'lucky college driver.' He took it out to the course the next day and smashed it up. His caddie disposed of it. Who's to find it now? It'll be in some Fife regional solid waste fill or something." I tapped my knuckles irritably against the window frame: If I hadn't flown to Hartford, I might have retrieved it. "They'll have to root through the rubbish, that's all. But I'm not sure I can convince Stewart to do it."

There was a long silence from Harry, who seemed to have immersed himself once more in his sketches. I sighed and looked out the window again.

"I doubt that it was discarded," he remarked at last.

"What do you mean?"

"Jack—Bryce's caddie—may not have thrown it away. He mentioned to me once that he likes doing repairs. Besides, it would be a memento. Not too many clients destroy clubs and then go on to lead the Open."

I turned from the window and grabbed my jacket. "Where does he live? I've got to talk to him."

"I don't know his address, but he has a little house on the other side of town. I went there to borrow some equipment to sketch."

"You could find the place, couldn't you?" Harry prides himself on his mastery of geography and on his sense of direction.

"Now? Anna, I've got work to do."

"Just point me in the right direction. How long can it take? Besides, if you hadn't told me, I wouldn't have had the idea. And we've got to get it. With the club, this is an open-and-shut case."

Harry fussed for a few minutes, but it was all bluff. He'd been working for three days straight on his illustrations, and I guessed it was time for a break. He unfolded his map of the town, then nodded briskly. "All right, let's go."

"You'll get some ideas for prints of St. Andrews at night,"

I suggested, but he wasn't mollified. We went downstairs in a heavy silence: Our holiday was certainly taking some peculiar turns.

It was close to eleven when we started for Jack's house, but there was still enough light to see easily. Children were running about the parks, and the sky had not so much darkened as whitened, losing color with the sunset to form a high, pale dome that softened the evening and blurred the edges of the landscape.

"Ahhh," said Harry, who began to smile to himself as if the unaccustomed light effects had been devised for his sole pleasure. He fiddled in his pocket for his small sketch pad, and I walked faster. "Jack may have gone to bed," I warned.

Harry nodded, but although he picked up his pace, I'm afraid he was paying more attention to the tints of the sky and the dark shapes of the stone work than to our destination. We walked between a pair of walls ten or twelve feet high and came out on a dark, tree-ringed park.

"Wrong turn," he said. "I don't remember this."

"Which way?"

He considered a moment. "We'll try this path."

More lanes followed, walled gardens, angular Victorian silhouettes, patches with cabbages and onions, greenhouses jammed with tomatoes, beds with roses a yard high, clumps of delphiniums, and meticulous borders of alyssum and lobelia and begonias. Where the walls were high, it was quite dark, and here and there, overgrown hedges arched over the spikes and wire that topped the stones to shade the path even more. We walked for another twenty minutes.

"What do you think?" I asked. "Are we going the right way?"

Harry didn't answer. My legs began to feel as if I'd been treading water. I'd forgotten how many hours it had been since I left the States, but the miracle of air travel was beginning to squash all sense of time out of the incidents in Thorston's and

188

Bryce's lives. Hartford, Michaelmas, the Sammy Davis Open, Louie's death, the robbery, Thorston's accident, the cottage— all seemed to have happened within a matter of hours, past and present intermingling. I wondered if it struck them the same way.

"Here we are," Harry said triumphantly. "I knew we'd come out all right."

We were back on one of the main streets.

"Is this where he lives?"

"Just a little way."

We set off again. The picturesque delights of St. Andrews wore thin, but after negotiating a dozen narrow pends and lanes, we reached a block of small houses with walled yards enclosing long narrow gardens.

"This is it. I knew I'd find it," Harry said. "His house is the third one down." He shot me a triumphant look, but I was unable to congratulate him, for parked on the street was Bryce's rented car.

I drew Harry back against the privet hedge. "Shhh. That's Bryce's."

Harry shrugged. "Strategy talk for tomorrow. At least you know Jack's still up."

A child of about ten ran out of a nearby house, stopped, gave us an odd look and ran on.

"We're conspicuous trying to hide here," Harry observed.

"Let's go around the block. Maybe we can climb into his garden."

My husband assumed a martyred expression but said nothing. We discovered a lane through to the next street and, after some false starts, found ourselves at the corner of the yard behind the caddie's house.

"Where does he work on his clubs?"

"He had some in the house, but his workshop's in the yard."

Just then, a door opened. "Good night, then. Twelve-thirty. Right you are," a Scottish voice said.

The reply was unintelligible; Bryce's speech was habitually low and indistinct.

"Sorry I canna give you that club."

"My fault. If I hadn't lost my temper—" His voice dropped again.

I couldn't resist nudging Harry. "What did I tell you—he's after the club, too. Damn. Jack must have discarded it after all."

We heard the men go out to the street and, after a brief interval, a car start.

"Ready?" Harry asked.

"I'm afraid there isn't much point."

"He may still have it. If Bryce ordered him to throw it away, he threw it away. Correct? The golfer is always right."

There was something to that. "But if he wouldn't give it to Bryce, he'd hardly give it to us. You'll have to talk to him while I take a look around."

"You can't rummage through his shed. Why don't we just ask him—pretend we're curious about how he repairs clubs—something like that," Harry suggested a trifle desperately.

"At this time of night? Don't be silly. Just say you've stopped by to wish him and Bryce luck for tomorrow. Talk for a few minutes and say good night. That's all. Nothing to it."

"Yes," said Harry, "while you're breaking and entering in the back."

"I'm merely going to climb over the wall and look in his shed." I switched on my pen-sized flashlight. "No problem."

Harry showed not the slightest enthusiasm.

"We'll miss our chance," I said. "It's late now. He'll be getting ready for bed soon. Please, Harry—I'll only take a minute."

"All right. But five minutes, no more." He looked aggrieved. "Then I'm heading for the hotel."

190

"You're a wonderful man," I said sincerely. "I'm amazed by my skill in husband selection."

When he set off toward the caddie's front door, I put my hands on the top of the stone wall and pulled myself up. Fortunately, Jack's garden was surrounded by one of the more modest fortifications, a thick fieldstone wall a mere five feet high. From the top, I watched Harry's head bob above the neighbor's hedge before he came into view under the streetlight. Then I let myself gracefully down into what turned out to be a well-manured rhubarb patch. I picked my way through the straw and plants, past a netted strawberry bed and a dovecote rustling with soft feathers, to the garden shed, a wooden construction halfway up the long narrow yard. Behind it was the vegetable garden, rich and odoriferous, and before it, a paved area bordered by neatly trimmed annuals. The kitchen door gave access to this area, and despite the growing chill of the evening, it stood open, revealing a warm rectangle of oranges and yellows against the lavender midsummer night. The caddie and his wife were sitting in the front room, and as I moved cautiously to the window of their shed, the doorbell rang. I waited a moment, heard Harry's greeting, and switched on my flashlight. Piercing the shed window, its lean white finger touched a garden hose, rakes, a mower, then a workbench, a vise, clamps, several odd decapitated lumps of wood—embryonic clubs, I supposed— and some chisels. A gleam of silver like the pipes of a miniature organ was revealed as a rack of shafts, and scattered about the bench were bits and pieces of leather, the straps and rivets of some discarded bag. I switched off the light and shoved at the sash of the rear window without success.

". . . just to wish you luck tomorrow," I heard Harry say.

"Good of you to stop by. This is my wife, Alison. Alison, this is Mr. Radford, the American artist."

A babble of small talk rose from the front room, and even at this distance, I could detect the strain in Harry's voice. He hated deception, and this sort of diversion, practiced on people he had no reason to dislike, was social torture of considerable refinement. I really owed him, I thought, as I tested the door to the shed. It refused to open, and the soft rattle of the ancient hardware told the tale.

"A cup of tea, Mr. Radford?"

"Oh, don't bother, Mrs. MacNab. I was just out for a walk. It's never light this late at home."

"It's no bother. Jack and me were just going to have a cup." I heard her footsteps on the kitchen linoleum and hastily stepped aside from the door. A knob clicked, then a whoosh as gas caught fire in a burner. How had they not heard the door rattle? "And where are you from in the States, Mr. Radford?"

The woman stood with her back to me, a neat compact silhouette, one hand resting lightly on the wall.

"Washington, D.C.," Harry said. "On the east coast."

"I have a sister in New Jersey," she said. "Outside of Paterson."

I fumbled for the piece of wire in my pocket and moved slowly back to the shed door.

"Married an American. A chap from Cleveland. He was over here for his company."

A scraping noise. The lock was old, its mechanism rusted. I put my shoulder against the door and pushed. Nothing. Again. This time the mechanism clicked.

"You'll have a scone, won't you, Mr. Radford?"

"Are you sure it isn't a bother?"

"None at all. Fresh baked today."

I slid back into the shadows as she returned to the kitchen, then when pots rattled out of sight, I edged to the door, turned the handle and pushed. There was a creak, then a deafening whistle that sent what little blood was still circulating in a dizzy rush to my head. The voices from within continued placidly, and the whistle ceased. Over my shoulder, I saw Mrs. MacNab pour boiling water into a teapot. I was edgier than I'd thought.

192

While she was busy at the stove, I entered the shed and shut the door.

Inside, a smell of earth and fertilizer, emerging from clay pots and wooden flats, reminded me of my own garden. I wondered if my begonias were surviving and whether I should have asked Harriet instead of feckless Baby to tend them. Across the room, the workbench countered with a pleasant scent of varnish and sawdust. Putting on my light, I ran my hand over a half dozen clubs in various states of repair and decay. None fitted Harry's description of Bryce's devastated driver. Below the bench were bins with boxes of nails and screws, some tins and jars, more scraps of leather—but no shattered club head. I flicked the light up across the ceiling. Nothing.

"You leave the light on in the shed, Jack?" Mrs. MacNab called.

I switched off the flashlight and squeezed into a spot between the rakes and the mower next to the door. Someone entered the kitchen, then a leather shoe tapped on the flagstones outside.

"Ach, it's all right. It's that reflection from the streetlight. I dinna know how many times I've come out—"

"It fooled me. Just like a wee light."

"Would it be fireflies?" I heard Harry ask. A discussion of those interesting insects ensued. I eased the door open and regained the safety of the bushy shadows to the side of the shed. Too bad Harry's heroic conversational efforts were doomed to naught. Jack really had thrown away the club, and if Bryce maintained his cool and Thorston his craziness, there wasn't much hope. Mrs. MacNab returned momentarily to the kitchen. "Another scone, Mr. Radford?"

"Please, they're delicious."

On second thought, I didn't feel too sorry for Harry. I was wandering around in the dark with manure on my shoes and grease on my hands and not a thing to show for either, while he was drinking tea and eating homemade scones. Mrs. Mac-Nab picked up a plate and switched off the overhead light. On her way out of the dark kitchen, she turned on a smaller light that illuminated the window to the right of the door. Underneath it were several squat, heavy garbage cans with conical lids and looping handles. I now noticed that one of the lids was ajar, and protruding from the opening was the unmistakable, leather-wrapped handgrip of a golf club. So! I took a deep breath and moved softly across the grass toward the patio. At the edge of the flower border, I stopped.

"That's what my sister says," Mrs. MacNab exclaimed. "The heat. She said, 'Alison, you wouldn't believe it.' Well, here you can always put on a sweater—"

The flowers were set in a bed raised from the patio and built up with a low wall. Very pretty. Some of the stones were loose. Potentially very noisy. I felt along the top, looking for the safest place to step, and touched something soft and slimy. I shook my hand in violent distaste as a large slug hit the pavement, and wiping my hand on my slacks, I decided to chance the path.

"Rain tomorrow," Jack MacNab remarked in the living room.

"Yeah?"

"What they say."

"Hope not," said Harry. "It's been so beautiful."

"You'll see some scores go up if it does."

"Not so good for your prospect?"

"No, I'm hoping for sun."

I walked down the path in full view of the house. Mrs. MacNab was sitting in a print dress with her back to the door. A pair of leather slippers told me where her husband sat. Harry was out of sight. Deceived by the shadows, I stepped too heavily onto the flagstones and froze.

"Oh, Mr. Bryce likes the warm weather," Mrs. MacNab said.

"Told me it was worth strokes off his round," her husband agreed.

"I didn't think much bothered him," Harry remarked.

"They're wrong about that. He's nervous about this one.

194

Still, it's the Open—and the Old Course," the caddie said, with quiet pride.

I crossed the patio, lifted the heavy lid of the can, and eased the club from its nest of tins and bottles and wrapped garbage as carefully as I could. It was almost free when something metallic settled noisily in the can's interior.

"Was that that cat? If it's after my pigeons—"

"Well, I think I should let you get to bed," Harry announced loudly. "Big day for everyone, tomorrow."

This caused a momentary distraction, and I was able to replace the lid. Then, club in hand, I clambered onto the raised lawn, squeezed between the shed and the wall, and without considering the geography of the block, scrambled over into the neighbor's yard as Jack MacNab reached the patio and switched on an outside light.

"I should shoot that bloody cat."

I crouched on the other side of the wall. This yard had a greenhouse and a stand of peas. It also had a small dog, which, scenting me, put its paws against the wire of its pen and started to yap.

"Aye, what did I tell you?" Jack said from the other yard. "Atta good pup, Angus. Too bad he's not loose. Yellow nuisance, that thing is. It'll have been after they pigeons."

I slunk along the wall. The rear of this yard was closed by a woven wooden fence, and shielded by a couple of fruit trees, I made my escape. Unfortunately, escape was only relative. From the air, the gardens and yards of the older parts of St. Andrews would resemble the honeycombs of a species of free-thinking bees: rows of irregular cells with stone walls, interrupted now and again by pends and lanes and streets. In my haste to evade discovery, I had clambered into a Chinese box of yards and gardens, none of which gave access to the street, and each of which seemed closed by a more formidable barrier than the one before. Finally, I stopped in the middle of a splendid collection of delphiniums and wet spider webs and searched the neighboring skyline for a streetlight. Beyond a stand of raspberry canes and a stone barrier higher than my head, I spotted a lonely white light. With this beacon, I negotiated around lighted windows and delicate annuals, avoided a yard with a mastiff the size of a small horse, and found myself in a damp, overgrown flower patch, facing six feet of massive Fife stonework, topped (such was the Victorians' admiration for the perseverance of the Scottish burglar) by bent metal brackets strung with four strands of barbed wire. Beyond lay the street. Before I risked disaster on the wire, I decided to switch on my light and examine the club: Bryce's name was stamped into the leather of the handgrip. This was undoubtedly the "lucky college driver." It was well worn and not the latest fashion. More important, the shaft was badly bent and both the wood and the metal plate facing the club were dented and cracked. MacNab had cleaned the dirt and mud from the head, but it had not been a meticulous job, the caddie soon realizing the damage was beyond repair. I hoped he hadn't used chemicals, but that question would have to wait; the wall was the first order of business. I wrapped the club in my jacket, and pushed the bundle onto the top of the wall where it caught safely under the wire. Then I looked around for something to stand on. Failing in this, I examined the wall itself and finally located a cut-off shrub that would provide a leg up. Grasping the top of the wall and struggling to keep my face away from the wire, I tried to lever the rest of my body onto the stonework. Now, naturally, there are certain commando types who could have managed this in a matter of seconds. Equipped with wire cutters and a rope, I would have done better myself. But the fact is that modern life does not equip us with rope and wire cutters and useful tools for an evening's stroll. Heroics—or even obstacle course athletics—are rarely called for; seldom anticipated. As the rough stones began to wear through the gabardine of my pants, I gained some sympathy for Wulf's point of view. Wulf lived, spiritually at least, in an era that believed in preparedness:

196

He traveled with his spear, his cudgel, his rations; he wore his topcoat and blanket in one; he was forewarned for encounters with the slings and arrows of outrageous fortune. He was, I decided, as—hands scraped raw—I achieved a precarious berth between the wall and the wire, a good shelter for a mind wounded by the treacheries of modern life. Wulf did not live under our illusion that comfort implies safety, and, presumably, the constant exercise of his imagination kept him from being surprised as I was when an awkward, but basically comic, situation turned sinister.

The wall compensated for its height by a considerable width. I was lying on it, considering how best to descend over the outward curving brackets, when I heard footsteps approaching on the sidewalk. Hastily, I pulled myself along, scraping my sides on the metal, until I reached the shadows of an enormous shrub with fuzzy purple blossoms. I tucked the bundle with the club under one arm and prepared, if worst came to worst, to sacrifice my struggle to reach the top and drop back into the garden. The footsteps rounded the corner and grew louder. Whoever was approaching was large and heavy and walking fast. A moment more and an opening in the leaves revealed Bryce, his hands in his pockets and his head down, walking quickly along the street. If he glanced to the side, he would surely spot me, and I thought it would be very difficult to frame a plausible lie. I pushed the bundle with the club over the side of the wall, ready to drop it out of sight, but the golfer was too absorbed in his own errand. He passed within a foot of me, his eyes nearly level with mine, without seeing a thing. I watched him until he turned up the side street and waited until I could no longer hear his footsteps. Possibly, he'd had the same idea as Harry and, like us, was finding it difficult to locate the back entrance to the MacNab establishment.

When I was sure Bryce couldn't hear me, I once again stuffed the coat and the club under the wire. Then I got on my hands and knees and checked several brackets until I found one that

197

looked as if it might hold my weight. Standing up on the wall, I stepped onto the wires, which rasped and creaked and sagged alarmingly, forcing me to cling to the bracket. I turned around and edged backward, balancing precariously on the metal and the wires. One foot waved into space, and holding the tip of the bracket, I let myself down. There was a shrill metallic screech, and, instead of dangling a safe foot or so above the ground, I found myself caught. The whole bracket bent, and the wire, released from its stanchion, entangled itself in my shirt and sweater. I was not badly hurt, but I was encased like a puppet in stiff, rusty wires, each barb an undoubted guarantee of tetanus. I struggled to disengage myself, and as each strand unwound, I was lowered toward the sidewalk, a jerky, uncomfortable progress that I had very nearly completed when a car turned onto the street. Frantically, I tried to escape from the remaining wire. With my exertions, the bracket tore loose completely and fell with a clatter, bringing the club and my coat with it. I picked myself up off the sidewalk and grabbed the bundle. But I had no chance to run, for the car stopped next to me, and Detective Inspector Stewart opened the back door and got out. I took a step toward him and tripped over a coil of wire.

"Let me help you," he said. "You seem to have gotten tangled here." He looked up at the damaged wire and added, "Not our recommended tourist activity, that."

I had nothing to say. Stewart ordered his assistant to tidy up the wire. Then to me: "Can I offer you a ride to the station?"

"Offer isn't quite the word, is it?"

"Trespassing, damage to property—"

"Throw in petty larceny," I said and, unwrapping my jacket, produced the club.

"What's this, then?"

"This is what killed Wilson Daintly."

Stewart's small, clever hands explored the damaged club with delicate curiosity. "You think so?"

198

"I'm sure of it. I'll stake my reputation on it."

"I'm glad you feel that way," Stewart said, gesturing toward the open door of the squad car, "because that's exactly what you are doing. For your sake, I hope the lab will turn something up."

16

BY THE TIME the church towers bonged out one o'clock, the pale pink and blue night was as dark as it was ever going to get. There was not a cab on the streets as we walked back from the police station, our feet making hollow echoes on the cobblestones.

" 'Dear Mom,' " Harry dictated. " 'Enjoying the surprising after-hours life of St. Andrews. Last night, Anna and I attended an entertainment by the local constabulary that lasted until the wee small hours.' "

"Lay off it, Harry. I'm sorry."

"Where's your sense of humor? Don't take it so seriously."

"I'm too tired to laugh."

" 'We also joined a local scavenger hunt and climbed half the garden walls in town.' "

"You're certainly getting a second wind," I said sourly. "You were grumpy enough earlier."

"Well, there are times when it's embarrassing to be married to an eccentric detective."

"Emphasis on eccentric or detective?"

"I mean, I'm the one who's supposed to be imaginative and Bohemian. When you show all that temperament, it puts me in the shade."

"I see nothing eccentric or Bohemian about wanting to get my hands on a murder weapon. That's one of the basic—"

"Besides, I begin to think you're right. A little unconventionality is good for the soul. Look at that sky, and the houses like ghosts—" He smiled benignly. So that was it: He had another picture in mind and all was forgotten and forgiven. He held his hands to frame the twin towers and the skeletal façade of the cathedral. "Lovely," he said, "and the same pink background is what I need behind the R and A. I know just the ink to use, and there's some Japanese paper with silver flecks in it—" He smiled again, absorbed in imagining his print, then added, as an afterthought, "Are you in very big trouble?"

"Not if that club killed Daintly."

"And if it didn't—or if you can't prove it?"

"Then I'm in hot water."

"Oh."

"We'll know tomorrow."

"I hope—" he began, but I cut him off.

"I'm too tired to hope," I said. When we reached our hotel, I collapsed in a quilt without getting undressed and immediately fell asleep.

*　　*　　*

The R and A Committee met at seven-thirty the next morning. Stewart had informed me, and Sutherland had left a message during the evening as a further reminder. This time we gathered upstairs at the clubhouse in a poky room as far from the eager eyes of the press as it was possible to get. The chill wind and scudding gray clouds that covered the feeble outbreaks of sunshine and blue sky seemed an apt reflection of the mood within. Everyone was nervous and irritable, and even the normally serene Irving and the practical Sir Malcolm Greene seemed on

201

edge. The complete and total success of the first days of the Open, the absence of trouble, and the delight of the crowds might all have been tokens of blackest gloom and disaster, to judge by the faces of the committee members. They sensed odd things afoot, and irrationally, if understandably, they were set to blame Stewart and me for their anxieties.

Greene called the meeting to order, lit the inevitable cigarette, and shook his gray mane out of his notes. "Gentlemen, Miss Peters, this is the busiest and most important day of the Open. We will get right to the point. What have you learned? And how is it going to help us?"

Stewart unfolded his note pad. I looked at him, and he nodded.

"We know," I said, "that Dr. Melvin Thorston, visiting lecturer in Scottish studies and medieval languages, damaged the courses."

"My God!" Sutherland exclaimed. There was a murmur of surprise and distaste. "We will have to notify the secretary."

Greene, a fellow academic, was more cautious. "Have you proof of this, Miss Peters?"

"I have his confession."

"There is little doubt, Sir Malcolm," Stewart added, "that the threat to Peter Bryce was typed on a machine in the university's history department. Dr. Thorston had access to that machine."

"And the professor served as an electronics expert in the U.S. Army," I continued. "He has the skill to set the explosive."

"This is all well and good, but what was his motive? Why would he do such a thing? And why would he admit it, Miss Peters?"

"Motivation is always speculative, Sir Malcolm, and Inspector Stewart and I have arrived at rather different conclusions," I said, tactfully. "We know for a fact, though, that he and Peter Bryce were former friends who had a serious quarrel. Professor Thorston blames Bryce for some great personal misfortune, a

202

circumstance that has led to increasingly aberrant behavior. Thorston has also suffered at least one complete breakdown, connected, I believe, with his military service."

"I see."

There was another murmur: Military service raised Thorston's stock slightly.

"Where is Dr. Thorston now?" Irving asked. "It seems to me that if this man is kept from the course and undertakes no more harassment, our problems are over."

This met general agreement, but like the short-lived sunlight outside, it was fleeting.

"No one knows," I said.

Stewart took up the matter. He described Thorston's departure from the hospital, his avoidance of his usual haunts, and his larcenous exit from the cottage. "Fortunately," he concluded, "Peter Bryce was also looking for his old friend, and he gave Miss Peters a lift home."

"He has a car, then," Sutherland said.

"Yes. We have put out an all-points bulletin: It's our best hope of apprehending him."

"But meanwhile"—Sutherland pursued—"he is free to drive the whole country—and to return here."

"That is the situation," Stewart admitted stolidly.

"Is this man dangerous?" Greene was always to the point.

"Possibly," Stewart said.

"That depends on who he is," I explained, and Stewart frowned.

"Now Miss Peters," Sutherland began, but Irving interrupted.

"Dr. Thorston is the fellow with the cape and the spear?"

"That's right. He is an actor of some talent. I suspect that's how he has managed to elude the police."

"He has gone beyond acting," Irving said. "Damn crazy nonsense for a professor, if you ask me. Traipsing around like a wild man."

"It—I should say Wulf—began as some sort of academic project." At this Greene nodded, as if he were well acquainted with scholarly exotica. "It is apparently a symptom of Dr. Thorston's emotional breakdown that Wulf has assumed a life of his own, beyond the professor's control."

"And Wulf damaged the course, you suggest?"

"No, Sir Malcolm. Dr. Thorston damaged the course. Wulf—"

"Yes?"

"Wulf has more dangerous games in mind."

"Be specific, please."

"Wulf may represent a danger for Peter Bryce. A serious danger."

"But it was Dr. Thorston who threatened Bryce," Frazer protested, in confusion. "Inspector Stewart said he tested the typewriter."

"It is Miss Peters's theory," Stewart replied, "on which I am reserving judgment, that Wulf represents the professor's dangerous impulses and hostile wishes. Am I correct?"

"Fair enough."

"The damage to the courses, however regrettable, is the warning of a modern rational mind. So is the note."

There was some discussion about this and considerable objection to the damage being in any way, shape, or form, "rational."

Stewart cut through the verbiage. "Whatever we may think about Dr. Thorston's conduct, it is Miss Peters's belief that the professor as such isn't dangerous. I'm inclined to disagree. What we both agree on, however, is that Wulf is a much greater threat—not to the course, but to Mr. Bryce."

"I'm beginning to lose your point, inspector," Sutherland said in a stuffy, haughty voice.

"The professor *may* present a problem. Wulf *will* present one."

"What sort of problem?" Greene asked. "When we began, we certainly did consider the vandalism a serious problem."

"The purpose of Wulf," I said, "has become the killing of Peter Bryce."

Alarm traveled the room with a whisper and crackle like summer lightning.

"That is a very serious accusation." Greene spoke severely.

"I'm afraid everything points to its truth," Stewart added in my defense. "That is why we must prevent Thorston from appearing at the tournament."

"All our officials must be notified. We'll need pictures of this chap," Irving declared. "But it is late in the day to alter our security arrangements."

"Bryce's group has been watched closely though?"

"Oh, yes, but under these circumstances—"

"We will have officers on the beach and access roads," Stewart said, "and watching the stations and the Golf Link buses. Remember the man has a broken right arm. I don't want to exaggerate his abilities. In addition to handicapping him, the cast will make him conspicuous. At this point, our real concern is any incident—"

"Certainly"—Sutherland interrupted—"that has been our concern from the first. That's the reason we hired Miss Peters." The lines on his face suggested regret for that decision.

"Who," Greene added, "has now told us more than we cared to know."

"It all goes back to organization," Frazer said, and the meeting threatened to break up in exclamations and whispered conversations.

"We wanted to inform you, gentlemen, of the situation and about what can and cannot be done." Stewart's voice was hoarse and exasperated.

Greene called the meeting back to order. After more discussion, Irving and Stewart came to an agreement about coordinating the course marshals and the constables, while I, in the unenviable position of knowing Thorston personally, was assigned to brief the officers stationed at the access points. The

205

meeting ended in much the same spirit as it had begun, with an uneasiness touched with embarrassment. The committee's alarm at Thorston's potential for disaster mingled with the fear that we might make ourselves look ridiculous with plans and alarms over this unconvincing assassin. An unbalanced professor with a broken wrist did not really seem so formidable, especially when he was an actor and poseur like Thorston. Yet there was no certainty. Thorston could set explosives and design and use a collapsible javelin. He was a man with many talents, and worse yet, he did not seem susceptible to pressures for conformity. Adding everything up, he was almost completely unpredictable.

"Ach," said Stewart when we reached the back door. The area behind the R and A was jammed with press cars and television trucks, with ticket holders and officials and members of the golfers' retinues. The first pair was set to tee off in less than fifteen minutes, and the excitement of the day was palpable.

"A no-win situation," I remarked.

"It wouldn't have bothered them half so much if Thorston were an ordinary type," Stewart observed. "A professional even. Anything but what we've got."

"No, he doesn't fit the image, but—"

"Inspector!" A young constable pushed her way through the crowd, red faced and excited.

"What is it, constable?"

"Message from headquarters, they've—"

"Inside, constable." He jutted his chin toward the crowd, many festooned with bright press badges.

I followed them into the building.

"What is it?"

"The car's been located."

"Thorston's? When?"

"Yes. Twenty minutes ago. It's been double-checked. We found it parked near the Sailing Club at the harbor."

"Then he's back. How did he manage without being seen?" Stewart exclaimed in frustration.

"The plate was covered with mud and some of the numbers blacked out. The traffic warden didn't think it was the right car at first. It's been parked there since early this morning, and—"

"Never mind. It's done now. I'd better tell them upstairs. Constable, get Miss Peters a radio. She'll need to keep in touch."

"Yes, sir," she said and went nipping out the door at top speed.

"Better spot him," Stewart said to me.

"And that golf club?" I asked. "Any word on that?"

"The lab doesn't expect anything until this afternoon."

"Nothing will happen until then anyway," I observed. I hadn't thought of that before, but it made sense: Bryce didn't tee off until one-thirty.

"Why not?"

"Dramatic irony. Bryce appreciates it, and Thorston is going to provide it."

"No more wild theories, please, Miss Peters. Just identify this man Thorston before he gets himself into trouble. And call us. Right? No individual initiative on this round. Remember, if nothing else, the inconveniences I could cause you."

"Inspector, I'm behind you all the way."

"Hmmph." He pulled a sour face. "Just remember what's behind you: trespassing, property damage, petty larceny, and interfering with evidence."

"Pretty good for a honeymoon."

Stewart turned on his heel and headed upstairs. "Bloody tourist," he muttered.

17

A DOZEN GOLFERS began the final round separated by no more than three strokes, and the excitement in the stands and galleries was immense. The stiff breezes sweeping off the bay and up the long heather-edged fairways from the river might have carried anticipation on their breath, for all over the old town there was a sense of expectation that grew more intense and concentrated as one approached the fat blue-and-white-striped exhibition tents, the jammed streets near the course, the canyon of spectator stands by the R and A, and the greens and tees already ringed with fans, red faced in the wind. Half of Britain seemed on hand, bringing with them the world's press. Cameras, cables, and microphones were everywhere; and a helicopter droned overhead with a cameraman hanging out the door, but there was no Melvin Thorston. No camera caught him in the galleries of the early starters, no microphone detected his voice among the bustle of fans streaming down from the town and straggling across the road from the railway shuttle.

Nor was a long ride out along the West Sands any more

productive. Families sought the capricious sun behind wind-breaks staked along the wide white beach. The patient donkeys stood with their tails to the wind awaiting clients, and children ran about with soccer balls and cricket bats, oblivious of the tournament beyond the gorse and grass of the courses. Thorston was nowhere in sight, and the constables stationed along the access roads shook their heads and shrugged their shoulders. On the estuary itself, nothing stirred but gulls and seals, and I stood for a moment by the car, peering down the wide mudflats to the silver sea bed, exposed by the tide.

"Is the wind going to be a factor, John? Some of the early starters seem to be having difficulties with these first holes. The front nine has not been a problem all week, but today looks like a different story."

"I think so, Desmond. They've had the wind with them going out the last three days, but it's blowing straight in today. They'll be fighting the wind all the way to the turn . . ."

The announcer's voice dropped. "This is Nakajima's second shot. He fell victim to the Road Hole yesterday after playing surprisingly consistent golf all week."

"He's selected a six iron. Oh, a lovely shot—"

The sand dunes and the rough, gorse-covered links behind the beach proved empty. Perhaps Thorston had changed his mind, hopped a bus, and disappeared. When I stopped Inspector Stewart for a moment at noon, he shook his head.

"Nothing?"

"Nothing at all."

"Is Bryce ready to tee off?" I asked.

"Yes. There will be plainclothesmen with him."

"Has he been told?"

"He asked if there was news. We informed him about the car's being recovered."

"How did he take it?"

"Pretty well for a man in his position. I wouldn't like to be only one up on Nicklaus with eighteen holes to go."

"Watson and Oosterhuis are in there, too."

"Nicklaus is my pick," said Stewart. "He can do it again." He compressed his lips as he hurried back to his car; if it had not been for Thorston, the Inspector could have picked himself a good spot along the eighteenth and dabbled in crowd control.

Peter Bryce teed off on schedule to a big cheer; he was five under for the tournament, with Watson and Oosterhuis, and in the words of the BBC commentator, "Easily the most exciting new player of this tournament." The cheers faded as his gallery trailed down the fairway, but Bryce's fortunes followed me through the press tent, where a television set recorded a mammoth drive off the second tee, and in and out of the exhibition, where I heard him rack up his first birdie of the round:

"He's within twelve, fifteen feet of the hole, but he's been making putts of that length all this week. The green at the second breaks a little to the left—" A hush, and then the commentator resumed, whispering in a birdie putt and another on the third. As I made my way behind the grandstand near the clubhouse, Bryce was crossing the immense green on the fifth, and the announcer was discussing in suitably subdued tones the treacherous pin placement.

"Bryce put a very good chip onto the green, but he's facing another long putt."

"I think they're all having a bit of trouble gauging the wind. The shots on the front nine are hanging."

"He's studying the lie, taking his time."

"This is a very careful, meticulous golfer, Mark."

"We should mention that the wind has really firmed up the greens. They've been watering every night, but with the wind, the greens are really hard by this time of day . . ."

"Bryce's hunched into that peculiar putting stance of his. Intense concentration—a long putt. Oh, it's a beauty. It's got a chance. Yes!" A long breath of satisfaction broke from the crowd, followed by applause.

"He's happy about that one."

210

"That was an important shot, Desmond. It salvaged a par after he ran into trouble with his approach shot. He hit a nice chip out of the bunker and then sank a difficult putt."

"So, Peter Bryce holds on to that two-stroke lead as we go to the sixth . . ."

Two holes later, the report came that the wind had dropped on the river. The holes at the turn all lay close to the estuary, and I figured that change of weather augured well for Bryce. I remembered his looking up at the clear twilight and predicting a victory. He'd hoped for good weather, and the sun was breaking through as if on cue. There was still no sign whatsoever of Thorston.

On the ninth, Bryce dropped a stroke after landing in a crater-sized bunker at the side of the green. I had checked in at the security crew's trailer, so I was able to see him, marching around at the bottom of the pit, his scarlet sweater vivid against the pale sand and the intense green grass.

"Going with the sand wedge," the commentator remarked. He proceeded to a judicious discussion of the choices and catastrophes of earlier victims of the hole's bunkers, but Bryce exploded the ball out of the sand, sending it up high and straight and dropping it onto the edge of the green. He two-putted to appreciative applause. Ahead of him on the course, Nicklaus had garnered another birdie on the tenth and now claimed a piece of the lead. The Golden Bear waved to the crowds, then the cameras cut back to Bryce, who was approaching his tee shot on the tenth. I sipped a cup of coffee and studied his intense, almost severe, face. In person, the power and egotism stamped there were unsettling. On the screen, lapped by the broadcasters' soothing blandness, the sheer force of his personality was undeniable. He adjusted his golf glove, consulted with his caddie, and stared down the lumpy contour of the tenth fairway, waiting for Crenshaw, who had already dropped two strokes, to slam a shot into the rough. The commentators murmured on, dedicated to understatement, restrained, even in

211

their soundproof booths, to whispers as delicate as a mortician's. Bryce flexed his legs, loosened his wrists, and hit a colossal drive: He was enormously strong and graceful, and I watched him stride down the fairway with a mixture of admiration and distaste. As he passed the applauding gallery, he raised his arm and nodded, almost curtly, to the fans. But if his aloof personality kept him from the unrestrained affection showered on a Palmer, a Nicklaus, or a Trevino, his great gifts brought respect.

"A very cool young man," the commentator remarked. "A golfer with remarkable maturity."

"Yes, he's all business out there."

"Someone remarked the other day that he's the Calvin Coolidge of golf."

Laughter from the booth. Then they returned to whisper that Aioki was in serious trouble on the twelfth. I left the trailer and began another weary circuit of the clubhouse area and the narrow gray streets nearby. There, even without my transistor, it would have been easy to follow the progress of the round. A radio in the secondhand bookstore brought the news that Aioki's troubles had escalated to disaster at the twelfth, while the television at the pub across the street showed the difficulties that had interrupted Nicklaus's strong play at the fifteenth. Like rumors rippling through a mob, the electronic familiars of the town whispered the news from open windows, from doors left ajar, from displays in shop windows, from passing cars. A good shot, a disaster in the rough, a drive to the green, another calamitous encounter with the Road Hole, all fluttered through the airwaves and reverberated from the solid stone buildings. If Thorston was listening, he gave no sign, and as the long afternoon wore on, it began to appear as if all the theatrics and excitement would be confined to the links. The security people began to feel better. When Bryce's group approached the final holes, the area of concern diminished, and Stewart called in the plainclothesmen stationed far down the course. Bryce was on the fifteenth, when I waved to the constable at the car park and received a cheery thumbs-up sign in return.

I felt only a shade less confident, as I started another turn through the crowd behind the clubhouse. I wandered along the street, checking the faces at the windows above, and looked in the bookstore for the second time that day without recognizing any of the browsers in its high, dusty stacks. Across the street, the same crowd were replenishing their resources at the pub. I waited for a moment to see Bryce's tee shot at the sixteenth.

"He's certainly playing very, very good golf today," the commentator remarked, as the camera followed the ball down a narrow fairway lined with fans and bunkers.

"Yes, Bryce has a lot of power, and he's putting well, too. He's now regained both the shots he dropped on the back nine, and he's one up on the field at this point, with three holes to play."

"Let's go up now to Nicklaus, who's getting ready for his tee shot at the Road Hole."

"He's bogeyed this hole in every round this week, Mark, so he'll undoubtedly be taking his time over this shot—"

I returned to the street. I was beginning to feel that I had outwalked the golfers, and I was ready to return to the security trailer for the final holes, when I noticed a group of shoppers enter the large woolen mill that abutted several golf and sporting goods shops. The mill was a crowded, noisy shop, jammed with tourists and woolen goods and reverberating with jangling jigs and reels. But, remembering that it overlooked the eighteenth and opened to the road along the course, I walked down the steps and into the cavernous space, hung floor to rafter with tartans, sweaters, and tweeds. The Open might be reaching its climax, but at least a portion of the day's tourists was more interested in bargains. A few discreet transistors informed the staff of the progress of the match, while dedicated shoppers plowed relentlessly through bins of seconds or admired the rows of pastel cashmeres stacked like tubs of sherbet in their

213

plastic envelopes. I ascended the narrow back stair to the tea-room, where the establishment lures its customers with prom-ises of free coffee and lemonade. This refreshment area was pretty well filled, its large rear windows providing excellent views of the eighteenth. I squeezed my way to the front, but no one concealed a cast under his tweeds or raincoat, and Wulf was not hidden behind one of the fiery blazers that marked the other visiting Americans.

Downstairs, I took up a position behind the racks of yard goods. I was reluctant, in truth, to admit that my last-minute hunch had been groundless and even more reluctant to continue my tiresome and unproductive circuits of the course, the town, and the beach. On the opposite side of the store, women's wear was set out on a raised area, and I noticed several men watching the tournament from behind the displays of shawls, kilts, and jumpers. One wore a poncho and a wide-brimmed hat that merited, I thought, a second look. Edging through the shoppers and the fans around the door, I mounted the steps, but the men at the window were talking together as I approached, and I was disappointed. Outside, a cheer rose from the stands, and every neck in the place craned for a glimpse of the fairway. I fiddled with the knob of the transistor: " . . . a beautiful shot. A shame Ben Crenshaw had such a poor front nine, because he has played beautiful golf over the last few holes."

"Yes, he's one under par now and looks to finish the day with a good round, despite losing those three strokes on the first ten holes. He's come back under pressure—"

"Like you, Miss Peters," a voice said softly in my ear. "I can rely on you to turn up. My old friend Duclos would endorse your character. You're a lesson in persistence for us all."

I half turned in the crowd, but there was a click and some-thing unmistakably sharp and metallic appeared just under my ribs.

"No need to attract attention. Please. My mind's made up. It's got to be done. Just start out the door," Thorston

214

commanded in a calm, remote voice and took my arm.

I didn't move.

"You're wondering how I did it and whether it's really dangerous? Let me explain. Simply a switchblade mechanism fixed onto my cast: good, solid plaster provided by the National Health. Gives me a free hand and I'm nearly ambidextrous. It's still possible. I warn you; I've decided."

I nodded and started slowly toward the door.

"I'm sick of this in-between life," Thorston remarked in the same quiet tone. "For years, I haven't been able to come to a decision. Nor to make plans. I really ought to thank you: You've brought everything to a head. Not so fast. Even if this is all your fault, I'd rather not involve you."

"I'm counting on that."

"Don't underestimate me," he said, his voice now tight and hoarse, and he gave me a push into the crowded street. I was sure that there would be constables around, but the road was packed with fans, and it was scarcely possible to move in the crush, far less to signal. With the excitement of the final holes, checks on access to the road and to the fence along the fairways had been abandoned. All eyes were now on the eighteenth, where Nicklaus, one shot out, was teeing up for the last time: He had conquered the Road Hole at last.

"Where's Bryce?" someone asked.

There were cheers for Nicklaus as Thorston and I moved slowly down the narrow road. The hotels and private homes and golf courses to our left were jammed with spectators, leaning out the windows, crowding balconies, balancing on the iron railings. One of them would notice.

"Turn up your radio," Thorston said.

"Approaching the seventeenth tee. A very big hand from the gallery."

"Well, John, Peter Bryce is up a stroke with two holes to play. What would your advice be?"

"Bryce has been playing exciting golf. He's been going for the long drive; he's been making the big shot. It's aggressive, attacking golf, and it's undeniably paid off for him so far."

"But this is the Road Hole."

"That's right. He's got to avoid the sheds and the hotel on the right and he has that line of bunkers to the left. With a stroke lead, I'd play this hole conservatively."

"Never," Thorston remarked.

"Sorry," I said as we jostled past a man with a cane. "Where are we going?"

"Straight ahead. We're joining Peter's gallery. Do you know I've never seen him play? Never. Yet I made it all possible. But you guessed that."

I nodded.

"It began—excuse us—official—you must be more aggressive if we are to get through, Miss Peters. Remember a lack of conviction on your part could be fatal. I've come too far. I realized that after our last meeting."

With this warning, I squeezed into the throng where my badge, combined with the shifting of the crowd that was moving up and down the road to gain sight of Nicklaus or the first glimpse of Bryce's attack on the seventeenth, speeded our progress. Thorston talked as we descended the slope along the eighteenth. He sounded quite calm, but closer attention revealed that this impression was deceptive. He was not so much serene as detached, as though he had succeeded in bringing some of the same objectivity to the passions and affairs of Melvin Thorston, Ph.D., that he had hitherto shown to Wulf. There was, after all, something comparable in him and Bryce; they had both been wired in odd ways, so that at a certain point their emotions shunted out, to reappear again, if Thorston were any indication, in bizarre and frightening forms.

"The beginning, Miss Peters. I was going to say that it began on a purely theoretical level. A problem in electronics and voice modification. Safe cracking is rather an ironic use of advanced knowledge in speech and technology, isn't it? But the Brain-

216

withe lock was a fascinating thing. When Wilson first mentioned it, I naturally assumed it was just his way of showing an interest in my work. Our current problem in the lab had concerned—but that's beside the point. Begun in innocence along the primrose path, Miss Peters. Of course, once I had the problem of the lock solved, there was pressure to put that knowledge to work. I pretended I didn't understand that."

We reached the foot of the lane and squeezed onto the short walled road that runs along the big seventeenth green to the Old Course Hotel. At first glance, I thought that the celebrated Road Hole looked rather commonplace.

"I can't honestly say I didn't guess what they had in mind. Perhaps not at first, but later I knew. I just didn't believe it would come to anything. Perhaps that's not quite true either. I was afraid to tackle Peter about it; I thought it best to leave the matter alone. I didn't understand the activist psychology."

There were course marshals along the road, keeping the spectators off the grass and organizing the gallery that was streaming up the fairway. Thorston whispered on: a proposition about guilt and innocence and memory that seemed increasingly indecent when I considered the outcome. The press photographs, the reports, the shock.

". . . have liked to ruin Wilson. He'd made a good thing of it, hadn't he? Believe it or not, I found it hard to run through enough money. Even with the books—you've seen my collection. I simply wasn't cut out for dissipation. Maybe it was an awareness of bad faith. I never took a share, you see. Never. I wouldn't have touched the money. But I borrowed from Wilson —as much as he'd lend me. Is that a significant difference? I thought it was, once. Still, that ought to clear me of Wilson's death. I had no claims. Peter did. Wilson had handled all the money—saw it got into circulation properly, that sort of thing. He fiddled Peter's share, I suppose. Cheated him in some way and paid the price."

Thinking he was absorbed in his story, I tried to signal the official nearest us, but Thorston was alert. He tightened his grip on my arm. "Careful, Miss Peters. I *have* decided."

Was that true? The crowd was packed between the green and the wall. If Thorston lost control of himself, he could do a lot of damage. To me, first of all.

"The spinal cord, Miss Peters. A very vulnerable spot. I know my anatomy. It went with the other part of my specialty, the voice. Voice boxes. Caroline was impressed. She was dedicated, although not very bright. But so charming, so nice. I had foolish hopes," he added, his voice strained. "Stay toward the front. We must be in the front."

I wondered if I should call his bluff. Make a break for it. Announce to the official not three feet away that the noted scholar and madman, Professor Thorston, was about to endanger play on the seventeenth. But the officials were absorbed in the match, and the crowds, likewise. They did not see the blade nor wonder why the man in the hat and the poncho was whispering continually and crazily in my ear. Perhaps he would do nothing more. Perhaps the event would be as anti-climactic as Thorston's appearance.

"The coins, of course, you noticed. I never wanted one. They insisted, *he* insisted—Peter, I mean. It was to involve me deeper, to make me admit my complicity. Typical of Peter's sadistic streak. Why did I accept it? Why haven't I thrown it into the North Sea? Surely you can guess. A sense of guilt, atonement, recompense. He never understood, of course."

"Who?"

"Peter, naturally. He never understood. Now, Wilson—Wilson was afraid of him afterward. Always. He must have known how it could come out. I wasn't afraid. He made a mistake there. He made a few, although he didn't realize it at the time. I didn't know till the morning after, you realize. No. Heard it on the radio. I'd gone to bed. It was all on the news."

That was a nasty touch, and his voice dropped even lower, rapt and self-absorbed. If the official would only turn toward the crowd. If one of the constables would appear. A glance would tell. There was one on the road. Another minute, I thought, but when Bryce slammed his tee shot straight down the center of the fairway, I was out of luck. The crowd pressed closer, and even the officials struggled to see where the shot had landed.

"The bastard's going to do it," Thorston exclaimed, and mingled with the hatred was a kind of pride. His long monologue ceased, and he turned his attention to the transistor.

"What are they saying?"

The announcer's voice rolled smooth as oil, ". . . avoiding the bunkers . . ."

"Is Peter in the bunker?" Tension ran like static electricity between Thorston's hand and the point of the knife. Something would happen. I swallowed and tried to consider what he might do and how I should react.

"No, I don't think so." It was important to be calm. To follow the game. To hope the game, the crowd, the weight of media and tradition and expectation would deaden the professor's manic impulse. The transistor kept us informed: "Beautiful placement—I'd think one of the irons, a six or a seven, Desmond . . ." the commentator said. "It's a question of holding his game together now. He's had trouble at this hole, but Nicklaus came off three bogeys here to make par."

"He's getting set for his second shot," I said.

Then there was a sound from the gallery, a sudden inhalation of breath, like a great sigh, and then a groan and a burble of voices. We did not need the commentator to tell us what had happened. We had seen Bryce's second shot arch gracefully from just beside the shed screens. Tiny, pellet-sized, it hung against the blue sky and then descended with a rush; and all the exclamations of the spectators, the crammed galleries, the towering stands, the faces pressed against windows, the drinkers at the pubs, and the salesclerks with radios under their counters could not alter its course. Determined by physics and by fate, it dropped out of the firmament, past the serried white-and-buff rows of distant spectators, and into a pot-shaped bunker at the side of the seventeenth green.

Thorston began to tremble as though his conflicting emotions were going to shake him apart, and I realized I still had no clue to what he intended. Perhaps he was not sure himself. Totally dominated by his emotions, he seemed unaware of the fans, the course, or of anything but the scarlet-clad figure striding up the narrow fairway. I tried again to edge aside, but he automatically tightened his grip on my arm, and the pressure of the crowd pushed the point of his knife through my jacket and my sweater. If he had, indeed, decided to attack Bryce, he would have to release me, and then he would be vulnerable. Unless he took a more ruthless course and dispatched me first.

"Tough shot coming up," I said.

The spectators around us began to applaud.

"Clap," Thorston said. "Or it will look strange."

Bryce and Crenshaw led the trailing gallery up the seventeenth. Crenshaw's shot had fallen short, but he was in a good position for a chip onto the green; and while he consulted with his caddie, Bryce marched over to examine the bunker. The lie represented a tricky shot, although he had made others as difficult and could still save a par. The crowd fell quiet in anticipation, and I turned down the transistor. Bryce studied the bunker until Crenshaw had played onto the green. Then he took his nine iron and readied himself for the shot with two practice swings. Facing the green and the road, he addressed the ball, his face blank with the indifference of absolute concentration. Thorston waited until Bryce had begun his backswing, then he cried out, his resonant actor's voice full of anguish.

"You lied to me, Peter. Why did you do it? Why did you have to kill them?"

The crowd stirred and turned, the officials froze, open mouthed; and Bryce, who may or may not have looked up, may or may not have seen us, rocketed his shot out of the bunker.

220

It cleared the green, bounced through the crowd onto the road, and came to rest on a trampled bit of grass an inch from the game's most infamous wall. Bryce stepped onto the green, and Thorston shouted again. "Tell us, Peter. We all want an answer."

The golfer's smooth face twisted with anger and tension, but he did not appeal to the marshals or send his caddie for an official. He stood across from us on the edge of the grass and stared at Thorston, as though awakened, surprised, from another life.

"Why, Peter?" Thorston cried, and shoving me violently aside, he started forward. I fell against the startled couple next to us, then dived for the professor, grabbing his cast and pulling him off balance when he lunged for the green. He stumbled, and as the marshals were suddenly restored to motion, I called, "Help him, he's been hit by the ball. Get the ambulance!"

Bryce crossed the green, the iron still in his hand; and there was a moment when I thought he was lost, when I thought that, like Thorston, he had disappeared from the course and the gallery, from the cheers, from his career, from the blue and green and sunny present to some other occasion, more violent, more vivid. He raised the club as if to strike both Thorston and me.

"How could you have hit her so many times? I've never understood," the professor cried, but oblivious to their own danger, the marshals stepped in front of us, calling loudly for the ambulance.

"Careful of his arm," I said, adding in a lower voice, "It's Thorston."

"My God!" one marshal exclaimed.

"Keep the crowd back. He's armed."

"Constable! Constable!"

There was a great commotion. Two police officers pushed their way through to us, waving on the ambulance men as they approached.

"Step back, please, step back."

"Can't see what's happened. What? I'm trying, Desmond," the broadcaster bellowed into his mike. "It looks as if a fan has been injured by that shot Peter Bryce hit out of the bunker here at the seventeenth. There was confusion on the shot. Perhaps you could hear someone shouting from the gallery. No, I don't know if Bryce heard the man or not—"

"Stand back, please. Clear a way for the stretcher."

"I'm all right," Thorston protested. "I'm all right. I didn't get hit. He hit—"

I held his injured arm firmly on the ground. "Stop it, you fool. Someone will get hurt." I felt for the switch on the knife and tried to retract it.

"We'll take him now," the ambulance attendant said.

I whispered to the constable, and he took a firm hold of the cast. "I see. Get on the stretcher, Dr. Thorston."

"He's insisting he's not injured," the broadcaster said, one hand on his earphone, the other on his bulbous mike. "I didn't see it happen. I thought it bounced off the road. Well, at the moment, the marshals are clearing the fans back from the ball. It's lying almost touching the wall. A very, very difficult—"

"Please stand back—"

"Notify Inspector Stewart right away."

"—shot. There's no room to swing. Some golfers have hit straight into the wall and used a ricochet here. It's an incredible situation—"

"Behind the lines, miss, please. We need room here—"

I ignored the official and followed the constables and the stretcher. Bryce was still standing on the very edge of the road. He had lowered the club and controlled the surge of livid anger without managing to restore his immersion in the game. In spite of the wind and sun, his face was white and tired, as though Thorston, for all his awkwardness, had struck a fatal blow.

"Mr. Bryce, Mr. Bryce," one of the officials called. "Are you ready, sir?"

222

He crossed the road like a sleepwalker. On my transistor, with a curious echo effect, the broadcaster began to whisper.

". . . clearly had an effect. I don't know what this will do to his concentration, Desmond, but it was very unfortunate. He's inspecting the shot now. If he takes a drop, he and Nicklaus will be tied, and unless he can put it in the hole, the match could be decided right here."

"The Road Hole's made the difference all week. It's taken out Ballesteros and Palmer. It destroyed Nakajima's round yesterday, and it ended the remarkably good run Simon Owen had this afternoon—"

"You've informed Inspector Stewart?" I asked the constable. They were loading Thorston into the back on an ambulance with two officers as escort.

"He wants you to meet him at the eighteenth."

"The knife?"

"They're taking care of that, now." He nodded toward the crowd. "As well to prevent panic."

"Yes, of course. The ambulance is the best idea."

"Yes, Desmond, it looks as if Bryce intends to take that shot. He's studying it from all angles—"

"Take that shot!" the constable exclaimed. "He'll be lucky to get out of there in six." He slammed the door and signaled the driver.

As I started to push my way up the road to the clubhouse, a solid wall of noise from around the eighteenth green announced that Nicklaus had held par on the last hole. They were even a moment later, when Bryce decided, after all, that he had an unplayable lie, and the Golden Bear went one up when he carded a six.

". . . could certainly have been much worse," the commentator murmured. ". . . sure to be controversy over just what happened on that bunker shot."

Behind me, Bryce was teeing up on the eighteenth. I struggled through the crowd, turning back in time to see his drive rise over the S curve of Swilcan Burn, sweep straight and beautiful all the way over the road that bisects the fairways, and land with a high bounce on a level strip close to the green.

"A beautiful shot! An incredible shot. Disaster at the Road Hole and then Bryce hits a drive like that one. This is really a class player—"

The packed stands and galleries broke into applause. I stopped at the top of the road to watch him approach. He did not acknowledge the fans but strode straight ahead. The effortless absorption in the game that had seemed to insulate him from everything but the stroke of the moment had been lost, replaced by a tight, ruthless determination. The crowd shifted, revealing the inspector. He nodded stiffly, and I joined him without making any comment. When Bryce and his caddie reached the ball, the stands subsided to a soft, expectant murmur. Above the R and A, a blue-and-white St. Andrew's cross snapped noisily on its lanyard, and wind-borne gulls cried in the sun, which now flooded prodigally upon the course and on the long bleached curve of the shore. Stewart and I stood in the chilly blue shade of the stands and waited.

"We've got the lab report," he said.

Bryce's second shot looped up from the fairway to land close to the back of the green. The best he could do now was a tie.

I waited until the applause ended. "What were the results?"

Bryce stopped on the edge of the green to assess his situation. Although not one of the monstrous double greens that distinguish the Old Course, the eighteenth is plenty big enough. He had a very long putt to save the match, and his caddie looked worried. Bryce walked over to the ball, studied its lie for a moment, then glanced up and recognized Inspector Stewart and me. He stared at us for an instant before a shade passed over his tense face, and he raised his eyebrows in a gesture of irritation or resignation. Then, without hesitation, he bent over the ball, hunched his large shoulders, and set the putt over the rippling green carpet, as bright and smooth as an emerald, but

224

rolling and capricious as the gray water in the bay beyond. There was a moment of silence, the fans, the golfers, the caddies, the press stood suspended, their next breath waiting on the white ball, which sped imperiously toward the hole, straight, perfect, gaining a treacherous momentum from the grade, curving slightly at a depression, slowing at a barely perceptible rise on the green. Unstoppable, like the remote consequences of a half-forgotten event, it rolled the long yards to the very lip of the cup. And stopped.

The crowd groaned.

"It's the weapon," Stewart said. "There's blood, and the types match."

Bryce walked to the cup and impassively tapped in the shot. Jack Nicklaus had won the Open by a single stroke, and a great wave of applause surged from the stands, the windows overhead, the road, the balconies of the Old Course Hotel, the crush around the clubhouse.

"He knows," I remarked to Stewart. "He knew when he saw us."

"Yet he made a splendid shot," the inspector said as the fans poured onto the course. "A really gallant end. Remarkable."

"A gamble."

"Oh, he had to hit long. It was a chance. Nicklaus drove the green here once."

"I meant staying for the final round."

"What else was he to do?" Stewart asked. "He had everything to gain."

"Except freedom."

Nicklaus had come out onto the eighteenth to shake hands with Bryce. The roar of his ovation was like a rush of water, turbulent enough to sweep both golfers away.

"How many men experience this?" Stewart asked as we moved through the crowd.

Reporters swarmed: "How did it feel, Jack?" "Just a word, please, Peter." "Congratulations." "Your third British Open!"

225

"Hard luck, Mr. Bryce." "What happened there at the seventeenth?" "Your second at St. Andrews." "Did you see?" "When did you think you had the match won?" "Did the wind make a difference today?" "A popular victory here." "Favorite of the Scottish crowds, Jack." "No one seemed to know." "Some disturbance." "Decided by the Road Hole—"

Stewart moved closer to Bryce, and two uniformed constables materialized from the mob. The swirl of victory and curiosity gradually focused entirely on Nicklaus, encompassing him like a mantle, separating him from all the rest. Bryce pulled on his Windbreaker and started to leave. Stewart fell into step with him.

"You were supposed to get that crazy bastard," Bryce said.

"We have him," Stewart replied.

"A bit late. You could have found him a hole earlier." There was a furious anger in his low voice, audible despite his self-control.

"No, Mr. Bryce," the inspector said. "The man we want timed his appearance to perfection. Most impressively, if I may say so."

There was a pause, and Bryce looked at me, then back at Stewart. The two constables moved unobtrusively to his side.

"I must ask you to come with me, Mr. Bryce."

Bryce didn't ask why; he was not a man to waste his time. He asked, "On what grounds?"

"We want to ask you some questions in connection with the death of Wilson Daintly."

"You have Thorston," he said. I could only admire his coolness. "Can't it wait?"

"I'm afraid not. Your flight leaves tonight."

"I'll have time to come by," Bryce said casually. He understood that he had left his departure rather late. Still, an hour's start, a fast car, plenty of cash: There's always a chance.

"We need you to make an identification," Stewart said.

"What of?" His low harsh voice dropped even lower.

"A golf club."

There was another moment, like the beat out of time when his putt had rolled smooth and straight toward the cup on the eighteenth. This time it was a private moment. A great stillness came to Bryce as he realized that his second gamble of the Open had failed him, too. It was not to be. Not the great victory today. Not the great career tomorrow. Thorston and his own fury had cut short his run. I saw his eyes shift to the horizon, the car park, the façade of the R and A, and his athlete's body tensed for flight, for violence: He was still carrying the putter. But, as Dr. Duclos had said, he was intelligent. Perhaps the other incidents had been aberrations; perhaps the other occasions had not appealed, as Thorston and Stewart had, to his sense of dramatic irony. With a faint, bitter smile, he handed the putter to one of the constables, nodded to Stewart, and started across the fairway toward town. As he passed me, he stopped for an instant.

"Miss Peters," he said, "you have provided inimitable protection."

Then he continued on his way, while Stewart and the two black-coated constables followed in a gloomy escort.

18

"And therefore, gentlemen, the Brainwithe robbery-murders in Connecticut ten years ago led eventually to the vandalism of the St. Andrews courses."

Silence preceded a murmur of surprise, doubt, and dissatisfaction that rolled about the circle of fat leather chairs and came lapping back like a slow tide on sand. The explanation seemed a trifle exotic to me, too. Melvin Thorston had left a trail of damage from the Jubilee ninth to the Old Course eighteenth, because his alter ego, Wulf, planned to murder Peter Bryce. By most normal standards of motivation, that was already unacceptable, although I noticed that the R and A committee had been quite willing to attribute eccentricity to Thorston. His Michaelmas friend, Dr. Duclos, was correct: The professor's character lacked something in both strength and plausibility. Perhaps that's why he had become an actor: His own personality did not carry enough weight.

What the committee balked at was the second part of the theory, that Wulf's hatred was the ultimate consequence of a caper that had run out of control ten years before and ended in a grisly multiple murder. Understandably, they did not like that at all. Even edited and without the police photographs, the Brainwithe case was unpleasant, and Bryce's alleged role in it reflected badly on The Game. The committee was inclined to resist the notion that Thorston fell apart because his friends had removed three witnesses to a robbery, a robbery perpetrated because the professor had figured out how to open a safe with some high-powered technology. To do the committee justice, it wasn't what you'd call a neat, tidy conclusion—especially since both witnesses and evidence had long since vanished.

"But you say there's no proof?" Frazer asked, his tone dubious.

"Not now and not here. Except for the club. Bryce did kill Wilson Daintly, most likely in an argument over the remaining money, and the club was the weapon."

"Unfortunate, that," Frazer remarked. "Even the other way around—"

"Remember, he very nearly won the tournament," I said.

They all blanched, although I'm sure they'd considered that calamity already.

"It does seem unsatisfactory," Sutherland said in a peeved tone. "And with Mr. Bryce claiming it happened in a quarrel —well, I think if your ideas had any substance there would be more charges. This is all fanciful."

"I disagree. The Crown has rightly decided to try Bryce on a sure thing. The prosecution can win this case. For the rest, witnesses in Connecticut have had years to forget what happened, and the key witness is dead, murdered while Bryce was playing a tournament in the area. Proving anything more than that Bryce struck Daintly a fatal blow will be difficult, especially given Thorston's mental state."

"How is the professor?" Greene asked.

"He is in a private sanitarium at the moment. Something Mrs. Gilchrist was able to arrange with the remaining trustees of the Gruen Foundation."

There were a few ripples at this. Irving knew the Gilchrists.

"A pleasant young woman but a bit giddy" was his characterization.

"His doctor has diagnosed a 'traumatic loss of memory,' " I explained. "Dr. Thorston has nothing to say about Bryce, the Open, or Wulf."

"A convenient loss," Greene said drily.

"But persistently maintained."

"He had symptoms enough," Frazer declared. "Daft from start to finish."

"They tell me he's working on electronic voice boxes again," I said. "Great things are expected."

"That's all very well and good," Sutherland interrupted. "But the fact remains, Miss Peters, that this is all unsatisfactory. What we've gotten is a great deal of information about the mental condition and inventiveness of Dr. Thorston—and a great deal of nuisance during the Open." He gave a shake of his head as though conscious of scoring points.

"Let me remind you," I said, "that I advised the committee to strengthen course security and to consult with the local constabulary. I specifically cautioned against an investigation of Wilson Daintly, believing from the first that it would be of limited value to you. On the other hand, if I had not met Daintly, I would not have gone to Hartford. Without what I learned there, I am confident Dr. Thorston would have died."

There was a stony silence. They did not look terribly pleased with their part in the salvation of Melvin Thorston: It would have suited them fine if Bryce had gotten away with murder— so long as they didn't have to know about it. They had the ruthlessness of true dedication.

"The costs of tampering with fate," Sir Malcolm observed philosophically.

"At the moment," I said, "I seem to have borne most of them. Including a very nasty bash on the head."

"Your check," he responded, sliding it deftly from beneath his notes and offering it with a quick, graceful gesture. "Our dissatisfaction has nothing to do with you personally, Miss Peters. Your ingenuity has been admirable, but, if I may say so, more than we had bargained for. We would have preferred—" He hesitated.

"Another murderer?"

"Certainly. And another victim."

"That does not come with the service, unfortunately."

On this we shook hands. Sir Malcolm Greene was urbane, his impeccable position secure. The unambitious Frazer was bluntly skeptical; while Irving, who had seen the wisdom of his original advice upheld, was cordial. Sutherland muttered about tact and bad publicity. I'd heard he was not to be on the R and A Committee for the coming Open. Perhaps not, for my stock with him had plummeted. A U.K. branch did not seem so likely as it had a month before, but as my plane began its long descent pattern into Dulles, I found I could accept that with equanimity. The committee's substantial check nestled in my wallet, but adding up everything, the British adventure had been a losing proposition, especially if I counted the additional time spent on police business since the tournament. The only good thing had been the holiday with Harry, and that had ended over a week ago, when he'd returned home to supervise the layout and the printing of his pictures.

The stewardess passed through with magazines for the last time, and I took a battered copy of the newest *Sports Illustrated* to check the follow-up stories of the Open. The headline above a brief account of Bryce's arrest read, "FALLEN STAR," and its author had exercised himself to cast the events in a suitably tragic mold. In this account, a sudden, violent, irrational quarrel had, like a stroke of evil fortune, stained an otherwise bright career. A few pages back, Harry's prints memorialized the Open. Bryce's scarlet sweater flamed a last time against the green fairways, and the gray bulk of the R and A loomed against the pinkish midnight sky like a mausoleum for hope and fame.

231

"Oh, you picked up a copy," Harry said when he met me in the terminal. "What do you think?"

"They're beautiful, although they can't compare with the originals."

"They were printed a shade too dark, but I'm satisfied. All things considered."

"You should be. It's a very handsome layout."

"It's brought a good response." His eyes were alight. After years of laboring in obscurity, a little fame and a large reward were more than welcome.

"Well deserved."

As we walked out into an evening pink, not with the northern twilight, but with city smog and rain, he asked, "How'd your report to the committee go?"

"Not too badly. They would have preferred to have had Daintly the killer, Thorston the victim, and Bryce the innocent bystander. Failing that, they wish they'd never heard of me. Poor Sutherland's trip up the social ladder has been cut short for the moment, and the committee has paid me in full."

"That's the key point."

"Yes. They agreed on further reflection that with me or without me, they'd have had some sort of mess."

"And the unknown terrifies."

"It gives cause for reflection, at least. Sir Malcolm was quite philosophical. I thought he was going to start quoting from the Gilgamesh epic or whatever his speciality entails."

"I'm glad it wasn't a total loss."

"Well, the trip had other aspects. Cases are a commonplace, but honeymoons—"

We exchanged a few compliments and a number of kisses, until the parking lot attendant came by and thumped on the roof of the car: He needed the lane open. Harry told him he had a soul without poetry and put the car in gear.

"I almost forgot," he said. "Baby handed me a note on the way out."

"Lucky." Baby never gave up.

"For you, my dear. Some fellow called about a job." He went through his pockets and came up with a memo. It consisted of the name of a prominent sporting goods company and the note, "Check for them, Matthew (The Fireman) Ferguson."

I laughed. "You've made this up deliberately."

"No way. Haven't you heard of The Fireman? I saw him in the NCAA's last spring. He's a tremendous guard. Big, fast, strong. They're saying he's the best pro guard prospect in years."

"Yeah? I've about had it with big prospects."

"The kid's terrific."

"And the sponsors want to know if he's clean, thrifty, and brave before he starts peddling their sneakers." God! Life was beginning to imitate artifice. I'll give up lying, I thought.

"You'll do it, though, won't you?"

"No way. I've developed a dislike for athletes. They're too damn big, for one thing. It's all right for you, but I'm sick of feeling like Detective Dwarf."

"You merely got off to a bad start. You'll love The Fireman. You know, of course, why he's called that?"

"No."

"He fires the ball from anywhere on the court. The most fantastic distance shooter. A twenty-five footer is nothing."

"That's what I mean. These are unnatural people."

"Besides, you owe me."

"Owe you what?"

"I took you to the Open."

"I remember."

"Monotypes, I think, for The Fireman. I'm trying to work out a technique that would catch both the speed and the pattern of basketball. It's an incredible game: the changes in tempo, the emotional preparation required before the action and during the time-outs. Seeing the players away from the game itself would help—"

233

"*Sports Illustrated* might commission more pictures."

"They're definitely interested. That's why I thought you might take on this job with The Fireman."

"You know, Harry, I'm really ready to get back to computer print-outs, financial forms, and bureaucratic snooping. They're a great deal easier, they pay a good deal better, and they don't involve nearly so much walking."

But Harry was paying no attention. ". . . a problem of balancing movement with clarity. The semi-abstract treatment has become a cliché. What I have in mind—"

I turned him off and watched the green and gray approaches to Washington. Perhaps that was why he was nicer than I. The patterns I'd seen had been less conclusive and much less beautiful, but they had some things in common with Harry's plans for the aesthetic transformation of Matthew Ferguson: a mixture of spontaneity and determinism. Daintly, Thorston, and Bryce had almost gotten away with robbery and murder. Had, in fact, until Thorston's breakdown destabilized a delicate set of relationships. There were still a lot of things I'd like to know—

". . . the preparations, I think. If you could show, by a repeated pattern, the link between preparation and execution—" He glanced at me. "I don't think you're listening."

"I don't need to. There are certain similarities in our businesses." I could just as easily have said, "in our obsessions."

"Do you think so?"

"I know so."

"Well?"

"Well, tell me something more about this Fireman character —just in case I change my mind."

234

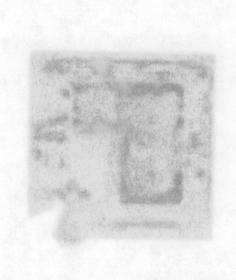